A HOME IN THE MIST IV

A Cades Cove Story

On Thin Ice

W.T. Ridenour

Author photo © 2020 by Kathy Ridenour.
Cover photo © Pixabay.com
Cover design © 2022 Timothy M. Ridenour
Woodburning © 2022 Tobe Licker

Edited and formatted by Cheryl S. Justice.

Published by WTR Books.

ISBN 978-1-7358587-6-0

TO

TIM & TOBE

And

AS ALWAYS

TO

KATHY

Table Of Contents

i

ONE

Fowl Business

STANDS TO REASON with the way the homestead was fillin' up that spring, I'd feel jiggled and jostled and wonderin' where all the elbow room had gone. Why, between Ma, Pa, Diver, Charlotte, Casey, Baby, and a slew of new farm critters to look after, a person could hardly turn around without bumping into someone or somethin'. Yet, truth be told, I was downright lonely.

Now don't get me wrong, Diver and Charlotte couldn't have been any closer to me than my own blood. And Casey, even though I was only a year old when he left home, and Pa was so riled about it that he refused to have his name mentioned around the place, I was plumb tickled to have him back. I can't say for true that I remembered him, but he was still my brother after all.

As for Diver. Well, I can't fault him none for not havin' much time. Between Charlotte, church duties, and parishioners who couldn't seem to make it through the week without needin' guidance from their shepherd. Well, let's just say, he was mighty preoccupied.

Then there was Second Chance. I didn't see much of him that spring either 'cause his ma was feelin' poorly and his pa wanted him to stay close to home in case she needed him. Course, seein's how Susan Beckett took an interest in carin' for Mrs. Fieldman, I don't reckon you could o' drove ol' Chance off if you'd o' tried to.

I reckon with Two Hand ailin' the way he was after that bear fight, Henry was in the same situation as Second Chance. I didn't see hide nor hair of him around our place for quite a spell.

Yeah, I gotta say, even with all the folks I had in my life that spring, I was still feelin' kinda low and lonely. Out of sorts you might say. And yet, no one seemed to notice—not Diver, not Pa, not even Ma—or so I thought.

Fact is, mothers don't miss much.

I's absentmindedly rockin' on the porch with a forgotten book layin' open on my lap, when I felt Ma's cool fingers brush through my hair.

"You're missin' her, ain't ya, son."

Her? I stopped rockin' and looked up at Ma so dumbfounded I didn't know what to say. How'd she know? I hadn't said nothin' to nobody 'bout Mary bein' gone. I don't know that I'd even admitted to myself that I was pinin' for her.

Ma's soft eyes twinkled as she smiled that tender, soul soothin' smile that only mothers can pull off. You know, the one that makes your heart feel all warm and tingly, like it's cradled in gossamer and silk. The one you're sure wasn't ever meant for no one else in the whole world—just you.

"I know it doesn't seem like it now, but she'll be back soon. You just need somethin' to keep yourself occupied in the meantime. And I think I know just the thing that'll do it. At least for a while."

"Yeah? What's that, Ma?" I asked.

She sat on the rocker next to mine and began sorting through a basket of quilting scraps she seemed to be endlessly collecting. I was always fascinated by the intricate patterns she came up with. Seems like she never sat down and had a conversation without sortin', cuttin', and stitchin' the whole time she talked. Then, come fall, Pa would set up her quilting rack and with the help of Sarah May and Charlotte, some lucky person would wide up with a brand-new patchwork quilt to warm their bed on them cold winter nights. Then all that work would be worth it.

"Well, me and Charlotte got to talkin'," she said. "We decided with all the extra mouths to feed around the place, we need to extend the garden."

I nodded and at the same time felt a bit of a flutter in my stomach.

"Okay," I said a bit warily.

"If we removed the fence from the south end of the garden and tilled the soil up to the Cove Trail, we could nearly double its size."

A knot began to develop in my gut--way down deep. I could see the work comin'. I was gonna be spending the next week or so digging up rocks, turning soil, and breakin' sod with a hoe.

Not that I would have complained about it. At least not out loud. But I reckon you might have figured out by now: I wasn't overly fond of chores.

Never have been.

I don't reckon me and the guy that came up with the idea of work will ever be bosom buddies.

Ma didn't look up from her sorting, but I saw a subtle grin flicker across her face, which told me she knew what I was thinkin' before she continued.

"I spoke with Sarah May about it, and she said that since Casey still isn't fit for that kind of work and Diver has his plate full..."

Here it comes, I thought.

"...that Forrest would be happy to come by next Saturday to help out. Figured he might could bring along Second Chance or the Tudwell boys too."

What? I breathed a sigh of relief.

Ma laughed. "Kinda funny how Sarah May offers Forrest's labor without mentioning it to him first. But you know he'll do it."

I was suddenly feelin' a whole lot better about the whole thing. A mess of fresh vegetables for the table, and I didn't have to do all the work.

"And that's where you come in," she said.

Uh-oh, I thought.

"With doubling the size of the garden, we're gonna need more fertilizer to fix the soil. That means more chickens. More chickens mean more eggs."

She must have been happy with her stacks of color sorted material because she began placing them in crisscrossed piles on her lap.

"More eggs than we need, but not enough to make sellin' 'em worthwhile," she continued. "So, I was thinking, why not build a new hen house big enough for a commercial flock. We could sell the extra eggs and pullets."

Ma sat there with a big grin on her face.

"It would be me and Charlotte's own business," she said.

I gotta say, it plumb tickled me to see how excited Ma was over the thought of havin' her own enterprise. How in the world she didn't see that she already did more'n her fair share around the place beats me?

"I think it sounds great, Ma," I said.

"And all I need you to do," she said as she placed the newly cross-stacked fabric scraps back into her basket, "is to build the new hen house."

"Me?" I said, dumbfounded.

"There's no one I'd rather trust to do the job," she said as she stood up, kissed me on the head, and went back into the house to check on Casey and start supper.

Me? Build Ma's new chicken house? I sat and pondered it a moment. *Well, why not me? I devised and built the fox trap on the existing one. It nearly worked too. Close enough. That ol' fox gave up on Ma's chickens and never came back.*

I got up and hopped off the porch, then walked across the yard to the old hen house.

Baby ambled along next to me, nearly gettin' tangled in my feet. She did that a lot of late in case that crazy red hen decided to go for round two.

I guess I hadn't thought about it before, but that old coop had stood there for quite a spell. And in all truth, it wasn't fairin' too well. The ravages of winter storms and gnawing raccoons were evident in its warped and splintered plank wood walls. Time demands a heavy toll in the Smokies.

Ma's big Leghorn rooster, perching high atop the coop, lazily shifted his weight, and showed total indifference to my inspection of his kingdom. I was a male and therefore of no threat, or interest, to him. If I was a female, he wouldn't have been quite so nonchalant. In fact, he would've been at full alert just in case a hasty retreat was required. I had to chuckle at the thought as I approached him.

"Got an attitude adjustment, didn't ya?"

Charlotte's lesson had sure made an impression.

He shook his comb and wattles and pecked at a pesky no-see-em that suddenly caught his attention.

Then, shifting his weight and turning his tail feathers my way, he feigned indifference. I suppose he figured no reply was necessary and chose to ignore me.

After looking over the old hen house, I searched around for a new building site. The old house sat right out in the yard and always had seemed out of place to me. It was the first thing a person saw when walkin' out the front door, and in my way o' thinkin', it ruined an otherwise stunning view. So, I was hopin' to find a less conspicuous location.

Walking around the yard, I weighed the pros and cons of several possibilities—mostly cons. Too far. Too steep. Too Rocky. Then, after circumnavigating the entire property, nearly back to the old coop, I found it. A horizontal slab of exposed bedrock at the base of a sixteen-foot vertical ledge near where Diver had built his ghost light blind.

The slab was a twenty-by-fourteen-foot rock shelf that slopped just enough to allow water to flow off it. There was a small, free flowing spring that dribbled down the vertical rock face and drained across it into a depression on the other side.

An eight-foot high, three walled, log structure with the cliff serving as the rear wall and a latched entranceway out front could be a varmint resistant safe haven. The heavy walls and slab floor would discourage burrowing critters, while a plank roof and lattice-work vents would not only let in plenty of light and air but prevent hawks and owls from decimating the flock. A series of multi-level roosting poles, plenty of double-stacked nesting boxes, and an enclosed sleeping area for the chicks, and all the girls should be quite comfortable and happy.

The site was far enough from the cabin to alleviate the smell of chicken waste on a hot summer's day, yet close enough to easily collect eggs, spread feed, and haul fertilizer to a nearby composting pile. The year round, natural spring alleviating the need to water the flock was a bonus all in itself.

A bit of quick sypherin', (Diver told me all that schoolin' would come in handy someday), and I figured at two to four square feet per chicken, an eighteen by twelve-foot coop with double stacked nesting boxes and chick pens below could eventually handle sixty to a hundred hens. Figure seventy to eighty percent laying and five percent brooding at twenty-one days per clutch of twelve to fourteen eggs and Ma and Charlotte should have all the egg and chick business they cared to handle.

But hopefully not enough that it need envolve me.

And seein' how there ain't nothin' a free ranging chicken likes better than a big juicy tick, the pest control factor alone would be mightily appreciated.

My biggest worry was being drafted into coop maintenance and egg candling.

As I was figurin' and calculatin' on Ma's hen house, Baby was frantically scratching and nosing around through last year's leaf litter. She'd jump first here, then there, then back again. Then shaking her floppy ears, and wagging her tail, she'd drive her nose back under one more time.

Small, tangled piles of dead debris were scattered along the muddy edges of the slow flowing spring-water brook, and she attacked each one as she came to it.

I didn't know what was of such interest to her, but I could see her tail and rear-end wagging and twisting as she dove into the leafy refuse, over and over again.

Twigs snapped and leaves flew. She growled and yapped, and all-in-all, seemed to be having a grand ol' time. I laughed at her antics and turned back to my plans.

If I use six-inch logs, I thought.

Suddenly, the wildest screeching and yelping I ever heard come from a half-grown pup, erupted behind me. I spun around and there was Baby, running backwards, shaking her head, and slapping at her muzzle with her paws. She'd crash into a tree tail first, flip over, leap back up, and start fishtailing around backward all over again, yelping the whole time.

I was afraid the poor thing had gone crazy. Rushing to her aid as quickly as possible, I dove in and grabbed a trembling rear leg, pulling her to me. Fowl smelling muddy water, thick with rotten leaf litter, splattered my arms and face as she struggled.

"What's wrong with you?" I gasped.

Still shaking her head, eyes wide with fright and emitting the most soulful whine I've ever heard, she looked me in the face.

There, hanging from her upper lip, tail curled under its body, was a large, black, hard-shelled crawdaddy.

Baby didn't seem to appreciate my laughter as I carefully worked the angry crustacean from her lip.

"Ain't nobody's fault but your own," I giggled.

Suddenly, I forgot the humor in the whole situation. That onery critter like to took off the tip of my little finger as I was trying to let it go.

I'm here to tell ya, that hurt!

I was sayin' "Wow! Ouch! Ow—ee!" and shakin' my hand like a willow in a windstorm.

It was kinda embarrassin' when I looked down and noticed Baby staring at me like I was the crazy one. I stopped fidgeting and placed my achin' fingers under my arm. It was then that Baby either snickered or sneezed. I can't say for certain which it was, but I'll call it a sneeze.

"Come and get it," Ma called for supper.

I reckon me and Baby were both more than happy to call it a day by then.

As we reached the porch, Pa walked up and stopped for just a moment looking at Baby and me. She stood there lookin' up at him with watery eyes and a big ol' puffed-out lip revealing a single exposed canine, and I was tryin' to avert my own watery eyes as I kept my hand clamped tight under my armpit.

He started to say something, then stopped and just shook his head. Opening the door, he went into the house.

Baby's whole body seemed to deflate as she turned and slunk off to her blanket.

"I feel for ya, girl," I said.

Then, bracing for a ribbing, I went inside too.

≈

Ma was plumb right about takin' my mind off o' my troubles for a while. Word spread through the Cove that us Banions were startin' another building project and come Saturday morning folks showed-up in droves askin' how they could help. I gotta tell ya, I was plumb baffled till Diver speculated that most o' them folks were ones that Pa's co-op helped out after that big flood.

To hear him tell it, it sounded like he had nothing to do with it.

"They's just tryin' to show their appreciation, and it wouldn't be Christian to deny 'em the chance," he said.

As they arrived, they just naturally turned to Pa to see what needed done. He told 'em Forrest was in charge of the garden, and as for the new hen house, well they'd have to talk to Ma's contractor. He acted like it weren't no big deal when he pointed my way.

Well, I don't reckon ya could o' squeezed my head into a fifty-gallon barrel if you'd o' used an apple press. A fifteen-year-old boy ain't often placed in charge of an adult work force.

Fact be told, it was a bit touch-and-go there for a moment. Then somebody shouted out that any youth who could face down an angry panther while bein' lost under a mountain could surely ramrod a buildin' project.

There was an awkward moment of silence followed by a big ol' cheer I reckon could o' been heard plumb to Knoxville. Pa got kinda tickled over all the back slappin' and hair touslin' and the way I was just a noddin', and shruggin', and beamin'.

"Like a possum in a slop bucket," was the way he later put it.

I ain't never been so relieved in all my born days as when Diver took pity on me and said, "Well boys, I reckon it's time we get to work."

Next thing I knowed, I was explaining designs, assigning work details, and ramroddin' that project like I was born to do it. And ya know what? Not a single double headed axe or blister inducing hammer ever touched my hand. I decided right then and there; that was my idea of buildin'.

Between that work crew on Saturday and a half dozen or so fellas that showed up after church on Sunday, we got the entire project done in a single weekend. Ma and Charlotte had a new hen house, a garden twice the size of the old one, and the old coop torn down and burned.

Pa even wound up with a small patch of fertile ground where the old coop used to stand to grow a little tobacco for barterin'.

Last thing before everyone loaded up to leave was placing a new wattle fence around both gardens to protect 'em from hungry critters.

"It's beautiful," pronounced Ma as she surveyed the new amenities. She hugged first me and then Pa.

"And Kenny Fishburn said to drop by his place when we get a chance," Pa said. "Said he's got some pullets he can part with to clear his debt."

Charlotte smiled up at Diver and kissed him on the cheek. The whole co-op thing had been his idea.

"We truly are blessed," said Diver.

"Amen to that, preacher," Pa replied.

TWO

Haggens

WHILE WE WERE ENJOYING our good fortune in the beautiful surroundings of our beloved Cove, a whole different reality was developing in the harsh lives of a hardscrabble family in the Ohio Valley of Northwestern Kentucky. A reality that would soon spread like a wildfire across our peaceful mountains and come mighty near to layin' me low beneath our home in the mist.

"What's wrong with you," Hiram Haggen thundered as he thumped his nineteen-year-old son on the back of his head. "Get rid of that saddle. The bridle too."

"Now, Pa, you can't be a thumpin' on me and treatin' me like that no more," whined Caleb. "I'm a growed man."

"You ain't so growed I can't knock some sense into ya," Hiram bellowed as he chased Caleb 'round an empty stock pen on their played-out dirt farm, all the while thumpin' him on the head.

Hiram was a hard man and never was one to take sass off any of his ten children. He ruled the roost as the missus and her brats could attest to, and they'd best abide by his say if they knew what was good for 'em. Only his middle girl, Ally, had a way of tamin' his ire on occasion, but even she dared not interfere when he was in a full-out frenzy.

He'd known for quite some time that his two oldest boys, twenty-one-year-old Barnabas, and nineteen-year-old Caleb, were both part of the infamous Ford's Ferry gang. Along with that Pott's Tavern bunch, about the meanest mess of misfits the Ohio Valley had ever spawned. Course, seein' how they were startin' families of their own, they had to do what they could to get by. If that meant tippin' the scales their own way a bit, then so be it.

On the other hand, with 'em both livin' in weaner cabins on his property, they'd live by his law or face the consequences—growed or not.

Couple years back, havin' family members in the Ford's Ferry gang weren't no frettin' matter. They kept their identities a well-guarded secret, and their victims were mostly just strangers passin' through anyway. Little effort was put into stopping 'em.

It wasn't a healthy endeavor for those who tried.

James Ford had been a bulldog of a man and a powerful local politician and businessman. He was considered by many to be "a pillar of the community." Despite running a network of highwaymen and river pirates, he had vigorously kept his public image clean and railed against thugs and lawlessness. Even though there were whispered rumors and innuendos about him, it came as a shock to the community when he was gunned down in '33. Word soon spread that he'd been the leader of the gang and his own men had done him in.

Since then, an ever growing, ever zealous band of self-appointed vigilantes had begun combing the countryside. They ran down possible gang members and terrorizing anyone who came under suspicion. It wasn't long before folks began to question which was worse, the gangs, or the vigilantes formed to stop 'em.

Either way, very few hardworking farmers slept soundly at night.

Hiram had warned the boys that if they chose to keep up their present livelihoods, they were to keep their dealings away from his farm.

Never bring stolen goods onto his property.

So, what does Caleb do? He comes chargin' in one evening all excited and busting at the seams wantin' to show his Pa a silver concho encrusted saddle and bridle he'd "acquired" from a feller who no longer needed it.

"Look at it, Pa," he said. "Bet ya ain't never laid eyes on nothin' so purty in all your born days."

Hiram was furious.

"What's wrong with you boy!" he roared as he boxed his second born upside the head. "You ain't got the sense of a mangy coyote. Even he knows to hide a ham hock in a hornet hole where nothing'll find the evidence. You reckon nobody's gonna notice somethin' that fancy?"

"But Pa," Caleb protested, "I thought . . ."

"No, you didn't," Hiram cut in. "I ain't plumb sure you got the brain power to form a thought in that hard head of yours. Now get that thing off o' my property."

As Caleb grumbled to himself, hauling his ill-gotten gains out the front door, Hiram stood shaking his head. How could a son of his be so dense as to bring a highly identifiable, one-of-a-kind piece of equine art like that onto his property? Somebody's gonna be lookin' for that mighty hard.

Sure enough, not a week went by before posters started appearing in every town from Vincennes to Elizabethtown and as far east as Louisville. They were offering a two-thousand-dollar reward, cash money, for information in the disappearance of a two term senator's son who was last seen traveling through the area. Sketches of the young man, his horse, and a finely tooled saddle and bridle decked out with silver conches were included.

"Yo, Pa," Clay interfered his father's thoughts as he sauntered into the house. Passing through the kitchen, he snatched an apple slice that his sister Avery was figurin' to use in a pie.

She slashed out with her paring knife coming mighty close to impaling his hand.

"I'm warning you," she said, poised for another jab. "And don't you be thinkin' you'll be gettin' a slice of pie when it's done neither."

He smirked as he sidestepped to stay well out of his sister's reach, knowin' from past experience that she could be deadly with that knife.

As soon as he reached what he felt was a safe distance, he glanced down at his fingers to make sure they were all there. He and Avery were both seventeen, but she was nine-and-a-half months older than him, and girl or not, she wasn't afraid to back her threats.

Satisfied no digits were missing, he turned to Pa.

"Mr. Billings is down at the stock pen lookin' to load that sow ya sold him last week," he said. "I told him she was holed-up in the barn and to go ahead and fetch her out."

Hiram looked up from where he was trying to patch a hole in his boot with a piece of raw hide and pine tar.

It rankled him somethin' fierce that he'd been compelled to sell his last hog to Billings. He wouldn't have done it if the extended draught they'd been facing weren't lookin' to drag on. If the fields didn't get rain soon, this year's meager harvest looked to be a bust, and then nobody'd be eatin'. Course, Billings could've offered a bit for the litter that sow was carryin', but he claimed there was no guarantee any of the piglets would survive the farrowing. Hiram bristled knowin' he'd never lost more than a few, *ever*.

Billings just said, "If you'd like to feed her 'til she farrows, we might work something out."

Course, he knew good and well, Hiram was only sellin' her cause he couldn't afford to feed her.

Hope she loses the whole litter, Hiram thought.

Looking at his son, Hiram said, "Okay, I'll go down and talk with him. Make sure he don't walk off with nothin' else."

He set the newly patched boot aside to dry, then yanked his other boot off along with a pair of threadbare socks he'd last changed back in December. Chucking the footwear into a corner, he traipsed across the kitchen floor, snatching a few apple cores off the table as he passed.

The cool white pine floorboards felt good underfoot as he walked out of the house in his bare feet.

Six dogs of varying shapes and sizes, descended from lineages not even the local vet could have deciphered, came rushing up as he rounded the corner of the house. Yapping and leaping, they nearly knocked him off his feet.

"Get back there," he shouted as he snatched up a stick to swat the mutts with.

That only made them jump all the higher, thinking he was playing with 'em.

Across a patch of dried grass, they called a yard, he saw his missus painfully stoop down to pick up another piece of faded-out laundry as she struggled to keep eighteen-month-old Hannah perched on her right hip. As she plucked a stained frock from her basket, Hannah reached out and yanked a pair of just hung breeches from the severely drooping clothesline and dropped it onto the dusty ground.

Hiram chuckled.

"Why don't ya go pester her for a change," he yelled as he tromped through the pack of squirming dogs. "Least-ways ya could be worryin' ol' man Billings down there pokin' through my barn."

Oddly enough, as Hiram was kickin' and fussin' with the dogs, he looked up and saw Billings come rushin' out of the barn, nearly falling as he hastily climbed into his wagon. He was sure Billings had seen him, but the man neither nodded nor waved. He snapped his reins and pulling his team around tight, whipped 'em into a full gallop down the long, dusty driveway.

Hiram scratched his head as he wondered what that was all about.

"Didn't even load the hog," he said to himself.

Plodding down the drive, taking care to avoid sharp pebbles with his tender feet, he soon arrived at the barn and stepped into the dark drive bay. Pausing for a bit to let his eyes adjust to the gloom, he inhaled a deep breath of the sweet earthy odor that permeated any well used barn. The sweet smell of old straw and weathered wood. He sure loved that scent.

The hog grunted as it scuffed its rough hide on the sides of a hard packed dust-wallow.

A big black rat scurried under the grain bin.

"What'd ya do, chase the ol' skinflint off?" Hiram asked the hog as he tossed it the apple cores.

Long shafts of sunlight filtered through poorly fitted wood plank walls and pierced the darkened room with bars of wavering dust motes.

Hiram stepped farther into the bay to look over his, "should already be gone," hog. As he did, a sharp glint of light caught his eye from the darkest recesses of the room. Puzzled, he went to investigate. There, along the back wall, slightly protruding above the age-worn lid of the empty grain bin, sat the cantle of the silver-edged saddle.

"What did you do, boy?" Hiram moaned.

Reaching over the bin, he pulled the saddle from its hiding place and watched as the bridle slithered out with it and coiled on the floor at his feet. With all them posters plastered about town, a man would have to be blind not to recognize that fancy leatherwork and all them sterling silver trimmin's. And no matter what else Billings might be, he certainly wasn't blind.

Having that two-thousand-dollar reward dancin' around in his brain went a long way to explainin' why he ran off without his hog.

With no time to waste, Hiram dropped the saddle on the dirt floor and rushed out the bay door. By his figuring, Billings had a three-and-a-half-hour ride ahead of him to get to town. Wouldn't get there till well after dark. It would prob'bly take another two or three hours to round up the vigilantes and a couple more to get back here to the farm.

Without any formal education to speak of, all of them figures got to rattlin' around in Hiram's brain makin' things a bit confusing. Near as he could figure, they wouldn't arrive till well after midnight. Even then, they'd be figuring on facing at least four guns between Hiram and his three oldest boys.

He snickered to himself, "Ain't a man in the county fool enough to be hankerin' to poke around at night on the Haggen place. Stands to reason they'll hole up till mornin' and hit us at first light. If we head out quick, we can get a whole night's jump on 'em before they even realize we've skedaddled."

As he ran toward the house, oohin' and ouchin' and high steppin' with every rock that gouged his tender feet, he bellowed out for Clay.

"Clay boy, get yer hide out here," he called.

As he neared the house, dogs jumpin' and yappin' and dodgin' his kicking feet, still thinkin' it was a game, Clay came rushin' 'round the corner.

The boy couldn't imagine what he'd done wrong.

"Pa, whatever it is," he stammered with both hands stuck out in front of him as if warding off a charging beast, "I didn't do it."

"Shush up boy," Hiram yelled over the clamor. "We got trouble comin'. We gotta make tracks fast. I want you to run tell your brothers the vigilantes is headin' this way. Tell 'em to load up only what they need and leave what they can do without. I want to be out o' here by dark and we ain't comin' back."

"We're runnin', Pa?" Clay asked in disbelief.

"No, we're savin' a bunch a fellas from wastin' their perfectly good ropes. Now get at it and do what I told ya."

"Yes, sir, Pa," Clay said. He headed out at a run to tell his brothers.

In short order, Hiram explained the situation to his wife as he stomped into his boots without puttin' on socks. He then rushed out and commenced to hitchin' up his team of massive draft horses to the big farm wagon.

Bedlam spread throughout the house as eight kids and their mother searched and grabbed and fought over what was absolutely necessary to take along and what wasn't.

More than a few tears were lost at items left.

"I don't want to go," Ally whined. "Sammy Rollins said he's takin' me to the ho-down come Saturday."

"You better stay shush 'bout you bein' sweet on that Rollins boy," said Avery. "Pa hears ya and you're gonna get a tannin' sure."

"I'm fifteen-years-old," snapped Ally. "I ain't no baby no more. I can have me a beau if I wanna."

"Well, first it was Kenny Hedrick, then Quincy Cox, now Sammy Rollins," said Avery. "Don't ya think you might could leave at least one poor fella for the other gals?

"You're just jealous cuz you gotta spend your time helpin' Ma with the twins and the baby 'stead of goin' out and findin' a beau of your own," Ally smirked.

She then stuck her tongue out.

"Lookin' after Hannah and the twins ain't half the pain that lookin' after you is," said Avery.

"Well, who asked ya?" shouted Ally as she left the room.

≈

A dusky sun sank below the western horizon as Hiram pulled the clattering farm wagon away from the only home most of his children had ever known.

In the distance he could barely make out the shadowy forms of Barnabas' and Caleb's wagons waiting alongside the rutted driveway. As he came alongside the barn he reined in his team and set the brake. Climbing down he entered the drive bay and soon returned with the saddle and bridle. Hefting them into the wagon bed, he returned back inside. With a squeal, a snort, and a few resounding, openhanded smacks, he reappeared leading the hog by a hemp rope leash.

"May as well take her along," he said, "seein's how Billings didn't see fit to take her."

After tying the leash off to the tailgate and climbing back onto his blanket covered seat, the entire Haggen clan set out for a new, healthier climate.

THREE

Camp

PA AND DIVER sowed a new crop of corn on the sloped field, repairing and revising the ingenious irrigation system as required. Under Diver's guidance, they then spent several tortured hours splitting the beehive to create two new sources of pollinators which would greatly increase the potential honey harvest. They situated one hive in a hollow black gum log attached to a nearby covered ledge, well out of the reach of the most industrious of black bears. The other they placed on tall poles in the old apple orchard. With luck, that one could be split several times in the coming years.

Diver divided the remainder of his time between church duties and what farm chores he could get to.

Pa kept busy with maintenance and repair of his traps, hide stretchers, tanning boards, and numerous Indian style bone scrappers, in preparation of next winter's fur season. In his spare time, he split firewood, (a never-ending chore every male on the place lent a hand to) and with my help, worked on extending the pasture fence to accommodate our ever-expanding herd of livestock. We now had four mules, one horse, two cows, and a calf on the way: six pigs, five ducks, eleven chickens—and of course, Baby.

Casey had recovered from his bout of the "viper vapers" as Mable Davis called it and was making impressive advances in the salt processing business. He'd fitted the old stone cabin with a window and door to use it as an office—and sometimes as a bedroom, rather than trekking through the forest at night after working late.

He'd hired the Deerborn brothers and Dean Tudwell (when the dairy business allowed him time) to work on a profit-sharing basis. They had cleared back a large section of scree, built a work platform from which to access the salt vein, erected a hoist beam with block and tackle to lift the load to a waiting wagon above, and cleared a trail to the Cove Road.

Jud Beckett was more than happy to purchase every load of salt they could deliver seein's how it was one of the most desired commodities in the region.

As for me, I was primarily left in charge of any farm chores that no one else could get to: milkin', feedin' livestock, sloppin' pigs, replacing warped wall boards on the necessary; you name it.

Though truth be told, I spent a large part of my time workin' hard to get out of work.

I justified that by figurin' it takes a heap o' time to check out them snares and fish traps I had. They was puttin' food on the table after all. And a feller's just naturally gotta take a break for a nap, or to do a bit of explorin' now and then.

The real workers on the homestead were Ma and Charlotte. They not only took care of both households' cleanin', cookin', sewin', and nursin'; but also worked the garden, did the cannin' and picklin', and stored the vegetables to get us through winter. Then there was makin' jams and preserves, churning butter, clarifying buttermilk, and fermenting yogurt. In there spare time, during season, they scoured the mountainsides and hidden valleys for nuts, berries, ramps, watercress, and any number of other wild nutrients they could feed the family. Not to mention their newly acquired enterprise: chickens. While it's true our chickens were open range, removing the need to feed and water them through the summer, there was collecting, candling, sorting, and selling eggs.

Candling was a time consuming, eye tiring process of using candlelight in a darkened room to "glow" an egg, trying to see whether it contained an infertile yolk or a viable embryo inside. It was done every five to seven days. An embryo showed as a dark spot with spider webbing and an air pocket at one end of the shell. When confirmed, if chosen to hatch, an egg would be placed under a brooding hen for twenty-one days.

The eggs collected for selling were stored and cooled for delivery to Beckett's Freight Store every Saturday, along with any extra chicks and pullets (a young hen up to a year old). Diver usually made the delivery along with whoever happened to have business in the Cove.

Once a week the entire hen house needed cleaning and fresh straw placed in the nesting boxes. As I feared, that became my job. Kind of embarrassing for someone who takes such pride in avoiding chores, if you know what I mean.

≈

While life was dealing the Banions and McCoys a fair hand, things weren't looking up for the Haggens.

Having loaded the hog into Caleb's wagon after dressing the boy down hard for not getting rid of that saddle, Hiram led the way as the small caravan fell in behind. After a lifetime lived in the Northwest corner of Kentucky, Hiram knew every trail and every two track in the region. He'd traveled every backwoods cut-through and knew every fordable stream. For all his faults, few men were more capable at keeping their families hidden from spying eyes. Not a quarter hour passed after leaving their farm behind then the heavy wagons faded into the densely wooded Ohio River floodplains.

The scattered cloud cover overhead thickened as the witching hour approached, blotting out the distant stars and crescent moon as if a great curtain had been drawn across the heavens above. On the mighty Ohio a gathering mist darkened as it transformed into a soupy veil of dense fog. Slowly climbing the river's banks, it overflowed into the woodlands beyond. Every shrub and creature of the night laid hushed and silent as long tendrils of swirling vaper drifted across the swampy lowlands. Only the creaking of muddy iron wheels and over-stressed timber axels disturbed the solitude of the night. As the mist enveloped the roadway and climbed to the hubs of the wagon's wheels a light rain began to fall.

Hiram pulled his team to a stop and set the brake.

Looking over at his wife, wrapped tight in an old wedding ring quilt against the cold rain, he shook his head as she shivered.

Woman's been chilled for three years, he thought.

The bleak winter after four-year-old Hiram Jr. was born saw some mighty lean times in Northern Kentucky. Crops failed across the region leading to the worst harvest in a decade. Banks were stressed and refused all loans while demanding prompt payment from farmers who had no funds to pay them. With no grain, and only poor-quality hay for his old milk cow, production suffered. Then he caught the dumb beast eating deadly Bracken Fern out of a clump of brush by the back fence. He lost her within weeks.

As if that wasn't enough, trying to stretch their meager stores, Avery and Pearle had sloshed around in a cold drizzle digging up half frozen turnips from their barren garden. Pearle ended up catching a cold that turned to pneumonia. Things were iffy the rest of that winter, but thankfully, her health improved with the coming spring. She just couldn't seem to get warm enough. After all this time, the slightest breeze still send shivers coursing through her body.

Annoyed by her shaking, Hiram told her to get under the tarp with the youngin's.

Snapping his whip behind him, he yelled, "Clay Boy, get out here. Let yer ma lay down a while."

A slight pause followed, then Clay's tousled head poked out from the corner of the sodden tarp.

"What'd ya say, Pa?" Clay asked.

"Get out o' there and come up here," Hiram ordered.

Clay rubbed his eyes and elbowed a sack of laundry he was using for a pillow.

"Aw, Pa," he grumbled to himself as he slithered out from under the tarp. Wrapping his arms across his chest, he carefully stepped over the wagon seat as his mother took his place out of the rain.

Sitting on the cold, wet plank, he glanced out over the swirling mist. A chill ran down his spine as his fertile imagination painted pictures of night creatures slithering and creeping just below the billowing blanket of fog. In his mind, they waiting to pull down any unsuspecting victims that stumbled into their ghostly domain. Clay had always feared the dark.

"Get down there and lead the horses," Hiram said.

"Wait?" cried Clay as a cold fist squeezed his innards.

"You heard me boy," Hiram grinned. "Get down there and lead them horses. I don't want 'em runnin' into fallen limbs or fallin' into unseen holes in this mess."

"Well, what if I fall in a hole?" pleaded Clay.

"If ya do, I'll pull ya out. If I can't, me and your ma'll make another one to replace ya. I done it ten times before," he smirked, "I can do it again. Now get down there like I said."

Icy fingers crept up Clay's legs as they sank into the murky vapor. Each hidden twig or sprig of long

Johnson grass made him jump as it brushed across his pant leg. He was sure they were harbingers of doom waiting to whisk him away. Finally, making his way around the big draft horses, he found a track in the road and began following it into the gloom.

Behind him Hiram released the brake and yipped the team into motion.

"Should be a clearing 'bout a mile up the way," Clay heard Hiram's bodyless voice drift out of the swirling fog. "We'll rest there."

To Clayton, it was a long, nerve-wracking mile.

After reaching the clearing and unharnessing the horses, they hobbled them so they could feed without straying. Being too dark to find a ridgepole for a tent, they rigged the canvasses tight across the wagons sideboards and divided the children amongst them to make room. Pearle and Avery did what they could to comfort the whining, cold, and hungry youngsters as Hiram and Barnabas made their way to the riverbank to gauge the possibility of it flooding. The rain had eased for the moment but would surely return.

"I'm sorry about all this, Pa," Barnabas said. "If I'd known he hadn't got rid of that saddle, I'd have done it myself."

"Yeah, that boy ain't got a lick of sense," said Hiram as he tossed a section of dead limb into the fog.

It clattered over several rocks before splashing into the river.

"Sounds like we got a good ten or fifteen feet before she overruns. Reckon we're good for tonight."

An unseen critter scurried away at the noise.

"I'm surprised you ain't bull whipped him to an inch of his life, costin' you the farm and all, the way he done."

Hiram stood stock-still with his hands clasped behind his back listening for any tell-tale sounds of pursuit in the dark. Noise travels a long way in the stillness of fog.

"Well, fact is," he said after being assured they were alone, "we've taken a loss for the last two years. Barely broke even since twenty-nine. Way this year was shapin' up there's not a chance I could have covered the note. Come November we'd have lost the place no matter what."

Barnabas was stunned. "I had no idea!" he said.

"Nothing you could have done if I'd told ya." Hiram looked over at the dark silhouette of his oldest.

"Well, I . . ." Barnabas started.

"No, let it lie," Hiram said. "But don't tell your brother what I told ya. He's still got a reckonin' comin' for defying me."

Barnabas nodded his head and grinned. *You're in for a hot time little brother*, he thought.

A Home in the Mist: On Thin Ice

"Let's turn in," Hiram said as he turned back to the wagons.

During the early morning hours, the rain intensified. Heavy drops of frigid water pelted the stretched canvas wagon covers driving the occupants deep into their scattered supplies trying to stave off the damp, creeping chill. No one witnessed the eerie light show that flashed glowing spider webs across the tempestuous skies, but they all felt the rumbling and crackling thunder as it vibrated the floorboards and jostled the glazed crocks of preserves and pickled vegetables. Hannah cried, frightened by the noise, as did Caleb's infant son, and Barnabas's toddler and baby. Finally, as the dark horizon softened with the coming of false dawn, the clouds began to disperse, and the storm slowly rolled away. Nature settled. The caravan drifted into a tenuous peace.

Morning broke cool, damp, and clear. Hiram and Barnabas were the first to arise. Climbing down from their wagons the two men nodded to each other, neither anxious to spoil the stillness of a new day. The first order of business was to check on the animals and build a fire. By working together, they turned over a fallen log giving them access to a supply of usable dry wood. As Barnabas chopped and stripped the fibrous fuel, he pitched it to his father who was soon standing over a crackling fire. Light grey smoke rose ten feet or more above the flames before slowly drifting away on a light breeze, creating a long dirty stream of smog through the dripping branches of the trees.

The sudden clamor of several agitated swallow-tailed kites drew their attention. Emitting a shrill, high-pitched whistle, they rose from their nesting trees and began frantically circling as if creating a barrier around their home grove.

"Over there," Hiram said as he pointed at a large bird skirting the river's edge at about tree level.

Walking to the riverbank, they saw a dark brown hawk with a white, speckled underbelly.

"Osprey," said Hiram.

As they watched, the large osprey seemed to pause in mid-flight before swiftly diving feet first, with splayed talons, into the chilly water. Moments later he popped up and flapping his mighty wings rose into the air with a freshwater drum clasped firmly in his grasp.

"Them things are known to snatch chicks outta their nests too," said Hiram. "Reckon that's what riled the kites."

In the distance, tucked into the base of a towering cliff on the Illinois side of the river, they could just make out the entrance to the infamous Cave-In-Rock cave. For decades river pirates and highwaymen had used the cave to lure unsuspecting travelers to their doom with the pretense of a wilderness trading post. They would hail passing barges, rafts, and keelboats with the offer of supplies and refreshments. When unfortunate wayfarers drew near, the outlaws quickly overwhelmed and robbed them. After disposing of the crew and stripping the vessel of all its valuables, they floated it a good distance downstream and sank it into the river's depths.

Though Hiram and Barnabas both recognized the landmark, they kept their thoughts to themselves. Many folks felt the river pirates still existed in the form of the Ford's Ferry and Pott's Tavern gangs.

Clattering pans and arguing kids drew their attention back to the wagons. The women were busy getting breakfast started over an ample pile of glowing coals and flickering flames.

Colton, Hiram's ten-year-old boy, stood off to the side by himself engrossed in the antics of the kites as they whistled back and forth high in the trees. He hadn't spoken a word since being lost in the woods alone for nearly a week when he was three years old. A neighbor boy who had witnessed his disappearance said a hairy man had picked Cole up and ran off with him. No one ever quite figured that one out, but it was assumed a bear had got him. Figured it had lost its young and wanted something to nurture. Whatever it was, Colton survived out there for a week with temperatures falling into the thirties at night. Then one day, he just walked up to a farmhouse some eight miles from home, unharmed, but mute. Soon after that, he became the brunt of every dirty trick his thirteen-year-old twin brothers could think of to play on him. As far as they were concerned, if he couldn't tell on 'em, he was fair game.

"I did to!"

"Did not!"

"Did so!"

Jonathan and Jaden came piling out of Caleb's wagon where they had slept, arguing as usual. Being twins, they were seldom far apart and yet seemed to be in a constant state of battle. Watching them, a person couldn't be faulted for thinking they were the worst of enemies, but just try pulling one of them off the other and punishing him. As Avery had learned; you'd soon have two out of control, red-headed wildcats attackin' ya screamin', "Don't you hit my brother!" as they hit, kicked, and bit the poor soul who had tried to stop the fight.

It was a losing proposition.

"You boys shut up!" yelled their mother as she vigorously rubbed her upper arms trying to warm up. "And every one of you, get over to that stream and clean up for breakfast."

A Home in the Mist: On Thin Ice

Near to camp was a fair-sized pond with several dead trees protruding from its murky waters. A rain swollen spillway flowed from its east end where it made its way across the clearing and washed over the muddy road before dumping a brown sludge into the Ohio River.

Not really knowing how he was gonna get clean in muddy water, Colton was nevertheless going to obediently try.

As Hiram and Barnabas strolled back toward the wagons, Caleb appeared out the bushes from where he'd walked off into the woods. Not looking up as he tried in vain to reconnect a damaged suspender clasp, he nearly ran into his dad.

"Come with me boy," Hiram grumbled.

Caleb's head snapped up as he came to a sudden stop. He first looked at the retreating back of his father, then at Barnabas. *What?,* he motioned to his brother.

Barnabas simply smirked, then shook his head and walked away.

Caleb's Adam's apple bobbed as he swallowed. He then hurried to catch up to his pa.

Hiram walked to his wagon and loosening a tiedown, threw back a section of tarp. Reaching inside, he rummaged around and pulled out a heavy bladed butcher knife which he tucked into his belt. He then grabbed the silver encrusted bridle and threw it over his shoulder.

"Grab the saddle and follow me," he said as he headed for the log from which he and Barnabas had earlier cut firewood.

"I'm mighty sorry 'bout not gettin' rid of this stuff, Pa," Caleb began, "but Yul Bayler said he knew a fella that was comin' by next week who'd pay right nice for it. I only needed . . ."

"Shush," said Hiram. "I oughta bullwhip ya for disobeying me. Not just about keepin' the saddle but for bein' boneheaded enough to tell Bayler ya did."

Arriving at the log, Hiram slapped the bridle down on it and motioned Caleb to do the same with the saddle.

"Now, I want you to use this knife," he said handing the butcher knife to Caleb, "and strip every bit of the silver off."

Caleb was stunned! "It'll ruin it," he whined.

"It just might keep the lot of us from bein' hung," Hiram spat.

As he talked, he noticed the twins across the way sneaking up behind Cole where he was stooped down vigorously trying to wash his hands in muddy water. They stretched their arms high over their heads, holding large rocks in their hands and with big smiles on their faces slammed them down hard in the mud on each side of their little brother.

Splat!

Hiram shook his head as the twins ran off laughing. Colton just stood there, clumps of mud and filthy water dripping from his face and arms.

Caleb, still staring at the most beautiful saddle he'd had ever seen was nearly crying.

"But, Pa," he said.

"Do it," ordered Hiram, "and when you're done, use that bridle to tie a big rock inside the saddle. I want you to sink the whole thing in the deepest part of that pond. And don't forget to bring me the silver."

"But the saddle alone, even without the silver is worth a fortune," gasped Caleb.

"With all that fancy leather work, it ain't worth nothin' but a horsehair rope if them vigilantes catch up with us. Why, that thing could be identified from here to King William's court. Now, do what I say and be sure you use a big enough stone. I don't want that thing ever comin' up."

Hiram disgustedly walked away.

One too dumb to talk, and one too dumb to listen to, he thought.

Leaving Caleb to work on the saddle, Hiram walked over to get his breakfast. As Pearle stood up with his plate, she noticed Colton standing there facing the pond with his arms stretched out and flapping like a bird.

"What's that boy doing?" she asked.

Hiram glanced over. "Does anybody ever know what that boy is doing?" He gave a slight shake of his head as several small globules plopped into the water at the boy's feet

Taking his plate, he asked, "Where was that your brother moved his family too?"

"Well, let me see," Pearle said as she walked over to the wagon and retrieved a small wooden box. Pulling a letter from it she struggled to sound out the words.

"Says Ca . . . Cad . . . Cades. Cades Cove. That's in Tennessee."

Hiram nodded. "Yeah," he said, scratching the three days growth of stubble on his chin. "Gotta go somewhere. May as well go where family is."

A sudden splash interrupted his reverie. It was Caleb looking like he was about to throw-up as the saddle sank into the dark pond-muck.

Hiram grinned at the boy's misery.

What he didn't know was that Caleb had a secret. One he treasured much higher than a silver trimmed saddle. One he was keeping all for himself. It was safely tucked away in the bottom of his saddle bag.

FOUR

Chicken Watcher

IT WAS A FINE EARLY summer's morning. My chores were done, breakfast was ate, and the sun was shining. I stood on the front porch surveying Pa's property and wondering where my dog, Baby, had got off to.

"Here girl!" I hollered and gave a whistle. I stood there for a bit. *Where could that dog be*?

Then, looking down the porch, past Ma's fancy furniture, I saw Baby's dirty snout come peekin' 'round the corner of the cabin. Her ears were droopin', her head was cocked to one side, and she was staring at me with some serious puppy eyes. Some folks might say I was seein' fairies 'stead of butterflies, but I reckoned she had a mighty guilty look on her face.

"What've you been up to, girl?" I asked.

She didn't answer.

"Oh well," I said as she stood there starin', "whatever you been doin', I reckon I'll hear about it soon enough."

Stooping down, I held out a piece of bacon.

"Got somethin' for ya."

Now that got her attention in a hurry. She came a bouncin' down that porch with her ears floppin' and her tail waggin' so vigorously it nearly threw her off balance as she ran. That dog sure loved bacon.

As she nipped, gulped, slurped, and threw her head back, as if to let the morsel slide down her gullet a bit quicker, I slipped a leash onto her collar. I don't reckon she minded the leash a bit as she kept jumpin', lickin' my hand, and lookin' to see if I had another piece of bacon for her.

"Got another surprise for ya," I said. "One you ain't gonna be so thrilled about."

She wasn't listenin' to a word I said. She just kept jumpin', yappin', and lickin' her chops.

"But like it or not," I pronounced as I stood up straight and pointed one finger at the sky, "by royal decree, from Ma herself; YOU STINK!"

I led her off the porch and down to a shallow pool in the stream. A pretty little spot we often soaked in on hot summer days.

"There ya go, girl," I said as I sat on a flat rock

with my feet in the water and tugged on the leash. "Get on in there and wash some of that stench off ya."

She paused for just a second, looking at the strip of mud along the edge of the waterline. Makin' sure there weren't any of those vicious crawdaddies, I imagine. When she didn't see any, she leapt right in. She always did enjoyed playing in water.

That's when I pulled the dreaded bar of lye soap outta my pocket.

Baby stopped splashin' and stood there, belly deep, lookin' at me and that bar of soap in my hand. She cocked her head, uncertainly. Her eyes kept drifting back and forth between my face and the soap. Hesitantly, she stepped forward and sniffed. Then she stepped back and looked up at me again.

"Sorry girl," I said, "but you're gettin' too ripe."

I dipped the soap in the water and sloshed it around a bit, then pulled it out and rubbed it into a good lather.

Baby just stood watching.

Then, getting a good grip on her collar, I pulled her up close and quickly swabbed a big ol' streak of suds from her flank to her tail.

There was a slight pause before that lye got to soakin' down through her coat and comin' into contact with her skin. I'm tellin' ya, that dog like to come unglued. She didn't like that soap one bit. She

48

went to hoppin', and yelpin', and tuggin', and pullin' so hard, she like to yanked me into the pool with her. I grabbed her and held on tight as I continued scrubbin' in that lye. She whined, yelped, thrashed, and carried on like I was skinnin' her alive.

Then she did something I'd never heard her do before. She bawled. Now don't get me wrong, she'd howled before. In fact, some nights it was downright intolerable the way she howled for hours on end. But this was more than a howl. It was an age-old, soul searchin', deep-throated, long-drawn-out, mournful yodel like I ain't never heard before. I reckon it would have done ol' Orion, the hunter himself, proud. And, as soon as it stopped, here came another one.

Ma came rushin' out of the house to see what was goin' on. Charlotte appeared at the breezeway door of the barn with a concerned look on her face. I saw chickens scatter, ducks take flight, and Aristotle threw back his head and whinnied before trottin' off to the back pasture. His mane was blowin' in the wind, and he had his tail held high as he raced to escape the maddening discord. And then, the oddest thing of all. I saw Baby lookin' around with her big brown eyes as if even she was tryin' to figure out where all the noise was coming from.

I couldn't help but laugh.

By then, I was so wet I went ahead and slipped down into the pool myself. I was soon suds up, and me and Baby took a bath together. Even did some laundry, seein's how I still had my clothes on.

Now, I ain't sayin' Baby came to likin' that bath none, but I guess as how I was in there with her, she come to toleratin' it. She just stood there with big sad eyes and her tail tucked between her legs as I quite vigorously scrubbed us both down.

Course, when I finally threw that bar into the yard and we began jumpin' around and playin' to rinse off, and all of them suds started floatin' away; well, she liked that just fine. It weren't long before all was forgiven, and we climbed from the water friends once again.

It was the day after me and Baby's bath, that Diver hitched up Aristotle and went vistin'. There always seemed to be folks that were ailin', or feelin' low about something, or simply needed a sympathetic ear in a time of uncertainty. I don't reckon there was a man in all them mountains more suited for the job of comfortin' a soul than Diver was. He was a mighty fine listener. But even Diver couldn't satisfy every need all by himself. Sometimes he brought 'em home.

Now, needin' wasn't always a bad thing, and that day turned out to be one of those exceptions.

"I hate to put you gals through all the trouble," Diver said to Ma and Charlotte as we sat around the dinner table, "but I'm afraid I volunteered your services today."

Ma and Charlotte glanced at each other. They'd not realized just how much work their new chicken enterprise was gonna be, much less the oversized garden. But they trusted Diver's impeccable character. If he thought their help was needed, it was needed.

Charlotte reached out to slice a piece of bread as she asked, "Volunteered us for what, dear?"

"Well, it seems the Grears are gonna spit-roast a half a steer, and I volunteered you gals to bake about a dozen pies or so."

"A dozen pies?" gasped Charlotte.

"Or so," said Diver.

Ma sat there a bit stunned. "What do they need a dozen pies for?" she asked. "Or so."

"Well for the gathering, of course," said Diver.

Pa put down his fork and sat back to watch the show. By the vague reply and nonchalant timbre in his voice, Diver was leadin' the gals on, and Pa knew it.

"What gatherin' might that be, dear?" Charlotte asked.

"The gatherin' after the wedding," said Diver. "Who ever heard of a wedding without a gatherin' afterwards?"

I could see an exasperated look startin' to build on Ma's face. I figured she was chewin' the inside of her cheek somethin' fierce tryin' not to butt in. Truth is, I was downright proud of her self-control.

Charlotte pursed her lips for just a moment and took in a soothing breath before saying, "Yes dear, most folks have a gatherin' after a wedding, but..."

I could see Ma was about to explode. If Diver didn't do some explainin' real quick, I didn't reckon her favorite wooden spoon was gonna survive the way she was twisting on it.

Charlotte's voice took on a bit of a lower pitch as she asked, "What . . . wedding . . . dear?"

I noticed the loaf of bread that Charlotte was slicing had begun to look a bit deflated where her fingers were digging into the fresh sourdough.

"Oh," said Diver as he reached over and plucked another slice of ham from the serving plate, "I suppose I should have started with that."

"Yes," Charlotte said, "you probably should have started with that."

Diver winked at me and grinned.

"Well, I wouldn't want you to think I was leading you on or some . . ."

"WHAT, WEDDING?" exploded Ma, accidentally slapping the table with her spoon.

Diver smiled knowing he'd done chucked that horseshoe 'bout as far as he dared to.

"Well, seems Hec Rucker and Charley Wrightman asked me to . . ."

Diver didn't get to finish his sentence before Ma and Charlotte were cheering the news. They immediately started discussing what kind of pies they would bake, how long it would take, how to best transport them to the Grear's ranch and, "Oh, my," what were they going to wear?

Me, Pa, and Diver, all sat back, and belly laughed as we enjoyed the gals' excitement.

"I had a feelin' they were gettin' sweet on each other," Pa said to Diver. "Couldn't hardly mention Charley 'round ol' Hec, that he didn't get a faraway look in his eye, but I didn't know it'd gone this far."

Diver smiled. "Well, they've both been peckin' around the bush with me for quite some time. Tryin' to see what I thought about the other without comin' right out and askin'. I held with, I thought they were both fine folks. And I do. Not to mention there ain't two better craftsman in the Cove."

"I'll attest to that," said Pa.

"Anyway," continued Diver, "I reckon when they finally got the flitters and whatnot outta the way, they figured they ain't spring chicks no more and may as well quit wasting time."

"Well, I'm real happy for 'em," said Pa. "I couldn't imagine a better couple."

The wedding was to take place after services on Sunday with the reception being held at the Grear Ranch afterwards. Mr. Grear sure held Charley in mighty high esteem and was goin' all out to put on a grand extravaganza.

"Everybody's welcome!" he'd declared.

He'd cleaned out his brand-new barn, so that between the main floor and the hayloft; there wasn't a person in the Cove that couldn't be accommodated for the wedding feast and the dance.

Saturday was the day Ma and Charlotte sent their eggs to market at the Beckett's Freight Store. Casey always brought home a wagon of salt on Friday evening and added Ma's goods to it. He and Diver then made the delivery in one load and picked up whatever supplies were needed at the homestead.

"Got a bit o' extra cargo for ya this week," Ma said to Casey. "Got four crates of chicks and pullets."

"That's fine," said Casey. "We got room."

"And pick me up fifty pounds of flour," she said.

It was another fine day as Casey and Diver pulled up outside the Freight Store. It had been a bit dry lately and a warm breeze kicked up a dust devil that dwindled after a hundred feet or so. Things were still fairin' pretty well around the Cove but a day or two of rain wouldn't hurt none.

As Casey set the brake and they clambered down from the hard oak seat, a young boy who'd been sitting on the raised sidewalk in front of the store ambled over and climbed up on the rear wheel of the wagon. He puckered his lips and shook his head as he studied the payload.

Casey and Diver glanced at each other, then back at the boy.

"Got ya some chickens there," he said.

Casey, a bit bewildered said, "Yeah, we got some chickens."

The boy scratched his head as if workin' out a problem.

"If'n you're goin' in the store; I reckon I could watch them chickens fer a piece of hard rock candy."

Casey snickered and said. "Them chickens don't need watchin'."

"Well, now," the kid said as he pointed across the road, "you see them woods yonder."

Casey glanced at the woods. "Yeah. What about 'em," he said.

"Just ain't no tellin' what might be in there eyeballing these chickens." The kid shook his head as if he'd relayed a dire warning that Casey hadn't thought of. "I'd sure hate to see ya take the chance of leavin' 'em out here unprotected."

Diver placed his hand over his mouth and smiled. "You gonna take a chance like that?" he asked Casey.

Still not willing to give into what he was beginnin' to see as a pint-sized extortionist, Casey said, "Tell me this, kid. Say a big ol' hungry, long-toothed coyote came stalkin' outta them woods and headed for my chickens; what would you do?"

"Well," the boy said with a serious look on his face. "I reckon I wouldn't get my hard rock candy. You can't expect me to face down no hungry long-toothed coyote. I'm only four-years-old. What kinda man are you?"

Diver liked to gagged. He was tryin' so hard not to laugh, his innards hurt.

"Yeah," he snickered to Casey. "What kinda man are you?"

Casey was so flustered he didn't know what to say. How had a four-year-old kid, standing on his wagon wheel, make him look like a callous ingrate? He was startin' to think it might be best to just go ahead and pay the price. Shut the kid up before he made him look even worse.

56

"Fine," he conceded, "you watch the chickens and I'll bring you a piece of hard rock candy."

Diver laughed and placed his arm over Casey's shoulder as they turned to go in the store.

"Hey, mister," the kid called.

Diver and Casey both stopped and looked back at the four-year-old.

"I been thinkin'," he said. "That's an awful lot of chickens to be watchin' for just *one* little piece of hard rock candy."

Diver cracked-up as he pulled a sputtering Casey into the store.

"Let it be," he said. "If words were weapons, he'd o' done laid ya low."

He picked up the counter bell and gave it a good jingle.

After a short wait they saw someone glance out of the half-closed door to the stock room and quickly pull away. Whispered voices could be heard as if an animated discussion were taking place. Finally, a fidgety little man wearing a pair of European Pince-Nez glasses clamped firmly to his impressive hawk's beak of a nose, came forward and stood behind the counter.

"Good morning, gentlemen," he said. "What can we do for you today?"

"Where's the other fella that usually works here?" Casey asked.

"Oh, ah, he no longer works here," the man said. "I believe he went over to the freight line. My name is Elias Gruber."

"Okay," said Casey. "That's strange that he didn't mention anything about changing jobs last week."

The man, with his eyes magnified abnormally large by his thick lenses just stood and stared at Casey without offering any further explanation.

"Well, we got a delivery to make," Casey said. "Eggs, chickens and salt. And we'll be needin' to pick up supplies."

"Ahem," Elias cleared his throat. He pulled a ledger from under the counter and placed it in a wooden bookstand. Opening it, he made a show of studying a row of figures.

"Well now," he said, "we can take all the salt you can deliver. And of course, we'll sell you any supplies you may need. But eggs and chickens? I'm afraid we've got all we can manage."

"Got all you can manage?" stammered Casey. "Jud always buys our eggs! Every Saturday."

Elias jumped a bit and had to straighten his glasses. A door in the stock room slammed shut and they heard receding footfalls rush down a long aisle in the warehouse out back.

"I'm sorry gentlemen," Elias said in a weak voice. "Preacher?" he reddened quite a bit in the jowls and the back of his neck. "Jud doesn't own the Freight Store any longer. Just the Freight Line. His boy Trace bought him out. He's the one who said we no longer need eggs or chickens."

Casey and Diver immediately understood. This entire ploy was about a vendetta Trace had against Forrest.

"And what are we supposed to do with all these eggs?" Casey shouted.

Diver laid a hand on Casey's shoulder. "It's not Mr. Gruber's fault," he said.

"And like I said," Elias muttered as he swabbed a rag over his balding head and the back of his neck, "we *will* take all the salt you can deliver."

Casey stared the man in the face.

"Reckon not," he said.

"Now, wait a minute," Elias stammered, "I happen to know that we've got a standing order to deliver that salt to our two largest customers." He looked like a man on the verge of a stroke. "We can't break that contract. Oh my, no. That wouldn't be good. Not good at all."

His oversized eyes blinked behind his glasses as he stood there in a near panic.

"I'm sure we can work something out gentlemen."

"So, you can take the eggs and chickens after all," stated Casey.

The man winced and stepped back as if Casey had physically struck him.

"I can't," he whined. Wiping the sodden rag across his quivering lips, he said, "I would if I could, but I just can't."

"Imagine that" Casey said before turning and walking out.

"We need that salt, preacher," Elias pleaded with Diver as he took off his glasses and smeared them, rather than cleaning them, on his rag. "Oh my, oh my," he fretted.

"Well now, I'm really sorry, Mr. Gruber," Diver said, "but I don't own that salt. The man you need to talk to just walked out that door."

Diver pulled a list from his pocket along with what money he had. Doing a bit of calculating, he scratched several items off the list and handed the slip of paper to Elias.

"I'll take what's there," he said. "Oh, and Mr. Gruber, add a bag of hard rock candy.

≈

When Diver came out of the store carrying a large wooden box of supplies, Casey was sitting stern-faced

60

on the driver's seat of the wagon looking straight ahead. His jaws were clinched so tight Diver could distinctly see the muscles quivering.

A young lady wearing a thread-bare gingham dress and a smudge of something on her right cheek was leaving a thin cloud of dust behind her as she hurried down the street kicking her hem as she came.

Diver placed the box in the wagon and pulled the bag of hard rock candy out of it.

"Where have you been?" the young lady huffed as she rushed up to the little boy who had offered to watch the chickens. She went down on her knees and grabbed the boy by his upper arms. "You like to've scared me half to death."

Diver stepped around the back of the wagon and walked over to them.

"Sorry if he ran off on ya ma'am," he said. "I reckon it was partially our fault."

She looked up at Diver, eyeing him through her disheveled dirty blond hair.

"He was watchin' chickens for us," Diver said.

The boy smiled as the girl stared at Diver with a blank look on her face. She pulled the boy close and hugged him with one arm. "He's only four," she said.

"So, he told us," chuckled Diver.

The girl's brow furrowed.

"Oh, I'm sorry," said Diver as he held out a hand. "I guess I should have introduced myself. My name is Homer McCoy, but folks 'round here call me Diver. I'm the preacher over at the Baptist church."

The girl's face showed obvious relief as she stood up and raised a hand to shield the sun from her eyes. She ignored a stray strand of hair that played about her face.

"Preacher man ya say?"

Diver lowered his hand and continued. "Yes. At the Baptist church. And this young man," he said, winking at the boy, "offered to watch our chickens for us so no hungry coyotes would get 'em. Only charged us a bag of hard rock candy."

The girl looked down at the boy and tapped him on the back of the head saying, "You didn't?"

The boy looked up and smiled, nodding his head.

"Looks like he did a good job too," Diver said. "Nary a chicken missing. Reckon he earned these."

Diver handed the bag to the young lady.

She smiled as she took it. "I'm thankin' ya, preacher," she said. "It's been a spell since Hiram Jr. and his siblings had any sugar snacks. I'm sure *they'll* enjoy 'em."

Diver couldn't help but notice the emphasis on "they." The boy shoved his hands into his pockets and grimaced.

"By the way, my name is Avery Haggen," she said, finally offering her hand, "and this little monster is my brother, Hiram-J." She tousled the boy's long hair as he wrinkled his nose and pulled away.

"Pleased to meet you, Avery," Diver said. "I ain't never seen ya'll 'round the Cove before."

"No, we just pulled in last night," said Avery. "Campin' over yonder past the mule yard. My ma's folks is supposed to live here 'bouts, but we don't know where."

"What's their name," asked Diver. "Maybe I can help you."

"Wheeler," said Avery. "Buck and Eunice Wheeler."

Diver remembered Pa telling him about getting bad milk from some Wheelers when little Wes died. They could be the same family.

"Don't know 'em myself," said Diver, "but I know someone who might. Tell ya what, why don't y'all come by the church on Sunday? We're havin' a wedding afterwards, then we'll all go to the reception over at the Grear Ranch. Gonna be some big doin's with a ton of fixin's. I'll introduce ya to a man who knows everybody for twenty miles 'round."

"I don't know," said Avery. "We got a heap of kin."

"The more, the merrier," said Diver. "Mr. Grear said everyone is welcome."

"Well, I'll tell Pa. We gotta get now. Thanks for the candy. The kids'll love it."

"Hope to see ya on Sunday," Diver said as Avery and Hiram-J. turned and headed back up the street.

Diver climbed up next to Casey on the wagon seat.

"Well, now what are we gonna do?" said Casey. "You know Trace is just doing this out of spite."

Diver reached over and placed his hand on Casey's shoulder. "Have faith," he said. "I reckon God's got a plan. Until then, I figure we're gonna be eatin' a lot of eggs. And if I know your ma and Charlotte, Hec and Charlie's reception's gonna have a heap o' cakes to go along with them dozen pies; or so."

Casey looked over at Diver and shook his head. "Already comin' up with positives for havin' too many eggs," he said.

Diver smiled. "Let's go home."

FIVE

Wedding

SUNDAY MORNING DAWNED with a beautiful display of orange-yellow hues in the eastern sky that heralded the coming of a perfect day in the Cove. A light but steady overnight shower had moistened the dry earth settling the dust and pollens. Only the refreshing fragrance of pine boughs and wildflowers wafted across the landscape on a gentle breeze that was crisp and clean.

As each of the congregants showed up at the Baptist church that morning, they couldn't help but admire the beautiful carriage parked out front.

It was a highly polished, four wheeled, one-horse carriage, made of white oak with maple wood trim. It carried a folding bellows top supported by hickory hoops, a double clasped trunk, and an ornate rein rail made of glistening bronze topped the dashboard. It had an over-stuffed seat for two with a lazyback, all made from deerskin tanned to pure white and worked soft as silk. The bellows top was elk hide smoked to a light tan, and the entire carriage rested on a heavy buffalo-strap suspension system. The fittings, carriage steps, and coach lights glistened with highly polished, hammered brass.

Standing before the vehicle was perhaps the finest mule the Cove had ever seen. (Omitting Orwell's Mammoth Jack of course.) A full sixteen hands high with a faultless midnight black coat, straight ears, and clear, long lashed eyes. The creature stood tall and proud in its well-oiled, brand-new harness, as if it understood its part in the coming festivities.

"Would ya look at that," Pa said as he bypassed the fine rig to pat the magnificent jack on its neck. "Ain't you a beauty?"

He looked the critter in the eyes as he went to pokin' through his pockets tryin' to find a piece of carrot or maybe a crab apple to feed it.

Ma shook her head knowin' if it weren't for her tending to his Sunday meetin' clothes, there's no tellin' what he might find in them.

Bein' a died-in-the-wool mule man, Pa fawned over that animal something fierce. And I could tell by the way its withers twitched as it lowered its head into Pa's chest, it felt the same way about him.

"Hec built that carriage from the ground up just for this occasion," Diver said as he climbed down from his own buggy and came over next to Pa. "Told me he'd been workin' on it for an entire year. Kept it under wraps the whole time wanting to get it done before he proposed to Charley." He ran his fingers along the slick varnished wood. "Said that's what he needed the buffalo and elk hides so badly for."

"I wish he'd told me," said Pa. "I'd o' hurried it up a bit."

"Oh, I reckon he had plenty to do," said Diver.

"A whole year?" mused Pa. "What would he have done if she'd said no?"

"I asked him that myself," snickered Diver. "He just stood there for a while with a blank look on his face, then said, "'Ya know, that just never occurred to me. I's so busy on the buildin', I reckon I forgot about the askin'.'"

Pa grinned. "Put off the hard part as long as possible is what he done."

The service that morning was about the sanctity of marriage and how it was a life-long covenant, not only between one another, but with God himself. A uniting of two to become one. A never-ending commitment that when renewed with a word of love every day will never wane but last throughout all time.

Following the service, Diver welcomed everyone to remain for the joining together of Charlotte Evalina Wrightman, affectionately known as Charley, with Hector Benjamin Rucker.

It was a fine ceremony. Hec was decked out in his very best Sunday clothes: a pair of full length dark blue trousers with the fly-front closure, a light-brown brocade waistcoat with a black velvet shawl collar over a light blue linen shirt, and a fashionable black cravat. He also wore a pair of clean, high-top, leather boots. I don't suppose he owned a stylish overcoat and hat since he chose to get married in shirt sleeves and bare headed.

He was followed down the aisle by his best man, Rolf Schmitt.

Shaking hands with Diver, but ignoring the gathered well-wishers as was common, he waited on his bride.

When Charlotte entered a gasp rose from those gathered. She glided down the aisle in a lilac-blue, full-length cotton print dress striped in a pink and white floral pattern. It had eggshell lace trim which rested on her shoulders and hung in delicate loops down her bellowing gigot sleeves. A black, six-inch, midriff belt gave the impression of a trim waistline over the conical double pleated skirt. A scattering of small pink and white silk bows seemed to shimmer as she walked.

Her fawn-color hair was worn in long wavy curls and was interlaced with fresh, sweet-smelling, white and pink mountain laurel flowers. A single strand of pearls hung arched above her brow line.

No one in the Cove, including Hec himself, had ever seen Charley in anything other than her work-clothes. Now, standing before them, it was hard to decide if she looked more like a Grecian goddess or an Amazon queen.

Sarah May and Miss Shelley, who had made the garments and dressed Charley, were thrilled when they saw Rolf suddenly grasp Hec under the arms as the man's legs began to buckle. Miss Shelley, as maid of honor, was beamin' 'bout as bright as Charley, if that was possible.

It didn't take no soothsayer to know ol' Hec wasn't disappointed.

The ceremony was short and sweet. The loving vows were recited, and Hec placed a gold band on

Charley's finger. Then the newlywed couple shared a quick peck on the lips that turned 'em both so red I reckon ya could have closed the shutters and still read a hymnal. They then nearly ran down the aisle, once again looking straight ahead and not acknowledging their guests. That was for later.

Rolf stayed behind to pay Diver for his services and thank him for such a fine job o' hitchin'.

"Hitchin' like that is gonna stay hitched," he said.

All in all, it was some pretty fine nuptials.

As we left the church, we stopped by the fancy carriage that Hec had just presented to Charley as a wedding gift and congratulated the groom. A group of women were making a fuss over Charley's dress and new hairstyle, but no one congratulated *her* on the wedding. That would have been like implying she was fortunate to find a man who would have her.

As the crowd thinned and headed to the Grear's Ranch for the reception, half a dozen young, single men of the Cove surrounded Hec and Charley's carriage. They reared their horses and spun them in circles, all the while shoutin', cheerin', and givin' 'em the loudest and rowdiest escort within their power. Of course, their shenanigans embarrassed Charley something fierce. She never had been comfortable bein' the center of attention. As for Hec, he just laughed, waved, and let the boys have their fun.

"I hope this is the end of it," said Ma as she watched the foolishness. "You don't think they're plannin' a shivaree, do ya?"

Pa laughed. "Seein's how Hec can throw any two men in the mountains, and some folks figure Charley could throw Hec, I don't think that's gonna be a concern. It'd take an awful brave man, or an awful foolish one, to interfere in that couple's wedding night."

Ma giggled and slapped Pa's shoulder. "That's a terrible thing to say about Charley." Then, as she thought about it, she cupped her hands over a big grin and laughed, "But I gotta say, they just might be right."

Arriving at Mr. Grear's new barn was comparable to attending one of Orwell Beckett's Independence Day celebrations. There was a half a steer roasting over a massive wrought iron spit and a whole pig with a dried apple in his mouth resting on a bed of ramps on a platter.

In the lower level of the barn sat four long tables loaded down with a wide variety of raw and cooked vegetables, three kinds of bread, sassafras tea, dark ale, strawberry wine, fresh cool milk and buttermilk.

A dessert table boasted pies to suit every taste, as well as; cakes, cookies, and cups of extra-large juicy strawberries topped with thick whipped cream.

Scattered throughout and around the barn were numerous tables, haybales, sitting stumps, and chairs. And if more seating was needed, there was always the long sturdy corral fence that the young men could sit on.

The hayloft had been cleared and swept clean, and a staircase had been built for easy access to the barn dance. The room was massive and would accommodate the band, caller, dancers, and spectators.

Of course, Mr. Grear wouldn't settle for anyone less than Cat Eye McGarity from over in Tuckaleechee Cove to do the calling. He could shuffle a square throughout the floor and return every dancer back to their original partner by the end of every tip without fail.

Mighty fine callin' if you ask me.

It wasn't long before Hec and Charley were seated in the place of honor with horseshoes, wishbones, and all sorts of lucky symbols hangin' above their heads.

Truth be told, it made me a bit nervous. I figured the luckiest part of that custom was that none of the twine holdin' up them horseshoes broke. Talk about a hard knocks way o' startin' your life together.

"Fine lookin' couple," said Pa as he and Diver stood drinking sassafras tea together.

"Yes, sir, it truly is," replied Diver.

They just stood there for a while, enjoyin' the crowd. There was folks there that seldom ever came in from the backwoods, mingling around with regular town's folk and everybody was having a grand ol' time.

Directly, Pa motioned with his chin toward a large group of people gathered 'round a few overloaded and very dirty farm wagons.

"Can't say I recognize them," he said.

There were a couple of fellas balancing heaping plates of food on the sideboards of a wagon as they talked, all the while keeping an eye on the crowd. By the looks of 'em, Pa took the whiskered older one to be a dirt farmer and the other to be his son. They were surrounded by several folks in various forms of repose on a big patch of green grass. Some sat cross legged, one knee hugged, and others were laying back on one or both elbows. Two were even leaning back against the filthy spokes of a wagon as if it were a living room chair.

The one thing they all had in common was, they were making short work of the weddin' fixin's.

As the adults in the group talked and ate, a half a dozen or so kids were left free to do whatever they wanted. Pa watched as they ran wild; shouting and hitting, stealing food and throwing it at each other, bumping into wedding guests without apologizing and being a general nuisance to anyone unfortunate enough to be sitting nearby.

There was one infant endlessly wailing, another somehow sleeping, and still another slightly older child blaring out a high-pitched screech that like to set Pa's teeth on edge. How in the world its mother could just sit there carrying on a conversation with the little polecat yankin' and a pawin' at her hair was hard to understand and worse to behold.

Then there was one young boy sittin' quietly by himself atop a nearby fence. He was kinda hunched over his plate as he picked at his food and seemed to be ignoring the chaos around him.

"Reckon that's the Haggen bunch," said Diver. "Me and Casey met that gal with the sandy hair over yonder, along with her little brother, Hiram, Jr."

Looking around he spotted him. "There he is over there, that one sneakin' up behind the kid on the fence."

They watched as the youngster stealthily crept up behind the fence sitter. Stopping, he placed one hand over his mouth as if stifling a giggle, then, from only six or seven feet away, he rushed in and pushed as hard as he could.

The fence sitter didn't have a chance. Throwing his arms out and kicking back with one leg that unfortunately stabbed between two fence rails, he was propelled forwards. Frantically grabbing for support, his body arched through the air and followed his plate of scattering food to the ground.

He landed hard.

Several of the adults looked on without response. The whiskered man by the wagon smeared grease from his lips with the back of his hand as he chewed on a thick piece of beef. He gave a smirk and shook his head at the shenanigans, then turned his back and looked the other way.

The perpetrator laughed as he ran off.

Seconds passed as the downed kid laid in the mess. He then rose and held both hands out away from his body as he stared at his food-stained clothing. His face was flushed as he wiped cornmill gravy from his cheek with a sleeve, but he didn't say a word. He just stood there, slowly plucking and brushing scraps of food from his shirt.

Diver started to go to the kid.

"Hold on," Pa said as he laid a hand on Diver's shoulder. "Some folks don't take kindly to an outsider butting into family affairs."

Finally, the girl Diver remembered was called Avery, got up and went to the boy. As she helped brush him off, she whispered something in his ear. He nodded but didn't say anything. He then hung his head and walked over to sit by a maple tree where he scratched at the stains in vain with a chipped and dirty fingernail.

"That boy didn't even acknowledge the one that pushed him," said Pa.

"Yeah, I noticed that," said Diver. "Kind o' like he's been trail broke so hard he ain't got no fight left in 'em."

"It's a shame is what it is," said Pa. "A youngster like that?" He shook his head. "A plumb shame."

Avery picked up the dirty plate and placed it in a washtub sitting near the barn. As she headed back to her seat, she noticed Diver standing next to Pa.

"Hello, preacher," she called as she headed his way. "I brung my family like ya told me. I hope it's okay."

The pushing incident had already been forgotten.

"Yes, just fine," Diver said, shaking her hand. "I want you to meet Zeb Banion," he indicated Pa. "He's the man I was telling you about."

It hadn't escaped Diver's notice how the Haggens had managed to bypass the church without stopping in on their way to the Grear's place, but he didn't mention it.

Avery looked up at Pa and nodded.

"The Haggens just arrived at the Cove the other day," Diver said. "They're camped over the other side of Jud's mule yard. Seems they got kinfolk here 'bouts, but don't know where. Couple called Buck and Eunice Wheeler. I told her if anybody would know how to find 'em, you would."

"Howdy, young lady," Pa said as he reached out his big hand. "Yeah, I know Buck and Eunice. When they first moved to the area, I was their nearest neighbor. Still am, I reckon, though you can't get no wagons back in there from my place. Them hollers is way too steep."

Pa thought about it for a moment or two.

"I reckon if you're wantin' to get up into that back country, you'll have to head out Parson's Branch. I guess it's about four miles or so, you'll come across a low stretch where the creek overflows the road. Just this side of that flat, there's an over-grown two-track that follows Gregory Ridge into the brush. It's rough goin' back in there, but it'll eventually get ya to their place. When ya get up on Craggy Top, if the mist is lifted, you'll be able to see a clearing off in the distance called The Sloping Field. That'll tell ya you're 'bout halfway."

"Well, I sure thank ya, Mr. Banion," the girl said with a look of embarrassment on her face, "but I never was so good with directions. Would it be too much trouble to explain all that to my dad?"

"Not at all," said Pa. "Lead the way."

Just as Pa and Diver started to fall in behind Avery, they heard a call.

"Preacher . . . Diver, can I have a moment?"

Looking back, they saw Orwell Beckett holding a drinking glass far out in front of him, trying hard not to slosh the liquid onto his cotton twill trousers as he ambled across the field.

"Sure," called Diver as he turned towards Orwell. "I'll catch up with you later," he told Pa.

As Pa went to talk with Mr. Haggen, Diver and Orwell slowly strolled among the magnolia trees near Grear's fishpond. Pa had no idea what their conversation was about, but seein's how it didn't involve him, he paid little attention to it; even when Casey and Rolf showed up and joined in. Nor did he notice how Casey seemed to stay back in the shadows of the trees keeping an eye on him and the Haggen's as he talked with Orwell.

As the feasting ebbed and folks began milling around, greeting seldom seen friends and acquaintances, a soft cacophony of plucks and squawks could be heard from the hayloft above. The musicians were tuning up and the dance would soon begin.

Hurryin' up the steps, I found myself a good spot near the open hay door from which to see the fun. Two fiddlers, a banjo picker, a hammered dulcimer player, and Mr. Wo with a ten-inch bamboo Jew's harp sat on hay bales placed on either side of a four-foot-square raised platform.

As folks stomped up the staircase and spread out along the pine board walls of the loft, Cat Eye McGarity stepped up on the stage and stood massaging his massive belly.

"Welcome all," he bellowed. "That was a fine mess o' vittles, weren't it?"

Everyone cheered.

"Why, just this mornin' I noticed I was gettin' so puny and fragile I nearly had to reach behind my back to button my shirt up. Look at me now."

Everyone laughed as Cat Eye turned sideways and held his fringed leather jacket open to show off his bulbous breadbasket. It had once been said that if Cat Eye ever set his mind to eatin' a whole hog by himself, there wouldn't be nothin' left but a memory.

"Now we're gonna get started with a reel, then form a square, and end out the day with a good ol' free steppin' round. What do ya say?"

Everyone cheered.

"Okay fellas, grab yer partners and form two lines."

When the lines were formed, guys on one side and gals on the other, Cat Eye explained what the figures would be. The head couple would start out with a come together and a bow, back to place, and then a dosido. A full eight figures followed while everyone else clapped and cheered. The head couple would then peel off behind their own lines, followed by the entire troupe, before forming a bridge for the others to go under. They then shuffled to the front, reforming the line with the second couple as the head.

The entire reel repeated and continued until every team had a turn as the head.

It was a great time for all, with the hoppin' and skippin', cheerin' and clappin', and the loud foot-stompin' music that couldn't help but thrill a crowd.

At some point during the reel, a pretty, young gal, with long wavy black hair and a sparkling smile, squeezed in next to me. She clapped and cheered the dancers on, and occasionally, accidentally rubbed her shoulder up against my arm.

At first, I didn't take notice, but after about the third 'accident', I don't reckon my focus was so much on the dance anymore. She then somehow went to side-steppin' with the music and tripped.

"Oh!" she gasped, as she grabbed my arm to keep from falling.

"Are you okay?" I asked as I helped her regain her feet.

"Yes, yes," she said. "I'm so sorry . . . and so embarrassed." She raised her fingers to her lower lip as she smiled. Her nose gave a small twitch, and I couldn't help but notice how her eyes twinkled.

"I can be down-right clumsy sometimes," she said. "I guess there must be a warped board or something I tripped on."

I looked down but didn't see a thing wrong with the floor. Brand new wood, just as smooth as it could be. I did notice though, that she hadn't let go of my arm.

Her smile widened to reveal beautiful white teeth and big, shimmering, brown eyes. "My name's Ally," she said.

My breath caught in my throat for just a bit before I croaked, "I'm Billy."

"Well, Billy, I'm plumb proud to meet ya." With that, she held my arm even tighter as she turned to watch the dancers.

I'm not real sure where the rest of the afternoon went after that. At least, not until they were forming the round dance. That's when Ally took me by the hand and said, "Come on, Billy. Dance with me."

Well now, I hadn't ever danced in public before. Fact is, other than Ma, there wasn't a person in the Cove that knew I *could* dance.

It was her that showed me how.

Now, Ma'd been a mighty fine dancer when she was young, but Pa just wasn't the type.

Figured it just didn't make a whole lot of sense to put that much effort into not goin' anywhere.

So, when Pa was off on his long-hunts, Ma taught me to dance. We'd push the furniture to the side and go to steppin' as we hummed to beat the band. I sure come to enjoyin' those cold winter days when Pa was out chasin' furbearers. And it weren't long before Ma said she'd never danced with a better partner.

Anyway, I didn't put up all that much of a fuss before I let Ally pull me out onto the dance floor. You should o' seen the faces on Pa, Diver, Forrest, and about everyone else in that barn. Not to toot my own horn, but I reckon by the grin on Ma's face, I did her proud. Me and Ally Haggen showed them folks what-for, and they sure enjoyed it.

Unfortunately, it wasn't long before Ally's big sister came over and said it was time to go. Ally tried to argue, but her sister said, "Pa says now!"

Ally stomped her foot, then turned to me and said, "I sure enjoyed our dance, Billy."

The way she got up real close and looked in my eyes, for a second there, I thought she was fixin' to kiss me. Or she figured I'd kiss her.

"Ah," I stammered as my heart was beat so loud, I reckon anybody within ten feet o' me could o' heard it.

Ally glanced around at all the people watching us and I guess decided to show me a little mercy. She settled for a clammy handshake. Then with a well-practiced twinkle in her eye and a most convincing bashful smile, she whispered, "It was quite wonderful. I can't wait till next time."

With that, she turned and brushed by her sister, only looking back for an instant to give me a wink just as she sank out of sight down the staircase.

I gotta say, I felt as shaky as a newborn lamb. My knees were weak, the back of my neck was hot, and I'd somehow developed a row of sweat beads on my upper lip.

Luckily, Ma came to my rescue. Between her and Sarah May trading places dancing with me, we finished off the night. I reckon Charlotte felt in her condition it was better to observe than participate. Her and Diver were both bein' mighty careful after what happened with Dennis.

While the dance was in full swing, and few people were 'round to take notice, Hec and Charley thanked Mr. and Mrs. Grear for everything and quietly rode away. The way I heard it, Charley was driving, and Hec was smiling and waving.

The men in the Cove got a kick out of that.

Hec's brother, Rupert, owned a nice cabin near Sevierville where they planned to spend their honeymoon. It was on secluded property overlooking the Little Pidgeon River.

Two whole weeks, all alone.

And we came to find out that Pa had been right. There wasn't a single person who dared to try a shivaree the entire time they were there.

SIX

Darlin' Lassie

AS SHADOWS LENGTHENED across the Cove and the light began to fade, Cat Eye signaled to the musicians it was time to wrap up the festivities. No lanterns or torches were allowed in the loft to forestall the gathering gloom as Mr. Grear was taking no chances with open flames in his new barn. I can't say as to how a person could fault him for that.

"Reckon that's all we got for now," Cat Eye announced to the throng as the musicians began packing away their instruments.

A few scattered moans and pleads for "one more" could be heard from the crowd.

Cat Eye raised both chubby hands, palms forward, and flashed a well-practiced, pearly-white smile.

"But I wanted y'all to know" he bellowed above the appeals, "Orwell Beckett is adding a hoedown to this year's July Fourth celebrations, and he asked me to call it."

He tucked his thumbs behind his suspender's straps and puffed out his chest.

"So y'all come on out and we'll continue this party. Wee doggies," he said, "we'll have us a grand 'ol time. I guarantee it."

He shook his big belly and grinned. "But as for now," he continued, "momma's home and supper's waitin', and these skinny bones is about to waste away."

As folks began to mill around and head for the staircase, he suddenly shook one finger in the air like a thought had just occurred to him. He said, "But now, if by chance some of you ladies might o' saved me a piece of pie?"

"Oh, you old phony," Mrs. Grear called from across the floor where she stood talkin' to Percy and Edith Blyth, the church caretakers. "You know we saved you a whole pie. Custard, I believe. And a bowl of strawberries and cream too. After all, that's the only way we could talk you into comin' all this way on short notice."

The entire crowd laughed.

Cat Eye's whole belly jiggled as he slapped his thigh at the joke and joined in the merriment.

"Ya can't blame a fella for holdin' out till a pretty filly makes him such a sweet offer now can ya?" he snickered.

The whole room suddenly went silent. Mrs. Grear, taken by complete surprise, covered her mouth with both hands while she reddened something fierce. For a married man to say such a thing to a married woman! She looked around at the hushed crowd.

"Wha . . . wha," she stammered, too shocked to formulate a snappy comeback. A rare and uncomfortable occurrence for the sharp tongued, Mrs. Grear. Finally, out of frustration, she loudly stomped her foot.

With that, everyone broke down in laughter once again and the tension faded.

Mrs. Grear hesitantly lowered her hands, then getting control of herself shouted, "Just go eat your pie Mr. McGarity. When you are done, ask Mr. Grear to loan you a second mule to help pull your buggy home. I'm sure the one you've got is bound to be played out by now, poor thing."

It was a mighty entertaining day, I can tell ya that.

As Casey helped me and Pa load up to head home he said, "Saw ya talkin' to some strangers earlier."

"Yep," said Pa, "kin of the Wheelers." He placed Ma's cake plates in the wagon bed. "Lookin' to settle down Parson's Branch way, I take it."

Casey didn't say anything for a moment, then lookin' over Pa's shoulder said, "Looks like Mr. Grear is headin' this way."

Pa turned as Mr. Grear drew near.

"Been meanin' to talk with ya," he said. He then tipped his hat to Ma. "Kate. Words been spreadin' 'bout how Trace Beckett done y'all." He shook his head and grimaced. "Just ain't right. Anyway, you put me down for three dozen eggs a week. Way I hear it, there's a lot more folks you're gonna be hearin' from too. And as for salt," he looked at Casey. "I need a ton a month. Can ya deliver it?"

"Yes, sir, I surely can," Casey said. "You name the day and it'll be there."

"Good," said Mr. Grear. "Unless I miss my guess, Tudwell's gonna be wantin' about the same. He ain't got but half the stock I do but them dairy cows need twice as much of that stuff."

"Well, I thank ya for true," Casey said. "And you can count on me."

"I know I can," Mr. Grear said in his naturally gruff voice. "Your Zeb's boy ain't ya?"

Grear then noticed one of his cows nibbling at a plate left on a fence post and rushed off to grab it. "Y'all have a good trip home now, ya hear?" he yelled.

We all climbed aboard, and Pa gave a short whistle as he flicked the reins. Diver did the same as he pulled his buggy in behind us. Mac and Cornpone got to stepping as if our old farm wagon was no encumbrance at all. Course, for those two massive beasts, I don't reckon it was.

"That was nice of him," Ma said as we clattered out of Grear's drive and onto Abrams Creek Trail. "The way he talks, we may have plenty of business after all."

"Yeah, and with no middleman to pay either," cut in Casey already workin' out who he'd have doing deliveries and how much more he would make by selling direct to the customers. "Diver said God had a plan. Reckon this must be it. Ya know, we just might be better off without Trace and his Freight Store."

"Well, let's not cut all ties just yet," Pa said. "There's still a heap of supplies we're gonna be needin'."

Casey grinned but sat back and said nothing more.

It was just as Mr. Grear had said. The old Cove Trail had never seen so much traffic. Seemed like folks must o' been under a mighty strain tryin' to think of ways to use eggs so's they could come buy 'em off o' Ma and Charlotte. And those that didn't need eggs needed chicks, or pullets, or even hens gettin' too old for layin', that they could use for roastin'. Ma even had to put back a gross of eggs every week special for the Tudwell's, just to be sure she didn't run out. As for us, we did run out. But that was okay. I like flapjacks.

Got to bein' so much racket from folks comin' and goin' up and down our ol' trail, that Pa finally threw up his hands and headed out to scout new traplines for next season. Said that's the only way he could find enough quiet to hear himself think.

Casey claimed it was the same way over at the salt works. Between mining the rock salt five days a week, winching it to the covered storage shed at the top of the cliff, and delivering it to several farms, ranches, and businesses, they had all work they could handle. Unfortunately, they could not fulfill the complete contract Trace's two largest customers wanted without shorting their neighbors in the Cove.

To his credit, Casey refused to do that.

But they did deliver enough each week to keep the orders coming.

Ma and Charlotte, for their part, were overjoyed. They brought in more money, be it cash, trade, or credit, in that first month than either one had earned in their entire lives.

Thank you, Trace!

Ma even hinted as to how I might ought to be lookin' around for another henhouse site. And who knows, she thought maybe we could start a line of Banion honey too?

It was during this time that three things happened.

First: Hec and Charley came home from their honeymoon with news that Doc Hickman's nephew, Tate Dulaney, had finished his medical apprenticeship. He was looking to leave Sevierville and hang his shingle in the Cove. He and his wife, Hailee, along with their young son, Toby, would be arriving by the end of the month. The Hickman and Dulaney names were highly thought of in the region, but Pa was still a bit concerned about how folks would accept a new doctor after what that quack, Kendree, did.

Second: Diver said Orwell had asked him to make a quick trip up North. Said he wasn't free to go into details at the moment, but he didn't figure to be gone more than two or three days at the most. Pa let the matter lie, but Ma's imagination immediately went to conjuring up all sorts of nefarious scenarios. It finally took Charlotte telling her that all was well and would come out in time to placate her curiosity. Even then, I could tell she wasn't pleased.

And third: On a warm, sunny Wednesday, just as I was finishing up my morning chores, Standing Elk's nephews, Spotted Crow and Sam Tullman came strolling up the Cove Trail.

"Hello, the Banion cabin," Sam called as they entered the yard.

Ma and Charlotte looked up from where they sat on the porch, cleaning leeks, lettuce, dandelion greens, and radishes for that night's salad.

Pa was in the pasture rubbing a honey-based salve he'd made into several nasty cuts on Cornpone's rear leg.

They'd been pullin' a mess of cedar fence posts out of a thick holler along the back property line when ol' Cornpone got a rear hoof tangled in a pile of hawthorn branches. Like to o' skinned his fetlock and pastern something fierce. I can tell ya, that ain't no pleasant ordeal. Them big ol' thorns on them hawthorn trees is some painful.

Course, Pa bein' a mule man and all, knew just what to do to patch ol' Cornpone up. When he was done he laid a gentle hand on Cornpone's rump.

"That oughta take care of ya, old boy," he said. "Reckon ya bought yourself a few days' rest."

He then headed out to see what the cousins were up to.

"Hi, Spotted Crow . . . Sam," I said as we all met in the front yard. "Y'all get Skeeter home okay?"

A Home in the Mist: On Thin Ice

Ma came over and took my upper arm in both her hands the way I'd seen her do with Pa many a time. Seemed once I'd growed taller than her, I'd become more of a man in her eyes. I kinda liked it.

"Don't ya think we should offer our guests some refreshments before we start quizzin' 'em," she asked.

Reckon that's just one of them female things. Even as inquisitive as Ma was, her first thought whenever someone showed up was fillin' their gullets. If it'd been up to me, a starvin' man would o' done perished and blown away before I'd a thought to give him somethin' to eat.

"Would y'all like some coffee and pie?" Ma asked.

Spotted Crow and Sam looked at each other with big smiles on their faces. Seems their last visit had introduced them to their new favorite drink. Coffee. Hot, and with plenty of sugar. Just like Two Hand liked it.

"We would," said Sam.

"With sugar," said Spotted Crow.

Ma laughed. "We have plenty of sugar," she said before leading the way into the dining room. Course now, plenty is a subjective word and Spotted Crow was fixin' to put it to the test.

Me and Pa followed and sat at the table making small talk with the cousins as Charlotte poured the coffee and Ma served the Honey Pecan Pie. Casey was at the salt works and Diver had not yet returned home from his mysterious journey, so we knew Ma and Charlotte would each have someone to fill in on all the gossip. Funny how reheatin' a tatter cake can make it even better than eatin' it fresh.

Spotted Crow jumped right in tryin' to stir ten ounces of sugar into an eight-ounce cup, so Sam Tullman began the tale.

"You'll remember how uncle Skeeter weren't in the best o' shape when we started out for Tellico Plains—where he'd left Aunt Standing Elk."

"Yeah, he was fairin' poorly," said Pa.

"Well, the wagon we hauled him in, it wasn't in the best shape either."

"Sounded like a passel of pigs fightin' over a freshly filled bucket of slop," cut in Spotted Crow. Taking a long slurping slug of hot coffee, provided sound effects for his statement.

"Course it weren't near as bad as Skeeter let on it was," continued Sam. "Why, you'd o' thought we had that thing loaded down with hot coals the way he whined, yelped, and cried the whole way. He acted like every little bump in the trail and squeak of the wheels was put there just to torture him. Must be a white man thing. You'd never hear an Indian carry on that way."

Pa grinned.

"No, it's a Skeeter thing," Ma said. "And that's when he's havin' a good day."

While Ma and Sam shared a laugh at Skeeter's expense, I sat transfixed watching Spotted Crow nursing his coffee cup. He didn't notice the dribble of coffee colored sugar that was slowly making its way down his chin, nor the granular off-white streak plastered on the tip of his nose. He just licked his lips, smiled, and buried his face back in his cup.

I glanced at Pa, who nodded but said nothing.

"Anyway," continued Sam, "Uncle Skeeter put up such a fuss that we had to stop every five miles or so to let him take a break. And river crossings? Why, they were an ordeal like you ain't never seen."

He shook his head and shrugged his shoulders as if the memory alone was physically painful. "I begun to think we were never gonna get there."

"And when we did," cut in Spotted Crow as he looked up from his empty coffee cup, "it turned out Aunt Standing Elk had got so tired of waitin' that she'd done left and went on home by herself. So, we had no choice but to take Uncle Skeeter all the way to Cranmore Cove."

Sam popped the last of his pie into his mouth and washed it down with a swig of coffee. He then placed his empty cup in front of him and sat in silence as if waiting for more.

Charlotte refilled his cup. She then motioned to Spotted Crow who held up one hand for her to hold off a moment.

"So, as you can imagine, what was supposed to be a simple trip to Tellico Plains, turned into a grueling journey of three times the distance," Sam continued.

"With Uncle Skeeter complaining the whole way," Spotted Crow added as he tipped his cup over his open, upturned mouth and shook it. "An Irishman that never shut up," A thick drip hit his lip. "and a squeaky wheel."

The last of the stomach-churning glob of sugar oozed from the cup and plopped onto Spotted Crows extended tongue. His cheeks sucked in as he swirled the concoction around in his mouth before swallowing. His eyes closed for a moment as he smiled. Then, spreading his jaws wide again, he tried for more.

Sam sat watching his cousin give the cup several more small jerks as if trying to displace the last few residual granules of sweetness. Not satisfied, he ran his index finger around the inside of the cup and then pulled it out to lick it off.

A stillness filled the room as we all watched him smack his lips. I can't say I've ever seen a person so obsessed with plain ol' cane sugar.

Suddenly, he became aware of the silence in the room. He looked around. We all sat staring at him. He shrugged his shoulders and grinned. "What?" he said.

No one spoke.

Then wiping a bit of drool from the corner of his mouth, he glanced at the cup still held tight in his hand, gently placed it on the table, and sat back.

"Sorry," he said with a sheepish smile. "It was good."

Looking at his cousin, he said, "Go on with your story."

Sam shifted on his bench. "Anyway," he said, pulling his eyes off his cousin, "as I was saying, one rear wheel on that old wagon was squeaking something fierce before we even started on our journey. We were just hoping it would make it to Tellico Plains. As for making it all the way to Cranmore Cove, well that was something else completely. Our best hope was that crossing a stream now and then might swell up the wood and tighten everything up. Of course, as old as that thing was, it did nothing but get soggy and started coming apart. First a spoke broke, then a rim came loose. Then, trying to knock the rim back on, we caused a wobble in the hub. Well, one thing led to another until a couple days this side of the Tennessee River the axle snapped."

He smiled as he shook his head in thought and absentmindedly stabbed at a few remaining pie crumbs with his fingertip. He licked the crumbs off his finger and slid his plate to the center of the table.

"Only thing going for us," he said, "is by then, we'd been on the road so long, Uncle Skeeter had got tired of ridin' and begun walkin' again. He never quit complainin', mind you; but he did start walkin'. We ended up just leavin' that old wagon where she sat and goin' on without her."

"Yeah," cut in Spotted Crow, "I found Skeeter a nice strong branch with a "Y" in it to use as a crutch and by takin' it slow and easy, we made it to the Tennessee in no time."

"Once we got there," continued Sam, "we talked a fisherman from Hiwassee Island into ferryin' us across the river and he ended up taking us up a small creek he knew about and right into Cranmore Cove itself."

Charlotte gestured with the large coffee pot toward Spotted Crow as if to ask if he wanted more, but after having seen her move the sugar bowl from the table to the countertop, he reluctantly declined.

Sam grinned as he watched the silent, mimed tragedy play out, then continued his story.

"Now, we was gettin' mighty close to Standing Elk's cabin by then and Uncle Skeeter was all decked out in them fine clothes of Diver's that you gave him." he said to Charlotte. Then he looked at Ma, "And he had that fancy haircut you gave him."

Ma covered her mouth and smiled as Charlotte giggled at the memory.

"But his whiskers had begun to grow out, ruinin' the whole effect," said Sam.

Sam reached behind himself grabbing his long black ponytail and bringing it up to his chin, so it stuck out like a fuzzy faced beaver pup having a bad hair day.

Everyone laughed.

"So, me and Spotted Crow told him he couldn't go no farther until he shaved. As you can imagine, he didn't like that one bit, but we stuck to it and even threatened to do the job ourselves."

"I'd a been happy to do it," Spotted Crow said. "But he up and decided to do it himself. Used his skinnin' knife. Did a pretty good job too."

"He did," said Sam. "He then led us down a well-used trail through some large shady hardwoods and into the prettiest little glade you ever saw. There, off in the distance, was a small log cabin with a few scattered outbuildings built near a cattail cluttered pond. And out front of the cabin sat Aunt Standing Elk. She was popping snap peas into a large earthenware bowl. Course, it didn't take her long to see us comin' across the clearing."

"We waved and called and tried to get Uncle Skeeter to hurry up, but he just kept hobblin' along," said Spotted Crow. "We finally gave up on him and hurried to greet Aunt Standing Elk."

"Once she recognized us," Sam continued, "she jumped up and laughed and rushed to us, just a huggin' and kissin' and carryin' on like we was her own sons. Course, seein's how she never had any sons of her own, maybe she did see us that away. But I noticed, the whole time we were gettin' reacquainted, she was lookin' past my shoulder, keepin' an eye on Skeeter as he hobbled across the field. The closer he got, the more tense she became. I didn't realize what the problem was at the time, but she'd never seen him in nothin' but buckskins and whiskers. She had no idea who he was. All she knew was some stranger was hobbling across her yard starin' her straight in the eye. As I glanced back and saw him gettin' close, I stepped aside. Standing Elk froze. Skeeter threw his arms up for a hug and Standing Elk's eyes widened. He rushed in and grabbed her, and she let out a yelp. Then he went one step too far; he kissed her right on the mouth.

"Wham! She hit him so hard he landed ten feet north and his crutch landed twenty feet south.

"'I'm a married woman!' she screamed.

"With that, she dumped out her snap peas right there in the yard and went after him with that big, heavy earthenware bowl just a flailing. Even from where I stood, I could see the look of pure terror in Uncle Skeeter's eyes. He may have been crippled when he first got there, but you wouldn't have known it with the way he leaped up and started out across that field. I reckon he could o' lapped that big ol' black horse y'all got in the quarter mile. And Standing Elk was right behind him the whole way.

"'I'm gonna skin you alive,' she was shouting as that bowl whistled mere inches behind his head. 'Treat a married woman that away.'"

"Now ya gotta understand," cut in Spotted Crow as he laughed at the telling, "me and Sam had no idea what was going on. We were planted there, dumbfounded, as Skeeter and Standing Elk raced around the property."

"'After I skin ya, I'll tan yer hide and hang it on my barn,' she continued."

Sam held both hands over his head like he was protecting it from hail strikes.

"Skeeter was running around with his hands up like this, shouting, 'But honey!'"

"'Don't you honey me!' she screamed."

"'But sweetheart!'

"'I ain't your sweetheart neither!'

"'But darlin' lassie!'

"That stopped Standing Elk in her tracks. She was still holding the bowl over her head, but as she huffed and puffed, she said, 'darlin' lassie?'

"Skeeter stopped running and with an audible gulp and a deep sigh, moaned, 'Yes, darlin' lassie. That's what I'm tryin' to tell ya. I'm yer own lovin' Skeeter.' He then collapsed."

"It was quite a show," Spotted Crow grinned. "But the funny thing is, even though Uncle Skeeter had raced around that yard like a coyote with his tail on fire while in a panic, he couldn't as much as stand up when the chase was over. Standing Elk picked him up her own self and carried him to the cabin."

"It's true," said Sam as he laughed out loud. "And my, how she pampered him the rest of the day. She acted like he was the cutest thing she'd ever seen. I don't reckon a week-old Whitetail would o' given her the warm and cuddlees the way Skeeter did right then. She couldn't walk past him without rubbing and pinching his cheeks with both hands as she giggled like a little girl. If he hadn't finally put a stop to it, I reckon she would have rubbed him plumb raw."

Ma and Charlotte loved it. They were beamin' like a couple of schoolgirls at their first dance.

After that we sat around for a bit laughin' and talkin' and enjoyin' good company. The cousins kept everyone in stitches repeatedly imitating Standing Elk's shock when Skeeter kissed her and Skeeter's terror when she went after him. With each retelling the exaggerated looks of dismay and panic got worse and worse.

Finally, as things calmed down, Sam said it was time to go.

"Dinner will be ready in a couple of hours, if you'd like to stay," said Ma.

Sam and Spotted Crow looked at each other, then shook their heads.

"We'd sure like to," said Sam, "but we want to make it to Long Star's before dark."

"Before the wolves come out," said Spotted Crow.

"What wolves?" asked Pa.

"The wolves that hang around Long Star's place," answered Spotted Crow. "Anyone that gets within three miles of her place at night are followed by wolves. Mostly the big male. Some folks say Two Hand summoned them to protect her and Henry."

"That's just superstition," said Sam.

"All I know is they didn't start showing up until Two Hand came to stay with them," Spotted Crow muttered. "And they don't shadow anyone at anybody else's property."

"That is strange," said Pa. "Mighty strange."

Before the cousins could leave, Ma slathered a bunch of honey on several biscuits and put them in a sack.

"Take this with you," she said, "and come back anytime."

"And tell Henry I'll be stopping by just as soon as I get a chance," I said.

"Tell Long Star we'll all be there for the Green Corn Ceremony," said Pa.

It was customary for several festival goers to stop somewhere along the way to rest during their travels. This year, Long Star had been honored with the hosting duties.

"We sure will," said Sam. "But heed what we said. Don't try comin' after dark. So far, them wolves haven't hurt nobody that we know of, but why take a chance?"

"We won't," I promised.

A shiver ran down my back as I watched the cousins trot across the field and into the dark forest beyond our far pasture. Could Two Hand truly summon wolves to watch over Long Star and Henry? Was it just a legend or was he truly a shaman and shapeshifter?

After having lived with him, I sure hoped Henry had some answers.

SEVEN

Maybell

WHILE THE BANIONS enjoyed their newfound prospects of financial security from furs, corn, honey, eggs, salt, poultry, hard work, and a moral compass led by my friend and mentor, Homer McCoy, the Haggens were struggling to overcome their Kentucky losses. The fruits of laziness, selfishness, malice, and greed.

Soon after arriving at the Wheeler holdings on Gregory Ridge, the Haggens' welcome ran dry. For sure, Buck was as pleased as punch to see his little sister, Pearle, after so many long years of absence, but the same couldn't be said for Hiram.

The relationship between Hiram and Buck had soured when as young men back in Kentucky, Hiram had "borrowed" Maybell.

Other than his wife, Eunice, and their daughter, Cheryl Renee, sweet Maybell was the love of Buck's life. She was the prettiest little black and white paint horse that Buck had ever seen. A real eye catcher and far too good for the likes of her owner, Les Kimball.

Les had come into possession of Maybell when his Uncle Stu died and left him the sole owner of a two-hundred-acre farm; livestock and the paint included. The only stipulation was that the farm, and all possessions thereof, whether livestock, equipment, or structures, could not be sold for a term of two years. It had to be maintained as a working, profitable holding.

Seein's how Les was a third-generation mortician, and the last person anyone who knew him would mistake for a farmer, it was obvious he needed help quick. That's where Buck came in.

According to a hand-shake agreement between Les and Buck, witnessed by a half dozen farmers down at the Galen Curtis Emporium and Feed, Buck and his family would live on and handle all affairs pertaining to the newly acquired Kimball Farm in exchange for two year's lodging and the paint horse.

Buck would become the proud owner of an animal he could have only dreamed of.

For the first year or so everyone was happy with the arrangement. Buck was providing a home for his family and Les was satisfying the stipulations of the inheritance. All was good.

Then Les Kimball's true nature began to show. Greed was his oldest and dearest friend.

As time grew short, he began to reconsider the wisdom of relinquishing ownership of the finest horse in the county to Buck Wheeler. After all, wasn't it enough that his whole family had received two years lodging in return for his work? Holding out for the pony also had been nothing short of blackmail. Taking advantage of a man while he was in need. The only way to stop such an injustice was to see to it that Buck's commitment went unfulfilled.

Being a man who had never been overly restrained by scruples, that last summer, Les did everything in his power to make Buck's life miserable.

He was determined to drive him from the farm.

He spread unsubstantiated rumors of negligent mismanagement and corruption. Made outlandish demands on Buck's work. He even claimed that Buck had somehow manipulated Uncle Stu into adding untenable stipulations to his will in order to cheat Les out of his inheritance.

Yet, even during the struggle to protect his family from Kimball's vicious and villainous attacks, Buck gave his all to make Kimball's farm the jewel of the county. Every farmer that passed that piece of land knew, "There lived a master of the soil."

Buck weathered every taunt and accusation that Les leveraged against him and twenty-four months after the handshake, the agreement was satisfied.

Even then, after the contract was complete, Kimball tried to finagle out of the deal by claiming Buck's work was unsatisfactory and the farm had not prospered. Not a man in the county bought into the ruse. Not only was Buck's work ethics well known, but his morals also. With growing pressure from the local community, and knowing the undertaker over in Jasper Flats would be more than happy to pick up some extra business, Les Kimball finally relented and turned over possession of Maybell to Buck.

Within weeks, Les sold the well-maintained farm to Judge Wilke at a substantial profit. As could be expected, none of the proceeds make their way into Buck's hands.

The Wheelers moved from the Kimball farm to a small but solid, one room log cabin in Buck's Aunt Thelma Lou's back pasture. Buck cared for his aunt's two milk cows and a half dozen or so chickens, but they mostly survived from temporary work he picked up on nearby farms. That, and whatever wild game and fish the surrounding countryside could provide.

It wasn't much, but they lived life to the fullest and enjoyed their time together. Come rain or shine, good times or bad, neither Buck nor Eunice ever contemplated selling Maybell. She was a symbol of their strength together. A reminder of all they could endure.

A Home in the Mist: On Thin Ice

≈

A sweet-smelling breeze played across the tops of knee-high corn leaves as Hiram Haggen swatted yet again the empty air near his right ear. A pestersome damselfly that insisted on using his ear as a perch dodged the flailing hand but refused to retreat. Its iridescent wings flashed in the evening sunlight like four sycamore seeds in the wind.

Hiram's trek across the cornfield to visit with his brother-in-law, Buck, was in fact more to escape his blathering wife, Pearle, and her squalling infant, Barney, than it was for need of male companionship.

Nearing Emerald Ash Slough, a flicker of white among the shadows of a dogwood tree caught his attention. He stopped to study the scene. Another flash. As his eyes adjusted to the speckled light, he realized he was looking at Buck's horse, Maybell, tethered to a low limb. She stood hipshot as her tail flicked at a cloud of gnats hovering near her black and white, pinto flank.

"Tell me about it," Hiram mumbled as he shook his head and slapped out with his hand, actually making contact with the pest that time.

The damselfly pulled back and hovered a moment about ten feet above the ground before finally turning on its axis and darting away.

With Maybell tied to a tree, Hiram knew Buck wouldn't be far away.

Probably fishing in the slough, he assumed. Climbing to the top of a nearby weedy knoll, he shaded his eyes from the glare of a receding western sun and scanned the bog.

A bullfrog burped out his baritone "jug-a-rum" mating call off in the distance.

As Hiram watched, the swaying tops of horsetail rushes soon betrayed Buck's progress well down the eastern shore of the crescent shaped pond. From hard earned experience Hiram knew Buck still had a good five minutes of slogging through the toe snagging rhizomes of the rushes and foot sucking swamp muck before reaching the honey hole—the best bluegill pocket in northwest Kentucky.

As Hiram watched, he could almost taste the feast to come. *Buck'll be eating good tonight*, he thought. *If I'd only known, I'd have brought my own pole. With an hour or so 'til dark and a pocketful of grasshoppers a man could do alright by himself.*

But he hadn't brought his pole.

He could always go down and keep Buck company. Moral support and all.

Nah, he thought. *Fightin' that bog just to watch someone else fish?* He snapped off a piece of dry reed and proceeded to chew on it. *Now what?*

Behind him, Maybell stomped her foot. Obviously getting a bit upset with the unrelenting gnats.

Maybell, he thought. Buck never let anyone ride Maybell. Not even his own brother-in-law. He said she had come far too dear to him. What amounted to two years of hard labor. But Hiram had coveted that fancy paint horse ever since he first laid eyes on her. And now, here she was. Saddled and ready to go. Buck would be at least another hour. Who would know? What could it possibly hurt if he took a little ride?

Glancing one last time down the slough, he saw that Buck had finally reached the honey hole and was busy trying to impale a writhing grasshopper on his hook.

A bluegill slowly rose from the depths and snatched a mosquito floating on the murky surface. Concentric circles distorted the mirrored plane as ripples raced across the water.

Buck bit his lower lip and dipped his line into the hole where the fish had disappeared. He was in his element; lost in his own world.

Slowly backing out of sight, Hiram gathered Maybell's reins and led her well out of earshot before mounting. He then urged her into a trot and slipped along between rows of new corn. It was like riding on air. That horse had a smoother gait than Hiram had ever dreamed of. Not knowing anything other than draft horses and mule stock, Maybell was like gliding on a cloud supported by satin breezes.

At the end of the cornfield, they hopped a ditch and took to a dirt farm road. Without the sharp-edged corn leaves to impede their progress, they picked up the pace and were soon slipping through a stiff breeze. Maybell was as eager to run as Hiram was.

Having lived in the area his whole life, Hiram knew all the roads that were free of spying eyes. He kept to the wagon rutted byways and farm field cut throughs that only boasted family dwellings and worker's shanties which sat well back off the road. He knew that being of the same general size, and with the same deep farmer's tan as Buck, from any real distance no one would be likely to tell them apart. After all, it was well known that Buck never let anyone else ride Maybell.

And who could blame him? She was a dream.

Hiram felt as one with the horse as roads and fields and game trails seemed to vanish beneath her pounding hooves. Blazing through thickets, jumping up startled cottontails, or splashing across shallow streams, she never shied and never seemed to tire. He could ride this horse to the ends of the earth.

Suddenly realizing he'd lost track of time, Hiram stretched forward and ran his hand along Maybell's neck. A light sheen of sweat tainted by the pungent though pleasant odor of horse came away with his hand. Had they truly been gone long enough for Maybell to break into a lather?

Looking about himself, Hiram became aware of lengthening shadows creeping across the newly planted fields. Where had the time gone?

And as far as that went, where were they?

Realizing he may have blown it, he considered his options. If they turned back the way they had come, they'd never make it to the slough before Buck realized Maybell was missing. Not an option.

If they went back by cutting through the edge of town? Maybe.

Hiram pictured Coulterville. If he took Front Street to Chase Blvd., he could turn left and cross the old Kettle Works Bridge. Not the route most folks would take through town, but not as much foot traffic either.

He thought about it for a moment. Nodding he said, "Yeah, that could work."

With any luck, he'd have Maybell tethered to that dogwood tree without Buck being any the wiser. Sure, she'd be a bit sweaty, but let Buck puzzle that one out. But if it was going to work, they had no time to waste.

"Ready, girl?" Hiram said. "Let's do it!"

Kicking Maybell in the flanks, he held on with all he had.

Time slipped by, but Hiram was too busy to notice. He'd always fancied himself a horseman, but he'd never experienced what a true sprinter could do. Everything was a blur to his watery eyes as he held on tight with white knuckles and clamped legs. If not for the urgency of the situation, he'd have never dared take such risks on that winding road.

Miles swept away like water plummeting down raging rapids. The town limits soon appeared. A straight shot down Front Street.

Thundering hoofbeats echoed off the closed storefronts as Maybell raced down the town's main thoroughfare. Pulling back hard and reining to the left, Hiram plowed Maybell around a sharp turn onto Chase Blvd. Churned up clods of dirt flung from iron clad hooves splattered shop windows and sullying wooden walkways as they passed. An elderly couple walking hand in hand screamed and raced for safety as the paint rushed by missing them by mere inches.

Hiram, not wanting to be recognized in the gathering gloom, kept his head down and his face turned away from spectators as much as possible. All was for naught if his identity was known.

The old bridge seemed to appear out of nowhere as Maybell clattered across its loose-fitting timbers. The evening stillness was shattered by the thundering beat of her shoes. All across town doors flew open and curtains were flung back as citizens glared out to see what was making the racket.

Hiram, drawing way too much attention, tucked his head further into his collar and leaned down close to Maybell's straining neck. From his huddled position, he didn't even see little Davey Bosner pass beneath Maybell's hooves.

Sitting on the bridge, dropping make-believe war canoes into the stream below, Davey had little time to react to the charging horse crashing down on him. He raised his left hand as if to ward off the half-ton of equine flesh and loosed a terrified scream that was lost in the clattering of timbers.

Maybell did all she could to avoid the child, nearly losing her footing in the process, but everything happened too quickly. Her left front leg clipped the boy's shoulder spinning him around and plunging him directly into the path of her powerful rear hooves.

Bones shattered and teeth cracked as Davey was flung, whirling like a discarded wooden top, into the abyss off the side of the bridge.

Hiram felt a moment of panic as he thought Maybell had lost her footing. He let out a yelp and desperately clinched his fingers tighter into her flowing mane. The world was suddenly hushed, and he felt a sensation like floating. Then, as if only a hitch in time, she regained her footing and swiftly left the horseshoe scarred bridge behind.

Hiram nervously laughed as he hung on tight and rode away, blissfully unaware of the tragedy that had just taken place.

By twilight, he had returned Maybell to her tether in the dogwood and taken shelter in a nearby patch of buckbrush to watch the show.

"This oughta be good," Hiram chuckled to himself.

Mere minutes passed before a whistling Buck Wheeler emerged from the growing dark. In his right hand he carried his pole with the line wound up tight and the hook safely secured. In his left was a stringer, heavy with big, fat, bluegill.

"How's it goin' girl?" he said to Maybell as he drew near.

The horse snickered and stood with her left front hoof slightly raised off the ground.

"I know, you want a get home and see if Mama's got some grain waitin' for ya."

He patted the horse on the neck. It was damp.

"What's this?" he said.

Dropping the stringer and pole, he rubbed the sweaty neck. *What's going on?* He reached back and pushed his hand under the saddle blanket, then along her flanks. His hand came back covered in froth.

"This ain't right," he mumbled to himself as he turned around and stared into the settling dark. Nothing disturbed the peaceful dusk except a sprinkling of fireflies and the nightly chorus of droning crickets.

Maybell pawed the air with her raised leg.

"You okay, girl?" Buck said. He knelt and gently squeezed her cannon. She flinched.

Swollen.

From his hideout, Hiram couldn't tell what Buck was doing. For some reason he was knelling in front of the horse. Then, after a moment, he stood and looked Maybell in the eye.

"You'll be alright girl," he said.

Then, taking her reins, he slowly led her away.

The pole and stringer laid abandoned where he'd dropped them.

Hiram waited in the dark until he felt certain Buck was not coming back. He then crawled from his hiding place and retrieved Buck's fish and gear.

Turning for home he smiled. "Best day ever," he chuckled.

≈

John and Sadie Bryce were not counted among the more respected members of Coulterville's elite. In fact, far from it.

Many long years ago, Sadie had been a debutante and the favorite daughter of Mayer Hastings. She had a life spread out in front of her that most girls could only dream about: education, wealth, and leisure. But to the dismay of everyone who knew her, she chose the wild and exciting John Bryce to be her beau.

With much cajoling and pleading and raving, her parents had warned her, he would do nothing but lead her to ruin. He had no position, no drive, and no prospects—no way imaginable to give her the life she was accustomed to.

Of course, being a bright girl, she understood her parents' concerns. They were trying their best to do right by her. But she believed that true love could overcome all obstacles. Well intentioned or not, parents aren't always right.

Unfortunately, fairytale fantasies and happy endings are much more often realized in a good book than in real life. And more often than not, a parent's hard-earned knowledge is well worth taking the time to consider.

All these years later, John and Sadie lived in a pieced together shanty on Little Half Fork Creek, two miles south of Kettle Works Bridge. John tended to take a nip a bit too often and Sadie wasn't quite dressed to the standards of the respectable citizenry of Coulterville. But they got by. In fact, with the creek providing most things a person required, John figured they was doing fine.

If you needed something, you could usually walk the streambank and find items that would make do. Why, if you waited a bit, it often floated right to ya.

And that's why John was in the right place at the right time to rescue little Davey Bosner.

Late one evening, Sadie went to collect eggs, and saw a spotted skunk with his head and shoulders crammed tight into a hole in the side of the chicken coop. She managed to thump him with a clothesline pole and chase him off without gettin' sprayed, but she decided it was for the last time. She told John if he didn't get that coop fixed, she'd be fryin' his bacon—and not in a good way either.

Grumblin' and mockin' Sadie's sassy voice to himself, John had spent the better part of an hour walkin' along the muddy banks of the Little Half Fork lookin' for a good piece of lumber. He'd pulled a number of useful items from the mossy water and left 'em scattered along his route to retrieve on his way home. It was turning into a profitable day. A couple hundred feet to go and he'd be to his turning around point at the bridge.

Suddenly, he straightened up from where he was pulling a broken chairback spindle from the muck and nearly fell on his rump. It sounded like the old bridge was collapsing. Stumbling back from the racket, he looked up to see a black and white paint horse charge across the expanse. As it passed, a dark object flew out from under the bridge railing and tumbled into the stream below.

"Lunatic!" John mumbled.

In an instant, the horse was beyond the lip of the bank and out of sight. Only the rhythmic beat of rapidly receding iron shoes on the hardpack roadway could be heard.

Continuing towards the bridge, John strained in the dimming light to see what had fallen into the water. Whatever it was had landed partially on a sandy sediment bar preventing it from floating down stream.

As he drew near, he could see a waving motion, like fabric swaying in the current. A shirt perhaps, caught on a moss-covered rock.

Had somebody pitch a bag of laundry?

John toed up to the water's edge, being careful not to slip down the slick mudbank. His shoes were already damp, but he preferred not getting them soaked. Standing high and cocking his head a bit sideways, he got a better look.

It *was* laundry. A faded red shirt. And slightly downstream a kid's brown shoe bobbed in the rapids where it was snagged on a half-buried tree limb.

Strange, he thought, *with the high cost of textiles, folks seldom chose to discard old clothes which could always be reused in some fashion.*

Looking back at the shirt, he noticed a pale object protruding from the sleeve. Small fingers bobbed in the water's surface. A hand?

That's not laundry, he thought, *That's a child*!

The moss-covered rock was in fact a head of stringy brown hair.

John leapt into the creek and swiftly sloshed his way across a thigh deep channel. His heart was beating so hard he thought he might be having an attack. Drawing near, he knelt in the cold water and gently brushed the hair out of the child's face. It was a boy. Couldn't be more than four or five years old. Only his head, shoulders, and one hand were above the waterline. If not for the sandbar, he'd have drowned for sure—assuming he was alive.

The kid's limbs were protruding out at awkward angles. The poor lad was broken up somethin' fierce.

Placing one wet palm in front of the child's nose and mouth, John held his breath. He waited. For several long seconds, nothing but the gentle burble of nearby rippling currents and the caw of a far-off crow could be heard. The air near John's hand was as still as death.

Then . . . there it was. He was almost certain. Another pause. Yes, there it was again. A very weak but unmistakable breath. The boy was alive.

"Over here!" John yelled. "In the creek!"

He knew he was too far below street level to be heard in town, but he was desperate. Neither courage nor responsibility was John's strong suit. Fact is, he had to admit, he wasn't sure he *had* a strong suit.

Leave him here and go get help? he wondered. *Or take him with me?*

John was about ready to bolt when the boy's eyes fluttered, then opened. A bubble extended from his left nostril and swelled as he whispered, "I'm Davey." A slight smile crossed his lips then his eyes gradually slid shut once more. His lips parted and the bubble deflated.

John couldn't bring himself to leave the kid and have him wake-up down here in the cold and dark all alone. He just couldn't imagine the terror of it. And what if the worst happened. What if he passed, all alone and afraid?

Tears washed down John's distraught face as he did something he had not done since he was seven. He closed his eyes and prayed.

"Dear Lord," he said, "I know you ain't got no reason to listen to me, but this boy ain't never did you no harm. Please give me the strength to get him home to his Ma."

He opened his eyes and looked straight into the heavens not even realizing he had picked the child up.

"You do that," he continued, "and I'll change. I ain't sayin' I'll ever amount to nothin'. Reckon I'm too old for that, but I'll sure try to do right by Ya. And that preacher of Yourn down at that church house too. Why, when I shake that man's hand, he'll know it's been shook. You just wait and see if he don't."

The entire time John had been praying, he'd been inching his way up the embankment with Davey cradled in his arms.

"You just take care o' this boy, Lord," he said, "and you ain't never gonna have no troubles with ol' John Bryce no more."

By the time John was finished, he'd climbed out onto the roadway and saw a crowd gathered 'round an old couple down the way.

"He like to've killed us, Gus," the old man was saying. "Came barrelin' through here like a madman."

They looked up and saw John carrying the boy.

"Now what?" Gus Kilroy, who had recently been elected to the new position of town marshal asked.

"Near as I can figure, he was knocked off the bridge by a wild man on a black and white pinto," said John.

"Sounds like the same one that nearly killed Mr. and Mrs. Fry," said Gus as the old couple nodded.

"Rick, run get the doc, then round up young Davey's folks. John, take the boy over yonder to my house. We'll put him in my son, Galen's room. Does anyone know who has a black and white pinto?"

Half a dozen people shouted, "Buck Wheeler!"

Les Kimball, who had stopped on his way home from the mortuary, stood up straight. His eyes lit up.

"That's right Marshal," he said. "Buck Wheeler fleeced me out o' my paint filly. Finest horse in the county. Got black and white pinto coloring. And I know for a fact, he won't let another soul ride her."

After Davey was placed in Galen's bed, and the doc was looking after him, Gus had John show him where he had found the boy.

"It was right there, Marshal," John said pointing down at the creek. "Right where that sand bar is."

Gus knelt on the bridge with a torch in hand. He examined several freshly marred spots and deep scratches in the weathered wood. One board was even chipped with long splinters protruding. Gus ran his hand along a fresh crack in the lower railing.

"Looks like there was a collision here alright," he said. "I reckon we know who our man is."

Standing up, he brushed off his knees. "I'd like six men to ride with me. If that boy dies, Buck is in for a hangin'. If he lives, Judge Wilke can decide what to do with him."

Several men stepped forward.

"We're with ya, Marshal," they said.

Clive Patterson grimaced. "Guess I am too. It's a shame though. I've always put a heap o' stock in that boy. Reckon he had me buffaloed all along."

By full dark, the posse had saddled up and with torches blazing set out to arrest a totally oblivious Buck Wheeler.

EIGHT

Well Of Deceit

HE PICKED UP THE BOWL of lukewarm soup and placed it on a small birchbark serving tray next to his special remedy. Heat lightning crackled in the distance hinting at another Smoky Mountain thunderstorm that would not materialize.

"Buck . . . Buck, are you out there?"

Eunice was once again so weak he feared her congestive condition would surely put her under. Day after day she languished on her sweat-stained mattress, listless and pallid, unresponsive to most of Buck's ministrations. She suffered through long stifling days yearning for night's cooling relief only to end up curled into a ball, shivering from the slightest of breezes.

Only on occasion, when complete exhaustion overwhelmed her, did she finally succumb to a lingering, semi-comatose state—her only true form of relief.

"I'm right here, darlin'," Buck said as he entered the room. "I went down to the springhouse and got ya some nice cold remedy."

Eunice grimaced as Buck placed the tray on a three-legged stool near the bed before sitting on the sheets next to her.

Buck's remedy was a concoction of ninety-five percent grain alcohol cut with a little ginger root and raw honey. A cure-all passed down from his aunt Thelma Lou's grandaddy. Buck wasn't really sure if it did any good for Eunice's malady, but it did seem to take away some of the pain.

Truth be told, Buck sampled the cure-all now and again himself whether he was indisposed or not. He attributed its cathartic effects as being a contributing factor to his uncommonly good health. The way he had it figured, if it gave Eunice any relief at all, it was better than doing nothin'. And nothin' was 'bout all else he had. He'd once fetched Doc Kendree from down there in the Cove to check on her, but the things he'd wanted to do, Buck wouldn't do to a rabid polecat.

Eunice looked up with sunken, red rimmed eyes and slowly shook her head from side to side.

"No," she whispered. "I can't drink that stuff."

Buck dribbled a bit of cure-all into a discolored tablespoon. He then reached across and tucked his hand behind Eunice's damp, stringy hair to helped her lift her head up.

"Just one spoonful," he said. "Then I've got some nice pigeon soup for ya."

Eunice puckered her cheeks as she clamped her toothless jaws tight and shook her head. Tears clouded her dull grey eyes.

Buck laid the spoon on their scarred, pinewood nightstand and lowered his earthenware jug to the floor.

"I'm sorry, honey," he said. "I won't force you to drink anything you don't want."

He settled her head back and took her thin hand in his. "I just need ya to get better." A tear coursed down his cheek. "I need ya."

Eunice just stared.

"Why don't I just sit here with ya for a while, and we'll talk." He lifted his wife's hand and kissed her on the knuckles.

She gave a slight nod.

Eunice's troubles had begun many long years ago when they had newly arrived in the Cove. Having fled unwarranted animosity from his onetime friends and neighbors back in Kentucky, they had come here looking for a new and better life. A life free of accusing eyes and sharp-tongued rebukes. Living each day without having to prove he was innocent of the crime he'd been accused of.

Even serving time for another man's sins had not lifted the stigma of guilt from his brow. Out of desperation, he had fled with his wife, daughter, and aunt, to these distant mountains. To this beautiful refuge in the Smokies.

Unfortunately, he'd unknowingly brought an Ohio Valley pestilence with them in the form of a wagon load of half dry hay contaminated with the white snakeroot plant.

Unable to procure safer, pasture cut hay, before their swift exodus from their Kentucky homeland, Buck had traded a chicken to ol' Chet Waters for a load of newly cut fodder gathered in the surrounding woodlands.

Chet was a recluse who made ends meet however he could. At the time he was clearing land for a local farmer and along with a stipend, he was allowed to sell whatever he cut.

Buck figured scrub hay was better than none at all. At least in the short-term. After all, he didn't know what the future would bring, and Aunt Thelma Lou's cows needed to eat.

Course, if he'd known what he was buying, he'd have opted for finding what he could along the way.

It wasn't till many years later, in the mid-thirties, that Dr. Anna Bixby convinced her neighbors to eradicate the white snakeroot plant. It was a common flowering weed that grew wild in the Ohio Valley woodlands. She'd first learned about it from an old Shawnee woman she met while hiking. After devising several tests, she proved the weed caused the dreaded milk sickness that was ravaging the area. Years later, her discovery was credited with saving countless lives.

Unfortunately, her discovery came far too late to help Buck. One of Thelma Lou's cows ate the plant.

As it so happened, Ma was sick at the time and couldn't nurse Weston, so Pa bartered a bushel of nuts and berries with Buck for some cow's milk. Weston took ill, as did the cow and her calf. None of them survived more than a few days.

It was about that time that Eunice drank some tainted milk also. It didn't kill her, but she did become deathly ill. All through that long winter she suffered.

Buck feared the worst.

Then come spring, she improved. That started a regular cycle. She'd falter in winter, (some worse than others) and improve with the gentle breezes of spring.

Until now.

Buck wasn't sure if the recuring illnesses where the ongoing effects of milk sickness, or simply exposure to the elements by a weakened constitution.

Whatever it was, he was helpless to do anything about it, and it frightened him.

"Remember that little flower garden you had back on the Kimball farm?" he asked Eunice as he gently massaged her hand.

He thought he saw a weak sparkle in her eyes.

"I sure thought that was somethin' fine."

As he talked, he dipped the spoon in her pigeon soup and held it to her lips.

"I don't reckon there bein' another girl in that whole county that could o' growed such a pretty mess o' flowers. It made me plumb proud to see how them other farmers eyed your garden as they passed by."

He had no doubt; there was a sparkle in Eunice's eyes. She sipped the broth.

"And remember when you caught Maybell nibbling on your black-eyed Susans?"

He chuckled as he refilled the spoon. This time he took care that instead of just broth, there was a bit of pigeon meat floating in the golden liquid. She needed something solid in her system.

"Why, I thought you were gonna skin that horse alive. If you recall, I kept her in the far pasture for a full week."

Eunice giggled as she chewed on a piece of tender, dark breast meat. She swallowed and opened her mouth for more.

"Yeah girl, we had us some mighty fine times, we did."

It was then that Buck's dogs began to bark. It wasn't uncommon for them to fitch out after a deer or 'possom or whatnot, but Buck knew his dogs and that didn't sound like no huntin' barks. No sir, that bark was a warning. It was how they sounded when they were protecting their territory.

"Wonder what that's all about," he said.

Soon, he heard a clattering noise coming up the old ridge trail from Parson's Branch.

"Sounds like we got company comin'," he said.

Propping pillows against the bed's headboard, he carefully helped Eunice sit up. Then, handing her the soup, he watched as she sloshed half a spoonful onto her old night dress before getting some into her mouth.

That's okay, he thought. He could clean her up later. For now, at least she was eating.

"I'll go see who it is. You go ahead and eat your soup." He patted her on the leg. "I'll be right back."

Just as he started to exit the room, he stopped and looked back. "I love ya, honey," he said.

Eunice glanced up for just a second and smiled. She then went back to concentrating on the bowl in front of her.

Her appetite seemed to have returned.

A Home in the Mist: On Thin Ice

As Buck crossed through the kitchen to the front door he considered reaching for his rifle. It wasn't often anyone came riding up his trail. On the other hand, they sure weren't tryin' to sneak up on the place. It sounded like the entire Cove was out there. He let the weapon be.

Walking down the way, several of Buck's dogs gathered 'round him. They were a fierce and protective bunch, when need be, but knew to take their cues from him. If Buck showed no alarm, they were docile as house cats. But if he commanded, not even an adult black bear would stand a chance against their fury.

Coming to the first dip in the trail, where a half-acre meadow of gamagrass and buckbrush skirted the east side of the roadway, Buck stopped and surveyed the meandering ridge top. In the distance he could see movement passing in and out of the tree line coming up his drive.

He pulled off his hat and used it to block the sun.

Light glinted off stone scoured wagon wheels and dangling copper housewares as they swayed and clattered on the sides of three heavy farm wagons. Even at a distance, Buck could see the wagons jostle and shudder as they slowly made their way over rock strewn hard pan and through thick stands of thorny brush. As they sloshed their way through a shallow stream and entered the sunny patch on the other side, a team of poorly paired draft horses could be seen pulling the first wagon. Mules were hitched to the ones behind. The last wagon had a couple of saddle horses on long leads tied to its tailgate.

From the best Buck could tell, there must have been a score or so of folks, young and old, perched on hard benches up front or sprawled in the overloaded cargo beds. Not a pleasant ride to Buck's way of thinkin'.

As they came to the bottom of the rise where Buck stood with his dogs, he replaced his sweat-stained hat and raised both hands out in front of him.

"Hold up there," he called. "You're on private property. We ain't lookin' to take in boarders, and we ain't got no work, so y'all just turn around and head on out the way ya came."

The last thing he needed was a mess of strangers underfoot.

The wagons stopped.

Both drivers of the rear wagons climbed down and walked up to stand by the driver of the first.

The hair bristled on Buck's dogs as they growled and bared their teeth.

After a short discussion, a woman called out.

"Buck . . . is that you?" She shaded her eyes to see better.

Buck just stood there not knowing how these folks knew his name.

"Buck, it's me. It's your sister Pearle."

Buck was dumbfounded. Pearle? He hadn't seen Pearle since he'd left Kentucky all of them years ago. He'd written once to let her know he'd settled and then again when Aunt Thelma Lou passed away, but that had been ten years ago. Not a word had passed between them since.

Then a thought struck him like a spike through the heart.

The man sitting next to Pearle was her husband, Hiram Haggen. The man he loathed more than any other in this world.

A cold shiver ran through his soul as he realized if he'd brought his rifle along, he'd have ended it right here and now. He'd a put Hiram down right where he sat.

"Can I talk with ya, Buck?" Pearle called. "It's been way too long, and I've missed ya."

Buck paused for a moment then said, "Yeah Pearle, step down and come on up here."

He stared hard at Hiram.

"The rest of ya, pull on over into that meadow. You'll be leavin' come mornin'. Come any nearer to the house, and I'll set the dogs on ya."

One of the men standing next to the wagon came around and helped Pearle down. She then walked with a stilted gait up the rise and hugged Buck.

"They're my family," she said.

"They'll stay where they are," said Buck. Then looking in her eyes he said, "It's good to see ya Pearle. Come on up to the house."

As they walked, Buck warned Pearle about Eunice's poor health, and that she wasn't lookin' her best.

"Oh, fiddlesticks," said Pearle. "I didn't come here to play fancy pants. I come here to see my kin. You take me to her, and we'll be just fine."

"I sure hope so," said Buck. "And Pearle, it really is good to see ya." He placed his arm around her shoulders and hugged her.

"My girl, Cheryl Renee, married a cooper over in North Carolina 'bout six years ago and they're doing real good for themselves," he said. "Got three young uns and a fine home to hear the tellin' of it."

Funny how even after all these years they could just fall right into talkin' like they'd seen each other yesterday.

"They make it up here every chance they get but I'll tell ya, I sure miss havin' that girl around. After Eunice got sick, we didn't have no more children so she's all we got."

Pearle reached up and squeezed Buck's hand as it rested on her shoulder. It felt good to be in the arms of her big brother.

"I'm sorry to hear that," she said. "I know how much stock you and Eunice always put into having a large family."

She gave him an embarrassed grin. "Borne ten kids, myself."

"Ten?" said Buck. "Now that must be a houseful."

Pearle brushed a strand of grey hair from her sweaty cheek.

"Well, it don't give me much time to get lonely, I can tell ya that."

Buck laughed and led Pearle into the house and through to the bedroom.

"Got some company," he said to Eunice as he crossed the room to his wife.

Eunice sat with both hands clutching the soiled and disheveled blankets bunched up under her chin. The nearly empty soup bowl rested forgotten among the folds of the material where its contents slowly seeped out causing an elongating stain. Confusion deepened the dark creases around her glassy eyes. She reached out a trembling hand and took Buck's sleeve, drawing him close to her face.

"I ain't presentable for guests," she whispered in a weak voice.

138

Tilting her head, a bit, she peeked around Buck's arm at the stranger, then drew back.

Buck smiled and kissed her on the forehead.

"It's Pearle," he said, standing aside so Eunice could get a better view. "You remember my sister, Pearle?"

"Pearle?" Eunice uttered.

"Yes, sweety. It's me, Pearle," Pearle said as she crossed the room and took Eunice's hands in hers.

Eunice looked at Buck, then Pearle, then at her dingy blankets.

"Don't you be frettin' none on my account," said Pearle. "Puttin' on airs with me. Why, we been down the road a time or two, and that's a fact."

She reached up and smoothed back Eunice's lank hair, tucking it behind her ears.

"Now let's see what we can do about gettin' you cleaned up a bit. What do you say?"

Eunice just sat staring Pearle in the eyes for a moment, then gave a slight nod.

"Good," said Pearle. She stood up and said, "Buck, come with me." Then smiling at Eunice, she said, "We'll be right back, honey."

In the kitchen, Pearle instructed Buck to heat her up as much water as he could.

"I'm goin' down to my wagon for a bit, but I'll be back."

Buck kissed Pearle's cheek, grabbed two large kettles, and headed out to light a fire near his spring. He'd forgotten how easily she could walk right into a room and take over.

Within twenty minutes Pearle came walking back up the hill carrying two thick homemade quilts, a threadbare night dress, and a set of clean bed linens.

"My oldest girl, Avery, is takin' care of the kids and I told Hiram not to wait up for me," she told Buck. "How's the water coming?"

"I got a kettle sittin' on the kitchen table ready to go," he said, "and another by the fire. There's a bar of soap and some rags by the dry sink."

Pearle nodded and shifted her bulky load up tighter under her arm.

"The wash tub's full and I'll put some hot rocks in it when you're ready," he said.

"That's good," said Pearle. She headed for the door. "You go ahead with what you need to do. I'm sure there's things you've been neglecting. As for now, us girls got some freshenin' up to do."

Buck breathed the easiest he had in a month. He didn't know why Pearle had showed up just when he needed her most, but he felt blessed that she had.

Nearly an hour passed as Buck heated water, cut wood, fed his chickens; and not knowing what else to do, fried up a skillet of scrambled eggs.

140

Pearle came out twice. First to get a fresh kettle of hot water and dump Eunice's soiled things into the soapy wash tub, and a then to snatch Buck's plate of scrambled eggs for Eunice to eat.

Finally, after what seemed like hours to Buck, Pearle slipped out of the bedroom door and quietly pulled it shut.

"She's sleeping," she said. Then looking into Buck's concerned face, she added, "It'll be a long haul for sure, but she's gonna pull through just fine."

Buck let out a ragged breath. "I don't know how to thank you, sis," he said. "I been worried somethin' fierce."

Pearle's heart went out to her brother. He truly was a good man.

"How long's she been like this?" she asked.

Buck shook his head and said, "Sit down. I'll make us some coffee and vittles and tell ya all about it."

As he floated a dollop of sizzling bear fat in his largest skillet and added two deer steaks, he told Pearle how he had bought scrub hay in his haste to get away from Coulterville after becoming a pariah. And how it had been contaminated by a plant called white snakeroot that caused milk sickness.

"As you know," he said, "there's no cure for that stuff. Either you make it, or you don't."

Moisture swelled up in his eyes.

"I traded some of that milk to a neighbor of mine. Killed his boy, is what I done. Then my Eunice drank it."

He wiped at his damp cheeks with dirty, cracked fingers, then turned the steaks with a large two-pronged fork.

"I didn't know, Pearle. How could I have known?"

As he talked, Pearle paled. She realized it was her own husband's lies had brought on all this pain and suffering. Would the damage that man's deceit caused never end?

"I'm so sorry," she whispered. "If I could take it back, I would."

At first Buck thought Pearle was simply showing compassion. Then it struck him—what she was really saying.

He turned from his skillet and looked into her tortured eyes, "I know, Pearle. It's not your fault. After we moved here Aunt Thelma told me what you said about Hiram hurting that little boy and letting me take the blame."

Pearle clutched a fist to her breast and sat wide-eyed. "I never knew she told you. I'm surprised you didn't come back and settle the score."

"I wanted to, Pearle. For a long time, I surely did. But deep down, I just couldn't see what good taking away your husband and your son's father would do.

Not for a crime I already paid the price for. It's not like it would have restored what I lost."

He placed a plate of venison steaks and sliced tomatoes in front of her along with a cup of steaming coffee.

"But I'll not forgive him, Pearle. Never. That's why I can't have him staying on my property. I'm afraid I'd kill him."

He pulled off his hat and tossed it on the counter.

"I understand," said Pearle as she stirred a spoonful of honey into her coffee from a jar sitting on the table.

Buck retrieved his cup and plate and sat down across from his sister.

"But I reckon I know where y'all can go," he said. "There's an old homestead 'bout three miles from here. I believe Indians ran a family out of there long before we came to the Cove. It'll be a trek gettin' in there, but I think it'll suit ya fine. There's an old orchard not far from there, but I don't know that I'd mess with it. The family of the man that lost his son has been tending to it for the last few years. He don't know the debt Hiram owes him, but I reckon I'd stay shy of him all the same. That's one man you don't want to cross."

Pearle nodded and cut into her steak. The last thing they needed was more trouble.

"The house and outbuildings ain't fairin' so well, but there's a good spring for drinkin' water, and if you follow a steep trail down a cliff face, you'll come to a real nice fishin' hole."

"Sounds perfect," said Pearle.

"Tomorrow I'll tell ya how to get there. There's access from Parson's Branch. The road you took to get here."

As they ate, Buck remembered how pretty his little sister had been. It saddened him to see the toll the years had taken on her. The craggy face and slumped shoulders. Even the golden speckles he'd so admired in her eyes had faded.

He then thought back to that day he went fishin' only to come back and find Maybell in a mysterious sweat. The day that changed his life.

It had started out so perfect.

The honey hole had never been so generous. Buck could hardly get a grasshopper on his hook before a big, fat bluegill jumped up and tried to snatch it out of his hand. He reckoned if he'd brought a bucket along with him, he could have just sat back in the shade and whiled away the time as them fish fought one another over who was gonna be the first to hop in.

Almost didn't seem fair. Fact is, he was havin' so much fun he'd lost track of time until he pierced his thumb while trying to bait the hook in the dim light.

He then wound up his line, grabbed his heavy stringer of fish, and slogged his way back through the bog to his waiting horse.

He whistled and did a little jig as he reached Maybell.

"Eunice is gonna faint when she sees the fish I'm bringin' her," he told the horse.

It was then that he realized Maybell was lathered up as if she'd been running hard and her left front cannon bone was swollen and warm to the touch. Whether it was damaged tendons or bucked shins he didn't know but he was concerned enough to forget about his fish lying there on the ground.

The injury was a complete mystery to him until years later when Aunt Thelma Lou told him Hiram had hurt that boy in Coulterville. She said he had confessed to Pearle during one of his dark bouts of melancholy. According to Hiram, all he wanted to do was ride Maybell.

"He'd o' let Buck ride her if she was his," he told Pearle.

The accident had been just that, an accident. He didn't even know he'd run the kid down until he heard that Buck had been arrested for it. By then he figured with Buck's upstanding reputation in the community, they'd go easy on him. If they knew Hiram had done it, there'd be a hanging.

Buck had led Maybell into an open-faced shed he'd built for her and after lighting a lantern, gave her a good helping of grain. He then stripped her saddle and tack before brushing her down with a handful of straw. Finally, after getting her as comfortable as possible, he set to seein' what he could do about the swollen cannon.

First, he ripped up an old shirt and soaked it in spring water to use as a cold compress.

Maybell snickered and tossed her head but didn't try to pull her leg away as he wrapped it. She understood Buck was trying to help her. Several applications of cold water reduced the inflammation.

"That's a good girl," Buck said, patting her on the neck and scratching between her ears.

He then made a liniment from witch hazel and rosemary with a honey base to ease the pain. After rubbing it in, he gently wrapped the cannon with long strips of soft linen.

While he was busy tending to Maybell he heard several horses ride up out front.

Strange time of night for visitors, he thought.

"Buck Wheeler!" he heard someone call.

"Yeah, back here," he yelled. "In the shed."

He heard the clack of wood as someone opened and closed his gate then looked up from where he sat, tying a last knot in the compress.

Seven men came walking around the side of his shed.

"You Buck Wheeler?" one of them asked.

"That's what my mama calls me," he said.

Patting Maybell's rump, he stood up.

As the men came into the light, Buck looked around.

"Hey, Mr. Patterson," he said. "What's up?"

"I'll do the askin'", said Gus. "I'm Gus Kilroy. The new Marshal in Coulterville. We have reason to believe you may have killed a child today."

Buck was dumbfounded.

"What are you talkin' about?" He scanned the faces of the men tryin' to decide if this was a sick joke.

Clive Patterson hung his head and kicked at an old horse apple on the ground.

"We got witnesses saw you race this horse through town nearly killing an old couple as they crossed the street," the Marshal said. "Then you ran down Davey Bosner on Kettle Works Bridge and left him for dead."

As he talked Gus squeezed past Buck and looked down at Maybell's wrapped leg.

"I don't know what you're talkin' about," protested Buck. "I wasn't even in Coulterville today."

Gus lifted Maybell's hoof and after a close examination pulled a fresh splinter from her shoe.

"Care to tell us how this piece of bridge timber got stuck in your horse's hoof?" he asked.

Maybell blew and shook her head.

"I haven't the faintest idea," Buck said. "All I know is, I was fishing all evening over in Emerald Ash Slough and when I came out Maybell was lathered up and limping. How that could be, I have no idea. We just got back about an hour ago and I've been nursing her ever since."

"Say ya was fishin', huh?" asked Gus.

"That's right," said Buck. "All evening."

"They bitin'?"

"Ain't never seen the likes. Must have caught twenty of the fattest bluegills you ever saw."

Gus whistled. "I sure do like bluegill," he said. "Mind showin' 'em to me?"

Buck got a funny look on his face. "Now that I think about it, I left 'em lay near the slough when I noticed Maybell was hurt."

"Ya don't say?" said Gus. "Well, I reckon we oughta go get 'em. Be a shame to let a catch like that go to waste."

Buck led the posse to where he'd left his pole and the fish. They were nowhere to be found.

"I don't understand it," he said as he frantically swept his torch back and forth in the dark, searching the area near the dogwood tree.

148

"I left them right here. I swear it."

At a nod from the Marshal, the men spread out, surrounding Buck.

"Come with us," Gus said reaching for Buck's arm.

After that, things moved quickly. Davey lived but would spend months healing.

Doc Adams doubted he'd ever walk without a limp again.

Judge Wilke took Buck's reputation into consideration and gave him six months hard labor and restitutions.

Unable to pay the debt, Maybell was auctioned along with most of Thelma Lou's land.

Tongues wagged in hushed whispers when Hiram Haggen never once visited his brother-in-law in prison.

Even when Buck was released after serving his time, his neighbors weren't satisfied. A man who could do that to a child could never be trusted again.

Buck had no choice. Unjustly disgraced, but with no conceivable way of proving his innocence, he packed up his family and meager belongings and moved to Tennessee.

NINE

Porch Ornament

RECKON I WAS SLIPPIN' a bit, 'cause it was Charlotte who first heard Diver comin' up the Cove Trail. She'd been out back hangin' laundry while me and Baby were busy tryin' to rid the pasture bridge of an oversized copperhead snake.

Seems Charlotte and Ma had both been startled on occasion when the viper poked his head up through the bridge decking as they walked by. Scared 'em both is what it done. I can't rightly say if it was the deck boards rattling that caused him to do such a thing or if he took offense at folks strolling across the roof of his home, but Ma wasn't havin' no more of it.

"Either that bridge is gonna be rid of snakes," she said, "or I'll burn it down and be rid of that bridge."

Pa laughed at what he thought was a hollow threat until he saw Ma gathering up a torch and a bucket full of pig lard. Now, buildin' that bridge had took some doin', and I reckon he wanted to keep it, because he decided right then and there—that snake had to go!

Pulling me to the side, he said, "See what you can do about it, Billy."

I never in my life heard Pa say it outright, but I don't think he was all that fond of snakes his own self. Now I'm not talkin' Skeeter scared, mind you; he just wasn't exactly warm and cuddly with 'em.

"Just be careful, and don't get bit," he said after lookin' around to be sure Ma wasn't listenin'. Satisfied he'd taken care of the problem, he settled into his rocking chair and began whistlin' about that old wooden bucket while he whittled on a tulipwood flute, he was makin' for young Forrest Weston's birthday.

As I walked toward the bridge, I could feel his eyes on my back. He may have sent me to do a man's job, but I knew he'd keep watch over me.

It wasn't but a few minutes before I had a plan.

"That's it, Baby," I said. "Keep her attention."

Baby was standing on the bridge, barking and snarling at the snake as it eyed her with cold, sinister, slit pupils. Looking straight ahead, still as death itself, only the flick of a forked tongue gave warning of impending danger. Unlike the more dangerous timber rattler, the copperhead was a silent killer.

No showboatin' with that one.

A Home in the Mist: On Thin Ice

As the standoff between canine and serpent continued, I'd crept underneath the bridge decking with a long-forked stick and a wooden bucket. I appreciated the fact that this could be the very same bucket that Pa was whistling about. I just hoped that my memories of it would turn out to be as fond as those in the song.

Peeking around through the timbers, trying hard to distinguish the copper-colored hourglass markings of the snake from the mottled shadows beneath the bridge, I felt the short hairs on the back of my neck suddenly begin to tingle. For some reason it hadn't occurred to me until just then that that snake could have friends down there with her. Of course, every schoolboy knows copperheads tend to be solitary critters. They don't den up together like rattlers . . . *usually*.

The flick of a tail drew my attention.

There you are, I thought. My eyes just naturally darted from side to side making sure we were alone.

So much for what schoolboys know.

Tightly grasping the forked stick in my sweaty right hand, I slowly reached up and gently wrapped my left fingers around the viper's tail. At first it didn't seem to notice. It was still concentrating on Baby. I then slowly pulled to ease it out of the timbers. I reckon you could say when I done that, she noticed.

That snake went to whippin' and pullin', and I went to yelpin' and yankin', and Baby went to barkin' and snappin', and I imagine Pa, up on the porch, like to had a heart attack.

A full four feet of writhing, angry snake came tumbling outta them timbers and slapped down on that muddy streambank at my feet like a flesh and bone bolt of lightning. Well, I mean to tell ya, I had my hands full in a hurry. That crazy thing went plumb loco.

I've heard folks talk about the lightning speed of them big 'ol timber rattlers, but I don't reckon they ever had a really disgruntled copperhead by the tail. I can tell ya firsthand, the one thing you don't want to do is turn loose of it.

Still clutching that tail for dear life, I was yankin' and pullin' and dodgin', and tryin' everything I could to keep them fangs pointed away from my tender legs.

Problem was, for every effort I made to avoid contact, that thing made a counter-effort to get to know me better. I did some mighty high steppin' for a few seconds there, I can tell ya.

Course, I'd like to tell ya I fended off all them strikes with my forked stick like Lancelot or Galahad did in days of old. But truth be told, it was more out of luck, desperation, and the desire for self-preservation that I finally pinned her head down.

A Home in the Mist: On Thin Ice

It was then, after I had the snake secured and no longer a danger, that Baby came bounding down into the stream, barking, and snapping, and acting like she was showin' that snake what for. Though, I noticed she never did get all that close to it.

More rattle than battle, as Pa would say.

Oh well, in her heart I know she was tryin' to help.

"Yeah, you done alright girl," I offered.

She calmed down and looked me in the face, then down at the water. Everything was fine for a moment. Then suddenly, her body stiffened. Her eyes got round. And to my surprise, Baby shot out of that stream in one great bound and landed on shore spinning like a top. I didn't know if she'd gotten bit or what was going on. She spun first, one way, then the other, trying to see along both sides of her body. When everything looked okay, she finally stopped and shook the water off. I was dumbfounded seein' her stand there trembling. Then it struck me. In all the excitement, she must of plumb forgotten about crawdaddies and lye soap baths.

I know it ain't right, but I had to laugh.

Heavy footfalls echoed on the decking above us.

"You all right boy?" I heard Pa ask.

"Yeah, I'm good," I said, "but if Baby was a cat, I reckon she'd o' just lost about a half a dozen lives."

"I'll be right up."

Placing a foot on the twisting body of the snake, I let go of the tail, drew my skinning knife, and quickly dispatched it of its gap-jawed head.

"Let it be," I warned Baby as I flicked the serpent's head into the stream where it could float away before someone stepped on the still dangerous fangs. The four-foot body made two full wraps around my forearm as I placed it in the bucket so Baby wouldn't ruin it.

"Reckon ya might could make me a copperhead belt?" I asked Pa as I looked up at his towering form still holding the half-carved flute and whittling knife in his big hands.

"Reckon," he said.

It was then that Charlotte came rushing around the house calling out that someone was coming up the trail. She was moving along a bit too quickly for her condition to my way of thinkin', but I reckon she just naturally knew it was Diver comin'. Something 'bout the connection between a man and wife, I suppose. I'd o' boohooed the notion, but many a time I'd seen Ma get all antsy for a day or two before Pa came home from one of his long hunts. Like she somehow knowed he was on his way.

Well, if that's what Charlotte was figurin', she was right. There came Diver, smiling big as you please, riding high on Aristotle and scattering chickens on the trail.

Aristotle was prancing along like he was carryin' Silly Billy himself (assuming he would have thought it an honor to haul about the king of England).

Pa and I both waved as Charlotte rushed across the yard to greet Diver.

"Kathryn, Diver's home," Pa called to the house.

When Diver climbed down, he and Charlotte greeted each other as me and Pa waited to let them have their moment. Ma came out and stood on the doorstep.

After a hug and a peck on the lips, Diver looked at Pa and said, "Howdy, Zeb. By the looks of them shavin's on the porch you must o' skinnied down that stick a bit."

Pa grinned. "A bit," he said.

I strolled up and shook Diver's hand.

"Have a nice trip, did ya?" I asked.

"That's about the size of it," he said. "Help me with my things and take care of Aristotle if ya would. Then we'll go in, and I'll tell ya all about it."

Diver unstrapped his travel bag and sleeping roll along with a sheathed rifle, powder horn and possibles bag.

Aristotle flicked his tail driving a biting horsefly from his rump.

Pa walked over and retrieved the rifle, pulling it from its scabbard. "Got yourself a Hawken," he said as he examined the weapon. ".54 caliber."

It was the same make and bore as Pa's, though not nearly as ornate. A fine rifle all the same.

"Didn't know you were in the market for one of these," Pa said. He worked the well-oiled action, both feeling and hearing the light, snick . . . snick, of the double hammer settings.

"I'm not," said Diver. "That's for Casey. He asked me to pick it up on my trip. I don't know what it was, but something seemed to have spooked him at Hec and Charlie's reception."

Pa shrugged and sighted down the barrel. "Well, whatever he wants it for, you done good by him. It's a fine weapon."

I hurried up and led Aristotle across the now snakeless bridge and into the barn where I stripped off his saddle and tack and fetched him a scoop of grain. I reckon that's what he'd been waitin' for, the way he nosed me outta the way so he could get at it. I then gave him a quick curryin' before trotting to the house. I sure didn't want to miss Diver's tellin' of his journey.

And miss it I could have, the way Ma was rushin' around, dishin' up strawberry pie, pourin' coffee and sweet milk, and passin' out forks and plates. Charlotte tried to help but I got the feeling she wasn't movin' quick enough for Ma. By her way of thinkin', the niceties had to be observed before the tellin' started, but there was no call to dillydallyin'.

We'd no more than sat down and said grace when Ma looked at Diver and said, "How's your pie?"

Diver chopped off a piece with his fork and made a show of tasting it. He grinned and closed his eyes as if relishing the perfect symphony of sweet and tartness.

"It's perfect," he said. "About the most..."

"How was your trip?" Ma cut in.

Everyone laughed but Ma. Her face was deadly serious as she sipped her milk.

"Well, first off," Diver said. He reached over and took Charlotte's hand. "We're moving."

Me, Ma and Pa, all 'bout hit the floor. We had no idea where that came from.

Charlotte smiled and reaching out her other hand, rested it on Diver's. "Not right away," she said.

We all looked at Charlotte, then back at Diver.

He smiled at our startled stares. "Like she said, it won't be right away," He winked at Charlotte. "But come fall, when Brother Wilson returns, I'll be out of work. We talked it over and decided we want to settle in the Cove permanently."

That brought smiles all around.

"You know you got a home here as long as you want," said Pa.

"Yeah, we know that" said Diver, "and it *is* truly appreciated. But we're starting a family of our own and we need a place of our own. Somewhere to grow."

"Fair enough," Pa said, giving Ma a quick look to forestall any objections. "So, what's your plans?"

"A mill," said Diver. "Casey is giving us that section of land from the falls out to Cades Cove Road. We're going to build a house and a grist mill."

"So, we'll still be neighbors," Charlotte said to Ma. "I'll be here to help with the chickens every day."

"Or, at least as long as she can," said Diver rubbing Charlotte's arm.

"And when I can't make it," Charlotte continued, "Jenny Schmitt and Lidia Tudwell said they'd be happy to fill in. Who knows, if things keep up the way they are, maybe we'll put them on permanently."

Ma was beaming. She'd been afraid Charlotte and Diver were going back to Kentucky.

"But that's not all," Diver said. "Orwell and Clarence are backing Rolf in a sawmill, and in return, he's going to supply Orwell with the lumber to build a store next to our place. The way he sees it, a nearby store would be mighty accommodatin' to all of them farmers waitin' around to have their grain milled. Kind of a community meetin' place."

"A store?" said Pa. "There's gonna be two Beckett stores?"

Diver grinned. "Well, Orwell's been unhappy for quite a spell now with the way his brother's been treatin' folks at the Beckett Freight Store. Bad for the family name. He said they've had words about it in the past. Now that Trace has taken over; well, let's just say he's decided enough is enough. He'll open a store of his own where folks will be treated like neighbors, not like debtors. He said he's envisioning a two-story frame building with the store on the first floor and the second to house his partner's family. It'll be called the B&C Emporium."

"B&C?" said Pa.

"Yep," said Diver as he mischievously grinned and gave Charlotte a one-handed hug around her waist.

"Oh, tell 'em already," Charlotte said as she gave Diver a playful opened handed slap on his chest. "Your long-winded way of gettin' to the point could make a person pull their hair out."

Diver winked at her, then turned to Ma and Pa. "Yep," he repeated, "The B&C. It stands for Beckett and Chapmere."

"Chapmere?" gasped Ma. "You mean Delma?"

Pa looked like he was about to faint.

"Yep," said Diver once again with a big smile on his face. "When Orwell first came to me with the idea of starting a new store, he asked if I knew anyone I'd trust to run it. Of course, Delma and James were the first that came to mind."

Diver chuckled.

"Seein's how they work for his brother, Orwell got plumb tickled over that. He said if Delma and James are half the workers her brother Forrest is, he knows the store will be in good hands. In fact, he liked the idea so well he said that if they agreed, he'd be willing to consider going into a full partnership with 'em. They could run the business as they see fit and he'd be the financial backer. All I had to do was get a firm commitment from them . . . face to face."

Diver sat back and did a small drum roll on the table with his fingers after popping the last of his pie into his mouth.

"And now, Kate," he grinned, "you know what my journey was for. Delma and James are coming home."

Well, as you can imagine it was a happy time around the Banion place that summer, what with Ma and Charlotte planning out every detail about how they were going to decorate Charlotte's new house and Pa and Diver figuring the ins and outs of building and working a grist mill.

And, of course, everyone countin' down the days till Delma came home.

As for me, well it was downright perplexin' how Diver once again was in the middle of bringing the Banion clan back together. I's scratchin' my head tryin' to figure if the credit goes to Diver for what he done for us, or to Pa, for pullin' Diver outta that pool in the first place.

Somethings just ain't for a mountain boy to understand.

≈

A few weeks after we heard the news about Delma coming home, I was out in the yard wrestling around with Baby while Ma and Pa sat on the porch talkin' with Casey. It was a clear, cool, mid-summer evening with a scattering of lightning bugs just starting to get their torches lit and some crickets tuning up down by the stream. One or two overachieving bees remained darting around Ma and Charlotte's garden trying to collect a last bit of nectar before nightfall. Every now and then, when the winds shifted just right, the far-off buzz of a large water powered circular saw could be heard ripping through massive timbers.

"Sounds like Rolf's working late tonight," Pa said.

Ma paused in her sewing and looked out across a distant valley where a flock of blackbirds were frettin' a chickenhawk which had flown too close to their nesting trees.

"Dean told me Rolf's about the most driven person he's ever seen," said Casey.

Dean and Casey had become the best of friends as of late with Casey spending a great deal of his free time at the oldest Tudwell boy's new house. Casey claimed it was because he and Dean had a checkers competition going, but most everybody suspected it was actually Dean's sister-in-law, Thelma Lou, who captivated his interest.

"He claims with the gristmill and store being built at the same time, even with Danny Harris and Chip Shelton helping mill lumber and Mr. Blyth runnin' deliveries, he can hardly keep up with demand," continued Casey.

He smiled. "Claims Jenny threatened to have a painting made of him, so she'd have somethin' to talk to."

Pa chuckled at that, but I could see in Ma's eyes, she knew how Jenny felt. Rather than say anything, she simply straightened her material and went back to stitching.

"Well, it won't be much longer," Pa said. "They're doing a fine job on those buildings. I just hope Diver's mill will be ready come harvest."

"Yeah, it'd be mighty handy, y'all grinding your own corn," said Casey.

"Cost effective too," Pa said as he shifted about, making little circles with his left shoulder while he closed and opened his fist.

"You alright?" asked Casey.

"Yeah, I keep sleepin' on my shoulder wrong."

"Reckon you'd o' figured it out by your age," smirked Casey.

Pa eyed him, and Casey decided to change the subject. "So, how's the corn lookin'?"

"Better'n I have the right to hope for," Pa said, workin' the kink out of his shoulder and reaching over to squeeze Ma's hand where it laid on the arm of her chair. "Lookin' like another bumper crop in a few weeks or so. If I can keep the coons out of it."

He looked at me and Baby and said, "Reckon it's about time you taught that lazy loafer of yourn that she's lived on handouts around here 'bout long enough. It's time we fetched Blue Boy and Ricket up here to teach her what that sniffer she's been haulin' around is all about."

"Sounds like fun," said Casey. "I wouldn't mind doin' some coon huntin' myself. I remember one time when me and Bobby Lee went over to . . ." He caught himself and seemed to think twice about telling that tale. "Well, anyway, a coon hunt sounds like fun."

Pa eyed Casey for a moment, then decided to let it go. "Course the hides ain't no good this time o' year," he said, "but we could sure make 'em think twice about hangin' 'round my corn field. I figure if Billy starts drag training tomorrow, we could do a hunt in about two weeks."

"Sounds good," said Casey, avoiding looking Pa in the eye.

I roughed up Baby's ears. "Looks like we're in for some trainin' whether we want it or not," I said. "And it's all your fault."

It hadn't escaped my notice that I'd been a witness to, rather than a participant in, the entire conversation.

Seen, but not heard. I couldn't rightly recollect where I'd heard that before, but I surely appreciated the sentiment. It just seemed to come natural when an older sibling was about. Truth be told, I didn't take offence. I liked havin' Casey home.

Before we turned in that night, Pa gave me a coon hide he'd doused with a jar of scent he kept in his tanning shed. He said he had scents from several furbearers, but Ma didn't need to hear about that. I thought that was a rather odd statement, but simply said, "Okay."

"First," he said, "I want you to get up early, while there's still dew on the ground. That'll help Baby focus on a single scent. Drag the hide around and let Baby occasionally catch it and play with it. But it's important you take it away before she gets tired of it. That's called, "putting it away hot." It'll make her want it even more. After a few days, lock her away while you drag the hide around the yard and leave it lay where she can find it. Put her on the trail and encourage her to get it. When she does, let her play with it for a bit and give her a treat, but again, be sure to take the hide away before she tires of it. Make the trail a bit longer and harder each day for a week or so but be sure she always finds the hide and gets her treat. The last day or so maybe even hang it in a tree. After that, she should be ready to go out with the old dogs. They'll train her from there.

Two weeks later, on a Friday evening, Baby's first coon hunt began. Along with me, Pa and Casey, there was Forrest, Chance, Second Chance, and a fella called Booker who was lookin' to train one of Baby's siblings; an overweight male called Root.

Booker said when Root was only a month or so old, he ran off chasing a rabbit and didn't come back. They hunted for him well into the night before giving up. The next morning, Booker found the dog with its collar snagged on a washed-out hemlock root down by Abrams Creek. He was fast asleep as if he didn't have a care in the world. Overhearing him tell his wife how the pup was found, their young daughter began calling it "Root". The name stuck. The dog's been called Root ever since.

The way Root scampered around jamming its nose into every nook and cranny it could find, I figured it was aptly named, even if not for the right reason.

"So, where ya wantin' to get this party started?" Chance asked Pa. Being the hound-man of the bunch, it was agreed, Chance would run the show.

"Over past that ridge yonder, at my cornfield," said Pa. "Hopefully we can make that porch ornament of Billy's understand I want her protecting the crop."

"It'll take some doin', but she'll catch on," Chance said. "She comes from the best team I ever owned. Who knows, with the right training, she could turn out to be even better than her parents."

Pa shifted his Hawken in the crock of his arm and looked at Baby with doubtful eyes. "That'd sure be somethin'," he said. "But you're the dog man here. If you're sellin' it, reckon I ain't got no choice but to be buyin'."

Now, to my way o' thinkin', Pa was as good as sayin' he believed Baby *could* be a better coonhound than her parents. And they were the best of the best. That was some mighty high praise for a so-called porch ornament.

I wanted to hear it again. "What'd you say?" I asked.

Pa's thick brows lowered as he locked a hard gaze onto my eyes. He knew what I was doing.

"I ain't used to chewin' my cabbage twice," he said. "Specially not for a pin-feathered poult tryin' to puff up his tail feathers like a struttin' Tom turkey."

"No, sir," I said, feelin' about as deflated as a boy can feel. Especially in front of a mess of adults and one of my own peers.

Pa's hard stare softened and he good naturedly shook my shoulder. "But if that little night yapper does learn to keep the coons outta my corn, she'll be livin' high on deer shins and ham hocks," he said.

I knew that was Pa's way of sayin', "We're good."

Shortly after we passed by the beehives and came to the base of the slope that the cornfield was on, Chance pointed out a rocky clearing.

"Let's set-up there," he said.

Set-up? I thought. I thought we were going to be hunting.

"Come on, Billy," Second Chance said. "We need to gather firewood."

As me and Second Chance scurried around in the underbrush, snapping off twigs and picking up fallen branches, he explained the plan.

"We build a fire and sit tight," he said. "That's one of the best parts of coon hunting. The dogs will scout out the area looking for coons. As they hunt, they will occasionally bawl out to let us know where they're at. We'll know where they are by the bark, they'll know where we are by the fire. If they come across an old coon sent, that's called a cold trail, they'll continue the occasional bawl, but it will be drawn out longer. If the trail gets hot and they're actually chasing a coon, they'll heat up. Their song will become continuous and louder. That's when we'll know to head their way. If they tree a coon they'll go into a frenzy with sharper snipped-off bawls and barking. That means hurry-up, we did our jobs, you come do yours."

"You make it sound like they're talking to us," I said.

"They are," said Second Chance. "Why I reckon a good coonhound is just about the smartest critter on earth. And if you think talkin' is something, you outta see 'em trackin'. If a really good dog loses a trail 'cause a coon went up a tree and crossed over to another one before coming back down, he don't give up. He starts circling. His circles get bigger and bigger 'til he finds where the coon came down, and off he goes after it. And if a coon goes into water, a good dog'll hold back and watch where it comes out before he continues the chase. He just naturally knows that a coon is a better swimmer than a dog. If a coon catches a dog in water, it'll circle 'round and climb up his back so it can sit on his head and drown him. The best dogs won't fall for that."

"Wow," I said. "I never knew there was so much to bringing home a coon hide."

"Yeah, there's a lot to learn," said Second Chance, obviously enjoying this rare moment of being the expert. "Maybe even more for Baby than you. That's why she needs to be with Blue Boy and Ricket. They'll teach her right."

By the time we got back, the dogs were already on the hunt. All but Root that is. No matter what Booker did, Root refused to follow his parents into the dark.

"I don't get it," said Booker watching his dog slink around, head hanging, and tail tucked between his legs.

"You put him back outside after that night snagged on the root?" asked Chance.

"No," said Booker. "The wife wouldn't hear of it. She said he'd be scared. He's slept with Sissy ever since."

"Well," said Chance, trying to be as diplomatic as possible. "I'd say you got a real fine house dog there."

Booker looked stunned. Down-right hurt even.

"Now, don't beat yourself up about it," said Chance. "Not every dog is cut out to be a hunter any more than every man is cut out to be a cobbler. If Root there is a comfort to your family as a watchdog and a companion, then so be it. Did you plan on having him out coon hunting every winter anyway?"

Booker looked rather perplexed. "No," he said. "Fact is, I ain't never been much of a hunter myself. Don't cotton much to the cold and damp and sleepin' out where ya could wake up with a bear cuddled up next to ya."

He looked at Root, cringing back at the edge of the firelight as if he were in trouble.

"Come here, boy," Booker called as he patted his leg.

Root leapt into Booker's lap, wagging his tail and licking Booker's chin.

"Yeah, you're alright," Booker laughed. "You ain't no hunter and I ain't no cobbler." He roughed the dog's ears. "But I reckon we'll be what we are together. And that's alright."

Most of that night we listened to the sounds of dogs singing. Chance pointed out the nuances of their voices until I could distinguish them apart. Once learned it was like listening to friends. Even Baby had a shriller but quite lovely voice herself. Three times they were on cold trails, and twice on hot. When a trail turned hot we hurried to catch-up to the dogs.

A Home in the Mist: On Thin Ice

The forest floor nearly glowed with its thick covering of moist leaves reflecting the moonlight.

Truth is, it's not half as hard to travel in the woods at night as a person might think.

Pa and Casey both carried rifles for protection from the forest denizens, but we were not after prey. We gave the coons a good scare and hoped they would flee at the first sign of Baby in the future. If so, we'd accomplished what we came to do. If not, we still had a great time.

All these years later, there's not much I enjoy more than laying in an overstuffed feather bed on a moonlit autumn night, listening to the far-off sound of coonhounds on a hot scent. Closing my eyes, I drift back to the days of my youth. A gentler time. A time of adventure and wonder. When all that laid before me were unwritten pages of infinite possibilities. I run free over the ridges and through the hollers of the Great Smoky Mountains, and as if out of the mists of my fondest desires, I see Baby running at my side.

TEN

Settling In

THREE MORE NIGHTS over the next week or so, Second Chance and I took Baby out and ran her with Blue Boy and Ricket. Pa assured Ma that Chance's dogs would keep us safe from the wilder creatures of our mountains, but I'm not sure she took a heap of comfort from his words.

Finally giving in, he admitted it was about time I had a rifle of my own. With a stern warning 'bout its safe use and a twinkle of pride in his eyes, he presented me with his precious Pennsylvania rifle.

I gotta say, I swelled up like the cat that ate the canary. Course, I tried not to show it, but I reckon it was pretty obvious. What, with the way I couldn't keep a grin off my face, and I got all choked-up, and took to shuddering and all.

Fact is, I doubt there was a man in them Smoky Mountains that wouldn't have given his eye teeth for the weapon Pa had carried all them years. It was 'bout as recognizable as he was. And it was mine!

Think about it. Pa may have owned a Hawken, but I owned the rifle that got it for him.

Anyway, me and Baby spent a whole lot of time patrollin' Pa's cornfield after that and come harvest time Pa reckoned we'd saved him a heap of grain. Said it made him proud to have a boy that could provide for his family the way I done.

Now some folks might say I deserved a cut o' the profits for them long nights I spent thrashin' my way through that corn out there in the dark. Well, I can tell them folks right here and now, there ain't never been a gold coin struck that could mean half as much to me as the praise I heard coming from Pa's lips. I don't rightly reckon I ever received a more generous paycheck in my life.

With the corn picked and stored: whether in the husk for eatin' fresh or shucked and cribbed to dry-out for meal and flour, Pa and Diver had time to move Charlotte's possessions to the new house.

The store, gristmill, and Diver's house were all complete and ready to be occupied.

While Ma and Charlotte went to work cleaning, arranging, and decorating, I helped out where I could.

We were all concerned about Charlotte doing too much in her delicate condition.

Pa and Diver prepared their wagons to move Delma, James, and little JJ from Maryville, and

Orwell sent along Forrest and Chance in two of his wagons to retrieve as many store goods as they could. All in all, I reckon them four heavy farm wagons was about the biggest parade Rich Mountain Road had ever seen.

Coming back, James' wagon would add yet another to the fray.

It was some mighty exciting times in the Cove.

That first night after Pa and Diver left, I was 'bout as tired as I could be. Them gals just didn't have no stop in 'em when they took to settin' up house.

I climbed up to my loft and crawled to my feather mattress. One nice thing about havin' all of them chickens was we no longer had hay stuffed mattress's on the homestead.

I didn't even remove my shoes before flopping down and closing my eyes. I may have been asleep before my head hit the pillow.

I soon dreamed:

A crisp, cool breeze was blowin' outta the north as I raced along a moonlit deer trail. Off in the distance I could hear Baby bawlin' and barkin'. Tellin' me to hurry it up, is what she was doing. I paid no heed to a wait-a-minute bush that was trying its best to slow me down. In my mind's eye I could already see that super-sized coon that Baby had treed. And I was fixin' to get it. Pa was sure gonna be surprised. It was a fifty pounder with a yellow mask, and fur as thick and soft as a baby chinchilla.

Now, I'd never seen a chinchilla mind you, but I'd heard tell of 'em. Fur so soft you could sink your fingers a full six inches into its fleece before you even realized you'd touched it.

That last hundred yards or so I don't believe I was actually running anymore. It was more like I had risen up and was swiftly floating through the underbrush. I reckon I gave quite a few night critters a pretty good scare. One I distinctly remember was a big ol' hoot owl. He was sitting with his back to me as I floated up and hovered just behind him. Many a night he'd asked me that same old question, so I felt it only fair to ask it right back at him. I got right up close and shouted, "WHO!"

Well, that owl like to messed his perch. I know he lost a dozen tail feathers tryin' to be shed of that area and I don't figure he was lookin' to be coming back.

Yeah, I'll tell ya true, if it was possible, that's the way I'd always travel.

It wasn't long before I settled into a clearing at the base of a burr oak tree. Baby was sitting back lookin' up at me as if to say I'd sure taken my time in gettin' there. Truth is, I was kind of embarrassed.

Who ever heard of a boy that had to prove himself to his own dog.

"Sorry," I said.

I didn't remember bringing it, but I suddenly had a blazing pine knot torch in my right hand. I raised it high to catch the glow from the coon's eyes.

A breeze rustled through the leaves. A limb swayed casting shadowy, spectral fingers across nearby foliage. The far-off screech of a night bird faded into a cloak of silence. Only the light sputtering of burning pine sap could be heard as the torch smoke gently wove its way through the overhanging greenery and dissipated into the void beyond.

I searched for the masked prey.

Circling the tree, I waved the torch back and forth, lighting every dark hollow and leaf obscured nook I could find. Knowing a coon will naturally gaze into the dim light of a torch, I watched for the yellow glow of his eyes.

"You sure there's a coon up there?" I asked Baby.

Continuing to search, I stepped closer to the tree, then back, then side-stepped, and did the whole thing over again. Fifteen minutes I searched. I'll tell ya, I was startin' to think Baby had blown this one big.

Then, just as I was about to give up, a long, white, toothy snout came peeking over a limb. As the beady eyes came into view, they glowed red.

Red? Everybody knows a raccoon's eyes glow yellow.

"Why, Baby, that ain't no coon," I said. "That's a possum." I looked at my dog and shook my head in disbelief.

"Here you got me spending the best part of the night chasing you halfway across the mountains and you ain't treed nothin' but a possum. Don't you know the difference between a coon and a possum?"

I pointed at the ugly marsupial and asked her again, "Now can't you see that's a possum?"

Baby looked at the critter in question, then at me. "Well, it may look like a possum," she said, "but it sure smelled like a coon."

The next mornin' Ma told me she'd been up late the previous night sewing curtains for Charlotte's windows. It was about ten o'clock and her candles were burning low when she heard a strange noise filtering through the ceiling. It raised the short hairs on the back of her neck. Strange night noises in the dark woods are expected, but when she realized the sounds were coming from the sleeping loft where her youngest son was all alone laughing to himself, somehow that gave her an even deeper case of the willies.

While Pa and the others were gone to Maryville, the Cove obtained a new resident. Doc Dulaney and his small family moved into Doc Kendree's old place.

Seein's how Kendree had left a lien-free house to
which no one laid claim, it was agreed the Dulaneys
could use the place rent free. It would be partial
payment for future medical services rendered to the
citizens of the Cove.

Now, I'm not saying everyone was thrilled about
having a new doctor in town. Kendree left a heap of
folks gun-shy of the profession and young Dulaney
had his work cut out for him gaining their trust. Fact
is, I reckon if not for Diver and a few other good
Samaritans in the Cove, them Dulaneys would have
starved in the first month or so of his practice.

While the Cove was abuzz with all the changes
taking place there, the backwoods wasn't quite so
anxious to disclose its secrets.

As Buck had told Pearle, that long-abandoned
homestead in the wilderness was about as perfect a
location as a body could imagine in that steep back
country. It sat on the west side of a four-acre natural
clearing high atop a knoll overlooking a rock-strewn
streamed in the valley below. Blueberries were
abundant in the meadow along with hickories and
several other wild edibles in the surrounding
woodlands.

A sturdy, two-room cabin with a stone fireplace
and a partially collapsed roof sat cradled among the
numerous outbuildings. A smokehouse, storage shed,

and corn crib occupied a patch of overgrown weeds with a severely tilting necessary nearby. A rock-lined walkway led to a stone springhouse with crystal clear, frigid water. Far enough away to avoid the odor sat the remains of a collapsed chickencoop and what appeared to be a partially shaded pigpen with a large wallow.

Nearly hidden by an overhanging patch of pawpaw trees, a narrow, rocky path followed two hundred yards down the contour of a steep walled cliff to a spring-fed pond teaming with fish. The path, shaded by a wall of thick rhododendrons and damp from numerous rivulets of seeping groundwater could be treacherous for the unwary with its slick outer edge plummeting thirty feet to the moss-covered rocks below. But with care, one could access a wonderland seldom seen outside the Smoky Mountains.

To Pearle's delight, Buck had pointed them to the very home she had dreamed of as a young girl. A place of beauty and sustenance. A healthy place to raise her family. A place to forget the endless expanse of dust clogged skies and plowed-under fields that had been their life on that drab and colorless dirt farm back in Kentucky.

Within six weeks, the boys had repaired the roof of the cabin, added a sleeping loft, and even built on a second bedroom with its own fireplace. The timeworn outbuildings were put back into usable order and a new necessary was constructed to replace the one that was falling into its own hole.

While the boys worked on the buildings, the girls gathered and stored wild edibles against the coming winter. Hiram fished and hunted to stock up the smokehouse larder. Two black bears, a whitetail deer and a young turkey had all fallen to his Kentucky rifle, along with several smaller critters that made do for their evening meals. Hiram had never seen such abundance. The amount of bear signs alone was staggering, especially around the blueberry patches.

As the Haggen clan sweated under the midday sun, a lone red-tailed hawk watched from a barren branch high above. His vigilant gaze followed their every move as they toiled below. Finally, seemingly satisfied, he gave one sharp screech and dove off his perch, gliding away through the treetops.

Caleb wiped his brow and watched the bird soar away. Barnabas, glancing up said, "You've seen hawks before, little brother. Let's get back to work."

Without replying, Caleb gripped his axe and returned to stripping a cedar fence post. He puzzled at feeling like a dark shadow had just crossed his soul.

For protection, Hiram always kept his rifle loaded and ready for action. Not the safest thing to do with a house full of young'uns, but between bears and Indians he figured on not taking any chances.

On two occasions he'd had to tan the hide of the twins and the dummy for playing with the dangerous weapon. He'd told 'em time and again to stay shy of it, but sure enough, he'd go to get it only to find it wasn't where he'd left it. Of course, no one was willing to take the blame, so they all got a switchin'.

It never occurred to him that Pearle or Avery may have moved the thing while cleaning. All he knew was, it was beyond him why their ma couldn't keep a handle on them brats. It was her job after all. That didn't sound like too much to ask? It's not like she sweated out there everyday fishing and hunting so's their bellies wouldn't be rubbin' their backsides.

Though it was far too late in the year to plant a garden, Pearle and Clay spent a bone jarring day bouncing along in Hiram's wagon to fetch Buck's plow in hopes of preparing the soil for next spring. Pearle had brought along her seed pots when they'd fled Kentucky, though unfortunately she'd learned neither of her daughters-in-law had done the same.

Pearle had promised Buck never to bring Hiram back onto his property, but he welcomed young Clay.

"How's the new home, sis?" Buck asked as he helped Pearle from her wagon and gave her a big hug.

He then shook Clay's hand.

"It's wonderful," she said. "Hiram never has told me why we had to flee Kentucky in the middle of the night, but I bless the day we did. I have a beautiful new home and live close to you and Eunice."

Her face paled as she looked Buck in the eye. "How is Eunice?" she asked.

"See for yourself," Buck said as he stepped to the side.

Eunice stood in the doorway, smiling and waving. "Come on in and sit a spell," she called.

Pearle laughed and waved back. "She looks great," she uttered to Buck under her breath. "Real good."

"I ain't never seen nothin' like it," said Buck. "Whatever you done put more life in the old gal than I've seen in twenty years."

Pearle shook her head in wonder. "Ain't nothin' I done," she said. "Must be that remedy you gave her."

Buck laughed. "Good luck convincing her of that. She thought I was tryin' to put her under with it."

"Well, whatever she thinks, I wouldn't mind having a jug of that stuff my own self," snickered Pearle.

Buck smiled as he gave Pearle another one-armed hug. "Reckon that could be arranged," he said. He shaded his eyes with his floppy hat as he looked up at the glaring sun. "Let's go in and have a nice cool spruce tea."

"That sounds mighty fine," Pearle said taking Clay's arm and starting toward the cabin.

Buck wiped sweat from his forehead then resettled his hat and fell in behind. He tried to ignore how much Clay looked like his father.

"Pearle," Eunice squealed as she hugged her sister-in-law. She rushed over and pulled a hickory pug from an earthenware jar of tea.

It was designed to keep the cool in while keeping the flies out.

"Have a seat. I'll pour you some tea."

She filled two egg shaped metal beakers and placed them on the table. For herself and Buck she used wooden cups.

"So, who's this young man," she asked smiling at Clay.

"This is my boy, Clay," Pearle said.

Clay nodded his head and said, "Ma'am."

"Fine lookin' boy," said Eunice. Like Buck, she was somewhat takin' aback by how much Clay looked like Hiram.

Sitting a fresh loaf of sourdough bread and lard spread on the table, she unwrapped a whittled down piece of salted ham that hung over the counter and began cutting several slices off it.

"Buck said you have a passel of kids," she laughed. "How many you got?"

Pearle reached out and took the proffered plate of ham. "I have ten," she said.

Eunice dropped into her chair. "Ten!" she said. Looking at Buck she said, "Ten."

Pearle smiled. "Yeah, I been blessed," she said. "Least ways those that ain't gotta change their diapers tell me so."

Eunice sat imagining what life would have been like with ten kids as she built her sandwich. She'd always wished she could have had more, but ten?

Feeling a cold sensation on her thumb, she looked at it and saw a large dollop of lard spread slowly sliding down to the web of her hand and dripping onto the table.

Looking up, she noticed everyone was staring at her. She must have missed something.

"I'm sorry," she said with an unsure grin. "I guess I was daydreaming. Ten kids!"

She patted Clay's hand and looked at Pearle. "So, what brings y'all our way?"

"I was hoping to borrow Buck's plow," said Pearle.

"Anything you need," said Buck.

Conversation went on after that, but Eunice only half listened. *Ten kids*, she thought. *Life would have sure been different*. Eunice knew that with her health she didn't have half the energy needed to take care of another soul beyond herself and Buck. *How could*

Pearle possibly do it? Of course, Pearle was quite a bit younger than her.

"Well, you know how he is," Pearle's voice interrupted her thoughts. "I don't reckon he'll ever file for homestead. He'll figure he settled the land so let 'em just try and take it."

"Mighty risky," said Buck.

Eunice realized she'd zoned out again but didn't mention it.

"Well, we gotta go," said Pearle. "We got a long ride back."

"I'll go load the plow for ya," said Buck.

"Nice meetin' ya," Clay told Eunice as he stood. "I'll help ya, Uncle Buck."

As he followed Buck out the door, Eunice and Pearle hugged.

"You come back anytime," Eunice said. "I've missed you something fierce."

"And I've missed you," said Pearle. "I figure I'll be bringing Buck's plow back in a few days. We can visit again then."

Pearle kissed Eunice on the cheek and faded into the glaring sun.

Eunice sat back down and wrapped her hands around her drinking cup. This wasn't the first time she'd drifted away during a conversation, but she believed it was the longest.

She hoped Buck hadn't noticed.

≈

With their parent's homestead restored to a livable condition, Barney and Caleb packed their horses and set out to find land of their own. Three families on the same plot would be too much for the surrounding woodlands to sustain.

Primarily following the streambed that Hiram's cabin overlooked, they slowly made their way north surveying each ridge and hollow as they came to it. Unknown to them, they were on the same stream that Buck's land bordered a few miles to the south. A stream the locals called Black Gum Shoal.

Two days they searched before finding a steep walled gap that led between a spruce covered peak and a craggy topped pinnacle. Following a narrow game trail that meandered through great patches of Catawba rhododendron and thornless blackberry bushes they exited the gap into a three-acre meadow that overlooked the distant, Sloping Fields, they had seen from Buck's trail.

Hearing flowing water nearby, they nudged their horses around a massive fallen boulder and came across a tumbling brook that plunged eight feet into a small pool of rippling water. At an outlet between two flat-topped rocks, it continued in a series of cascades to a wide, slow-moving creek a hundred yards below.

Looking across the valley, they could see it stretched far to the south.

"I bet that goes all the way to Parson's Branch," said Barnabas.

"My guess would be beyond," agreed Caleb.

Barnabas lowered his hat to his saddle horn, raked back his greasy hair with both hands and looked out across the expanse.

"Well, little brother," he said. "looks like I found my new home."

Caleb looked at the back of his brother's head and took note that he had said his home, not their home.

"I figure I'll find a useable trail down to that valley floor and have easy access to the Cove," Barney thought out loud. He then looked at Caleb and saw the steel in his eyes.

"Don't fret brother," he said nodding his chin back up the trail through the gap. "You find a place back there and I'll let ya come through my land to access the valley. Won't charge ya nothin' neither." He grinned. "We're brothers after all. I'll look out for ya."

Caleb reined his horse about a bit harsher than the gelding cared for, his hot temper flaring nearly out of control. *Calm down*, he warned himself. He knew he didn't stand a chance against his older sibling's fury.

Behind his stiff back he heard Barnabas chuckle.

"You go on now and find yourself a real nice piece of ground," he called. "I think I'll hang around here for a while and ponder on where I'm gonna build my new cabin."

Caleb prodded his horse into a canter and soon disappeared down the trail without giving a reply. The back of his neck heated up, and his jaw was clinched so tight he feared he might break a tooth.

One day, he thought. *One day!*

Upon reaching the far end of the gap, he reined to the right and settled into an easy walk traversing a narrow floodplain that stretched between the stream and a steep ridge. As he worked his way through tangled masses of undergrowth and climbed a series of ascending hillocks his temper cooled. His rage was placated by the sound of rippling water and a hundred whistles and tweets from multicolored songbirds in the sun-speckled, emerald canopy overhead.

For nearly an hour he followed the stream, occasionally being pushed into the channel's edge by an encroaching hillside and at other times straying far inland to circumvent a particularly swampy shoreline.

Finally, as the sun moved past its zenith and shadows gathered on the east side of trees, he pulled back on the gelding's reins. A sheer rock ledge had pushed up to the streambank alongside a series of rapids too turbulent to cross.

"Well, that sure put a stump in the field," he said.

As he sat pondering his next move, he caught the scent of frying liver. He'd never developed a taste for the dark meat himself, but he figured it had about the most appealing smell he'd ever come across.

"Now, what ya reckon that is?" he asked his horse as he climbed down and let it drink from a protruding gravel bar.

A long thin smudge of fragrant smoke hung about twelve feet above the water and lazily swirled around overhanging branches as it drifted downstream.

Caleb gave his horse a shocked look. "Go check it out you say?"

The horse raised his dripping muzzle from the stream and nickered.

"Well now, don't get pushy," he said.

Leading the horse well back into the thickets where it couldn't be seen from the water, he tied its reins to a young box elder tree.

"You just wait here. I'll do the hard part."

The horse lowered its head and nosed around in the lush vegetation. If it understood Caleb's quip it didn't seem to take offense.

Skirting around the prominence, Caleb found a brush clogged gully that led to the ridgetop. Half climbing and half crawling, he scratched and dug for every handhold he could find. Being blocked off from the cool breezes wafting off the watercourse, the air hung hot and heavy. Every few minutes he had to stop and swipe rivulets of perspiration from his eyes with the backs of his hands. He'd then lay back and gasp for air before turning over and continuing to climb.

No more than twenty minutes elapsed, though it felt like hours, before he came crawling through the leaf litter onto the top of the ridge. Propping himself up with his back against a tree, he nearly cried at the thought of all that cold water so nearby, yet none to soothe his parched and tormented throat. Brushing back a carpet of pine needles and dead twigs, he desperately scratched around until he found a smooth round stone about the size of his thumbnail. It wasn't chilled cider, he had to admit, but it would have to do. Popping the pebble into his mouth, he closed his eyes and waited for the saliva to flow.

The sun journeyed west as shadows lengthened to the east. Long tattered wisps of scattered clouds gave testament as the last remnants of a far-off storm. Time passed and Caleb dosed.

It's debatable who was frightened more. The fat chipmunk who was boldly sitting on Caleb's shoulder rustling through his beard for grubs, or Caleb himself when he opened his eyes to see tiny hands and beady eyes two inches in front of his nose.

A Home in the Mist: On Thin Ice

Caleb yelped and leapt up sending the small rodent scurrying over his shoulder and down his back to the burrow he had nearly decimated while scratching around at the base of the tree.

"Ooh, ooh," Caleb groaned as he shivered at the thought of a rat brushing through his beard. He scurried away from the tree frantically brushing off his shoulders. In the confusion, he had mistaken the chipmunk for a rat, though with his aversion to all rodents, it wouldn't have made much difference.

Several minutes passed before he remembered why he had climbed the ridge in the first place.

"Oh yeah, somebody was cookin' out here in the middle of nowhere," he mumbled.

Keeping an eye on the tree, he gave it a wide berth as he crept toward the edge of a cliff. When still ten feet away, he got down and crawled forward. Then he shimmied up to a vantage point next to a windblown cedar.

Across, and slightly upstream from where he laid, was a well-maintained log cabin with numerous outbuildings and animal shelters. A bare-chested lad of perhaps fifteen or sixteen years of age appeared to be braiding a rope he had attached to a wrist thick maple sapling. His long black hair and buckskin britches gave testament to his Indian heritage.

A half-dozen chickens squawked and pecked in the grassless dust of the front yard while beyond a wattle fence, several goats, a cow, and what Caleb took to be the oddest-looking donkey he had ever seen ambled around through well-defined paths in an overgrown pasture.

From the dark shadows of the cabin entrance a woman appeared carrying a large round woven-reed-platter with what appeared to be vegetable scraps piled on it. By her waist length black hair and long buckskin dress, Caleb assumed she must be the boy's mother. She stopped as they spoke for a moment then lifted a rawhide strap from the gate and walked to an unchinked structure where she dumped the scraps between the logs. Even from where Caleb laid, he could hear the squeal of fighting pigs.

All evening long Caleb watched the domestic routines of the homestead. Mother and son.

He had come to the conclusion that no one else was about when, shortly before dark, an old man with long white hair and a tall walking staff, exited the cabin and strolled down to the stream's edge. He just stood there for a long time, unmoving, gazing out across the water. It was as if he was communing with nature itself.

Then, with no forewarning, he looked straight up into Caleb's eyes.

Caleb quickly dropped his head and backed away from the cliff. His heart felt like it was going to pound out of his chest. *How had the old man known?*

Several minutes passed as Caleb laid there. Slowly, his pulse returned to normal. *He couldn't have known*, he thought. *Why, as old as that guy is, it's doubtful he can even see this far.*

Crawling back to the edge, Caleb slowly peeked over. The old man had disrobed and was sitting alone in the growing dark, neck deep in the cold water. He paid not the least bit of attention to the high ridge or the voyeur above him.

Caleb spent the night concealed on the ledge. Nothing was amiss except the fright he received when a large owl swooped down over his head and snatched the mischievous chipmunk that foolishly ambled out of its den after dark.

Forgoing breakfast, Caleb watched the homestead the next morning until he was convinced the small family were on their own. *With Andy Jackson clearing the mountains of Indians anyway*, he thought, *what could it hurt to speed the process along.*

"Yeah, you may have found yourself a homesite, brother," he muttered to himself. "But I got me a whole farm."

ELEVEN

Invasion

THERE AIN'T NO OTHER WAY to say it but that
it was one joyous day when all o' them wagons
pulled up in front of the B&C Emporium. I don't
reckon there'd ever been such an outpourin' of
welcomes and well-wishin' as what we witnessed from
every corner of the Cove. People seemed plumb
tickled to have another choice of where to spend their
money—or trade their goods, as the case may be.

'Course, I don't reckon the sentiment was shared
by some of them Becketts. Them, and a few folks who
worked for 'em which stood to lose a heap of business.
What, with the way they'd been treatin' folks, their
future didn't look real bright.

No more did the wagons pull up than Ma and
Charlotte went to makin' a fuss over little JJ like he
was the most perfect little man they'd ever laid eyes
on. For sure, they both gave Delma a peck on the
cheek, but I figure she'd a plumb felt left out if not for
me and Sarah May goin' all out to make her feel at

home. After all, she had been like a mother to me 'til I was eight years old, or so.

When James saw all the carryin' on over his son, why he got to struttin' around with his chest puffed out like he'd accomplished a mighty great deed when he'd sired the boy. Make ya think Delma didn't have a thing to do with it.

I noticed how Pa steered clear of his son-in-law. I reckon he'd heard 'bout all he was fixin' to on the long ride home. Even Diver seemed to become mighty busy when he saw James headed his way.

As for me, I was just plumb tickled to see all the folks that showed up out o' nowhere. They jumped right in, liftin' and totin' and carryin' stuff into the store or up to Delma's and James' apartment without even being asked to do so. Saved me a heap a work.

That's the neighborly sort o' thing that seemed more commonplace back then. Back when folks were tryin' hard to bring civilization to the backcountry and just natural like, looked out for one another.

Weren't no time at all before that store was stocked with everything from pickle barrels to garden seeds and linens to rock candy. If it was needed for the home, workshop, or farm, chances are it could be found at the B&C.

Barrels and wooden boxes displayed goods along nearly every wall. Tables and countertops were piled high with clothing, slates, candles, earthenware goods and bolts of material. Shelves were stocked with dry goods such as coffee, sugar, tea and flour along with needles, thread, medicinal herbs and plugs of tobacco. Walls were adorned with tools, weapons, tack, and coils of hemp rope. Even the open-beamed ceilings were strewn with large hooks supporting pots, pans, wash tubs, and a Charley Rucker rocking chair.

Of course, room was left for playin' checkers near the pot belly stove so the older fellers would have somewhere to congregate on a cold winter's day.

In the summer, long tournaments could be held out on the wide front porch when it wasn't being used for community meetings or political rallies.

Orwell had even got the B&C registered as the local post office.

Officially, Orwell and James owned the store, but there weren't no doubt who was runnin' it. That was Delma's domain.

James was to be in charge of making monthly trips to Maryville or Knoxville to resupply the place with non-local items such as fine porcelain China and nankeen cloth. Ma and Charlotte suppled eggs and pullets, while Pa and Diver brought in corn, cornmeal, and honey. A quickly prospering Casey, kept the store well supplied with salt and Clarence Tudwell sold 'em milk, cream and butter.

A Home in the Mist: On Thin Ice

From the day Delma propped open the front door and welcomed her first customer, that store was an establishment the Cove couldn't live without. And one Trace Beckett loathed with a passion.

It also, indirectly, like to o' cost me my young life.

≈

"We got a problem boy," Pa said as I helped him, and Clarence hitch a couple of unhappy stirk cows to the back of our wagon. Bein' yearlings, they were young enough to manage, but old enough to put up a fuss. I don't reckon they appreciated bein' rental payment for Pa's lower pasture. One was only going up the hill to our place. The other was headin' to the Rainwater homestead.

"As you know," Pa continued, "the Green Corn Ceremony's comin' up and I promised Long Star we'd be there. I figured on havin' Casey watch over the farm while were gone, but he's gonna be in Lexington at a livestock auction. He's tryin' to get himself a mammoth jack to work his salt hoist. Figures it'll speed things up, not having to depend on his wagon team to do the lifting too."

I knew what was coming and was disappointed to be missing the ceremony and seein' Henry.

"Seein's how Diver's gonna have all he can handle at the mill, well it just wouldn't be right to burden him with our chores," he continued. "What I'm sayin' is, I figure you're old enough to keep an eye on the place your own self."

That's when it struck me. Pa had never left me in charge of the place by myself before. That was a mighty big responsibility for a boy shy of his sixteenth birthday. Kind o' made me choke-up a bit just thinkin' 'bout it.

"I won't let ya down, Pa," I said.

He scraped a bit of cow slobber off his hand onto the wagon's tailgate then briskly rubbed his palm on his pant leg.

"I can have Forrest check on ya if you'd like."

"No, that won't be necessary," I said. "I can handle it."

He squeezed my shoulder. "I know ya can boy. Now let's see if we can get your ma to see things that away."

Them cows fought for a spell as we got under way, but they soon learned they were no match for Mac and Corn Pone. After that they calmed down and followed along like they done it every day of their lives.

When we got home, it was time to convince Ma.

"The way I see it," Pa said, using his most assertive voice, "I was a growed man, workin' side by side with your Pa before I was Billy's age."

I was takin' a completely different track. "Aw, come on, Ma," I was pleading, "I ain't no kid no more. I can do it."

Pa was giving me the stink eye apparently not seein' how grovelin' was a real convincing display of manhood.

"What I'm sayin'," continued Pa, "is . . ."

Ma laughed as she laid a hand on each of our chests. "Now shush," she said. "The both of ya. Y'all sound like the magpie that tried to steal his own shiny talon. Pecked all day and didn't get nothin' but a sore toe for his trouble. I think Billy watchin' the farm is a fine idea. Ain't a soul in the Cove I'd place more trust in."

Well now, me and Pa neither one knew what to do with that. We'd not even got to our most convincing arguments and suddenly there was nowhere to go with 'em. It was kinda discombobulatin' to have 'em squirmin' around in your brain like that and no way to let 'em out.

"Just do what you always do, and things will be fine," she said to me. "Charlotte and the Tudwell girls will come by mornin' and evenin' to take care of the chickens. You won't even know they're here."

Pa finally swallowed down his unused arguments and slapped me on the back. "Well, reckon it'll be your place till we get back," he said. "We'll be headin' out first thing Wednesday mornin'."

"Oh, and one more thing," said Ma. "I figure your orchard ought to be plumb droopin' with apples 'bout now." (How it had become *my* orchard I wasn't sure, but I wasn't 'bout to correct Ma just then.) "Why don't you take the buckboard and fetch a dozen or so bushels for the B&C while we're gone."

The corral had not yet been completed down at Diver and Charlotte's place, so their mules were still on our homestead. Ma and Pa were taking Mac and Joleen so that left Corn Pone and Gabby to pull the farm wagon.

"Sure, Ma," I said. "It'll give me a chance to visit with Delma too."

Seems kind o' funny now, but I was plumb lookin' forward to bein' home alone. Fact is, it meant I was gonna be doin' all the work by myself, but somehow that was okay. A man ought to work his own land.

That's how I wound up all alone for the first time in my life. If I'd o' only knowed what was headed my way, I'd o' turned the farm over to Forrest and jumped right up there behind Ma.

Ride the crest or sink into the depths: such are the fickle tides of fate. The best a man can hope to do is stay the course as he trims his sails to match whatever winds may blow.

Come Wednesday morning I saw Ma and Pa on their way then strolled to the barn to start my daily chores.

≈

"I'm tellin' ya, there won't be nothing to it."

Caleb had spent the last hour trying to convince his brother, Barnabas, to help him run off the family of Indians that were squatting on his new homestead.

"They ain't got no law here 'bouts that's gonna fret none about no backwoods cabin that ain't owned by regular citizens no how," he said.

Barnabas smiled and shook his head. "My, oh my, brother, you surely do have a way with words."

Barnabas was the only child in their family who ever had any formal educatin'. It wasn't but four and a half years in the one room Oak Valley schoolhouse (enrollment of twelve), but it was enough for him to realize that what Caleb had just said seemed to have an awful lot of negatives in it.

"And even if'n there was," Caleb continued, "Andy Jackson himself would be on our side."

Barnabas and Caleb, along with their families and younger brother, Clay, had spent the last two weeks camping on the land Barnabas claimed for his own. A cozy, two room pine log cabin, with thick shuttered windows and a stone fireplace, now sat overlooking the wooded valley below. Nestled in close to a large fallen boulder for protection against the west winds, it had a stunning view of the crystal-clear pond while also being forever bathed in the soothing murmur of the brook-fed waterfall.

Barnabas had scouted the area out and found a gentle slope to the valley floor where a shallow-water crossing gave him access to the lowlands and a route to Parson's Branch. All he needed was Caleb's help in clearing the way. Help he realized he wouldn't be getting without assisting his brother in claiming some Indian woman's homestead for his own.

"Well, so be it," he mumbled to himself.

Looking around, he noticed everyone staring at him. He hadn't realized he'd spoken out loud.

"Well, if we got it do, let's get it done with," he snapped at his brother.

Caleb smiled. "First thing tomorrow," he said. "Now where's this shallow-water ford you been talkin' about?"

"Follow me," said Barnabas. "I reckon we're gonna get plenty o' use outta it."

As Barney led his brothers down the long slope, the women sat on a smooth log nursing their babies and talking about plans for their new homes. The fact that another woman stood to lose everything she had the next day didn't enter their conversation. Being a

Haggen meant looking out for your own. If the other fella can't do the same: so be it.

Leaving a disappointed Clay to watch over their families, Barnabas fell in behind Caleb and gigged his horse into an easy trot. According to Cal, they should make the homestead by mid-afternoon, leaving them plenty of time to take care of business before settling in and enjoying the cozy cabin for the night.

"You'll be my first house guest," a smiling Caleb snickered.

Squirrels scurried to the far side of trees and potter wasps bolted into erratic flight as the horses disturbed purple flowering milkweed in their passing. Half-moon divots left etched across the forest floor by iron-shod hooves were soon investigated by sharp-eyed chickadees and quick-footed voles in search of handily displaced insects.

The weather was pleasant; the terrain largely unencumbered, and if not for the nefarious nature of their mission, one would have thought it a perfect day.

Several miles shy of the cabin they found a good place to ford the stream.

By Caleb's account of the swampy shoreline and whitewater rapids, Barnabas wanted no part of the cascades near the homestead.

A few miles more and Caleb reined in.

"I reckon it might be best to go on foot from here," he said.

Having ridden on many a raid together with the Ford gang, they understood the pertinence of caution. Both had seen men emboldened by the promise of an easy target, rush in, only to fall before the fury of a hidden contingency of vigilantes. How the vigilantes had known to expect the raid was never discovered, but the Haggen boys, having held back, simply faded into the countryside, leaving their compadres to fend for themselves. Some claimed it was an act of pure cowardice, but the fact remained, the brothers were still in the saddle while a couple of mouthy rivals weren't.

An hour or so later found the brothers entrenched behind a large fallen tree no more than fifty yards west of the cabin. They both emptied and reprimed the flash pans of their rifles while closely observing the peaceful homestead. Many a man had lost his life over a misfire due to a faulty charge.

"That's the kid there," whispered Caleb.

By all appearances, the normal daily routines on the farm were being carried out with no apparent apprehension or foreboding of the events about to unfold. No inkling of the perils that lay ahead.

Barnabas watched as the long-haired teen mixed farm chores with target practice. From a leather pouch at his side, he'd select a rock and quickly fling it at a broomcorn shield hanging from the limb of a tree. Barnabas couldn't help but admire the kid's speed and accuracy. A detail best kept in mind.

Suddenly, a long-tailed weasel poked its head out of and then leapt from a knothole in the smokehouse wall. The kid spun and fired. As hair exploded from the weasel's underbelly, it launched itself straight up and did a flip but came down running. It crossed a bare patch before diving into the tall grass, the kid right behind it. What he would have done with the sharp toothed critter had he caught it, Barnabas couldn't imagine.

Just as Caleb had described, a pretty little Indian gal came out front and emptied a watery substance from a clay bowl onto the dirt yard. In an instant she had chickens fluttering and squawking at her feet.

The old man hadn't appeared.

"You sure there's no one else about?" Barnabas asked Caleb.

"I spent an entire evening and most of the next day up there watching this place," Caleb said as he pointed at the ridgetop across the stream. "Didn't see a soul but the kid, the woman, and the old man I told you about."

"Could be someone's away for some reason," Barnabas reasoned.

"Could be," agreed Caleb. "But if so, we'll know when we check the place out. Any indication that someone else lives there and I'll know to keep an eye out. Sides, ain't no Indians gonna try and take a farm from a white man once he's settled into it. Not with federal troops right there in Knoxville."

Barnabas had to admit, his little brother was onto a good thing here. Why build when someone else has already done it for you. If all went well, he'd have to see about swapping fortunes. Let Caleb work his hands to the bone trying to pull a homestead out of that wilderness at the gap.

Looking back at the kid, he saw him go through a sagging gate and into an overgrown pasture. In the far corner of the field, near a cattail bordered stock pond, stood what Caleb had described as a crazy looking donkey. Barney chuckled. It was a hinny.

As the boy walked, he passed beyond the lip of a small hillock and disappeared from sight.

"Come on," Barnabas said, pulling on Caleb's shirt sleeve as he rose up and stepped over the log. "We'll check out the cabin while the kid's occupied and see if the old man's about."

Slinking through the underbrush, then along the side of a storage shed, they stopped for a moment to peek around the corner before bolting across the dirt yard. Several quick steps brought them up with their backs against the wall on either side of the cabin doorway. It was a warm day and the door stood open to get a nice cross-breeze with the kitchen window.

Barnabas held an open hand up to still his brother, then pointed as an indicator for Caleb to glance around and make sure the kid was still out of sight.

Caleb twisted to look past the corner. Turning back, he gave the okay sign.

From inside they could hear the clanking of cookware followed by a repetitive snick, snick, as if a knife was cutting vegetables on a wooden surface.

Reaching down and slowly easing his rifle's hammer back to full cock, Barnabas wrapped his finger around the trigger. Then, holding the weapon at half salute, he peered into the doorway before following his nose around. A quick scan of the single room revealed it to be empty except for the woman standing at a counter with her back to him.

Suddenly, the woman spun around, a startled look on her face and the knife grasped before her in both hands.

Barnabas lowered his barrel, pointing it at her midsection.

"Now, don't do nothin' stupid," he said. "I ain't never kilt no woman before so let's not make this the first time."

208

She stood there, looking him straight in the eye. In her tightly clinched hands, the knife made several involuntary gabbing motions.

"Easy there," Barnabas said taking a half step into the cabin and giving another quick glance around. "I'm sure you don't want my brother out there doing something unpleasant to that boy, now do ya?"

He saw the woman pale. One hand let go of the knife and grasped the countertop behind her as if her legs had become unsteady.

"That's right," said Barnabas, "Ol' Caleb ain't got my good nature." He made a fake shivering motion with his shoulders. "Why, it plumb makes me go all squeamish inside just thinking 'bout what he might do to that boy."

He could see the effect his words had on the woman. First defiance, then defeat registered on her pretty face. With one last look of seething hatred, she flung the knife into the corner of the room.

"That's a good girl," Barnabas said as he motioned her to the side with the barrel of his rifle. Glancing out the kitchen window he asked, "Where's the old man?"

Standing in silence, her gaze seemed to bore into his soul.

"I said where's the old man?" he shouted.

"Gone," she spat.

"How long?"

"He left early this morning, before first light."

Barnabas glanced out the window, then back at the woman. He could see something building behind her dark eyes—something he didn't understand but found oddly disturbing.

"How long will he be gone?"

"Until he comes back," she said with distain.

Barnabas pressed the cold barrel to her throat. "I said how long?"

She held his gaze. "He doesn't answer to me. He comes and goes as he pleases. He could return tonight or next week. As far as you are concerned, the longer he's gone, the longer you live."

Barnabas laughed. "I ain't scared of no old man."

She smiled. "Oh, you will be," she said. "The one thing I can promise you is, you will be."

The cold rigid certainty of her statement sent an unexpected shiver streaming down Barnabas's spine. He was no coward, but he had seen enough to know not to take the harbinger of death lightly. His right eye twitched slightly, and he licked his suddenly dry lips. How this wisp of a woman had so easily instilled dread into his very being he didn't know. But he did know Caleb was standing in the doorway watching. If there was one person he could never show cold feet in front of, it was his little brother.

"Outside," he said pushing Long Star roughly with his rifle barrel.

Caleb stood to the side as Barnabas ushered her past. They then went around the cabin and through the gate into the open pasture out back.

"Stop here," Barnabas said.

They all three stood facing the overgrown field the boy had disappeared into.

"The boy your son?" Barnabas asked the woman.

She said nothing.

"We could just kill him and not worry about it," Barnabas said.

"Yes, he's my son," the woman said.

"What's his name?"

She stood taller as she said, "Henry."

"That's good," said Barnabas, "real good."

Keeping his rifle pointed at the woman he shouted, "Henry! Henry! Boy, you hear me? Your ma needs to talk with you something fierce. I think she'd be real comforted if you's to come runnin' right quick."

Caleb slightly spread his legs and held his rifle unthreateningly in the crock of his arm but with his finger on the trigger.

A moment passed before Henry came walking over the hill, the hinny at his side. When he saw the two armed men, he stopped.

"Run, Henry!" screamed Long Star. "Run!"

Barnabas stepped to the side so Henry could see the rifle pointed at his mother's head.

"I don't think I'd do that, boy," he shouted.

Henry stayed frozen in place.

"We just got a proposition for y'all." Barnabas smiled. "A real estate auction, you might say. No reason for anybody to get hurt over it."

Caleb took a couple steps forward and laughed. "Yeah, an auction where we're the only bidders. But I guarantee, y'all will get the best offer we make. Now who could ask for more than that?"

Henry began slowly walking toward Caleb. Caleb shifting his rifle to half salute, did the same. As they came to within twenty feet of each other, Henry stopped near a massive oak tree. His hand idly drifted down toward the leather pouch on his side.

"Watch him, Cal," Barnabas shouted. "He's deadly with them rocks he carries."

Caleb raised his rifle. "Regular ol' King David, are ya?"

Henry's hand froze, his eyes boring into Caleb's.

"Get rid of them stones," Barnabas shouted.

Henry had all eyes planted directly on him. At the same time, his eyes never left Caleb's. Never wavered. Slowly he reached two fingers into his pouch and pulled out a single rock. Stretching his arm far out to the side, he held it for a moment, then dropped it.

"That's a good boy," said Caleb. "Now the rest of 'em."

Henry eased back into his pouch and once again pulled out a single stone. Eyes glued to Caleb's, he reached out, paused a bit longer than last time, and dropped it.

"Hurry it up, boy," called Barnabas.

"Yeah, business is waitin'," grinned Caleb.

"We ain't got . . ." Barnabas' words caught in his throat as a huge Bowie knife appeared over his right shoulder and pressed firmly against his windpipe. There was no need to look back. He could feel the presence of a giant behind him. The presence of death.

"I believe I'd drop that rifle," the woman said.

Barnabas' hands sprang open like he was holding a deadly viper. The Kentucky rifle fell to his feet.

Caleb, hearing the clatter, glanced back. To his shock, his brother stood weaponless with a giant Indian holding what looked like a short sword to his throat.

Thinking quick, he shouted, "Back off or I'll kill the boy!"

Problem was, when he looked back, Henry was gone.

A Home in the Mist: On Thin Ice

From the corner of his eye, Henry had seen Two Hand glide past the cabin. Rather than risk a shot with Long Star and Henry in the line of fire, he had left his Hawken leaning against a fence post and pulled his Bowie knife. Henry, taking care not to give Two Hand away by looking at him, made a show of slowly dispersing of his rocks, all the while keeping everyone's attention planted firmly on himself. When Two Hand disarmed Barnabas and Caleb glanced back to see wait was happening, Henry stepped behind the large oak tree.

As soon as Caleb started to step toward the tree, Barnabas felt a burning sensation followed by a warm trickle sliding down his throat.

"Stop, Caleb!" He screamed. "Throw down your rifle! He's gonna cut my head off!"

Caleb looked back at Barnabas and the bloody knife at his throat.

"Sorry bro," he said. "But I ain't lettin' 'em get their hands on me."

Turning back to the tree, he stood puzzled by an indistinct shadow hurling towards his eyes, he didn't even have time to register danger before a guinea egg sized rock bounced off his forehead.

Caleb took two steps backwards, went slack at the knees, and collapsed with no attempt to block his fall. He was fast asleep before he hit the ground.

TWELVE

Retribution

I HAD BEEN MIGHTY BUSY ever since I saw Ma and Pa on their way that Wednesday mornin'. I'd been bustin' out chores like I's tryin' to prove I could do 'em on my own, when in all truth, there just wasn't much I didn't do on my own every day of the week anyway. Must've been the fact that I didn't have no one else tellin' me what to do that drove me all the harder. Funny thing is, when I finished with what *needed* to be done, I found myself lookin' for what *could* be done.

Imagine that. Billy Banion lookin' for work.

I reckon if parents could bottle that kind of drive and sprinkle it on their youngins' hotcakes every mornin', they'd save a ton of money replacin' britches cause the seats wore out.

Now, for a fact, I wasn't the only one workin' hard that day. Diver was kept busy with farmers hauling in early harvests hoping to beat the fall rush. They were mostly little the guys who got pushed aside at most mills so the more profitable customers could be taken care of.

Diver did things different. He assured everyone that preferential treatment had no place at his mill.

As it turned out, having early crops worked out for everyone involved. Diver needed time to "learn his stones" before the rush hit, and the farmers were willin' to spend a little extra time if it meant a more favorable cut of the milled flour.

It's a mighty delicate operation tryin' to mill fine flour verses heavy, or cornmeal verses cracked corn. It takes a Master Miller to get it right, and that only comes with practice.

Diver needed to learn each setting of the runner stone as it settled on the bed stone in order to get the flour grade he desired. That's something a body just can't learn without a few loads of grain to practice on.

On the other hand, few farmers had cash money to pay the miller, so they recompensed him with a percentage of their finished product.

Grain for work, and work for grain.

It was a time-honored tradition.

It also allowed for a fair amount of haggling and gave the farmers some leverage while Diver was learning.

Take advantage while you can, if you know what I'm sayin'. Even if it's a preacher your tryin' to get one over on.

Besides, it was down-right fun watchin' to see who out quibbled the other. In most backwoods settlements, you took your entertainment where you found it.

While Diver was learning to be a proper miller, Delma was verging on exhaustion tryin' to keep up with the customers flowing through the B&C.

When Sarah May dropped by to get a cone of sugar and saw Delma's predicament, she immediately placed Darleen in charge of JJ, and jumped in to help wherever she could.

No one seemed to know where James got off to.

'Course, with all that was going on in the Cove, nobody gave me a second thought. And with Casey in Lexington and Ma and Pa not due back for three or four days: well, I felt plumb free, and happy about it.

By midday, Thursday, I'd done 'bout all I could think of to do so I decided to take Ma up on her suggestion and fetch a mess of apples for Delma.

As I hitched up the mules to head to the orchard, I kept an eye out for Baby. I even whistled a time or two. Not a sign of her. Reckon she must o' been out chasing a rabbit or something. Well, this was one outing she was gonna have to miss.

A Home in the Mist: On Thin Ice

I'd have been plumb embarrassed to be seen by the neighbors driving such a lop-sided team. Corn Pone stood a good four hands higher than Gabby did. 'Course, I didn't figure on meetin' nobody where I was headed anyway, so sometimes you just gotta make do with what you got.

It was a perfect day to take a ride. The kind of day that makes a fella want a pucker up and whistle along with the birds flutterin' through the treetops.

'Course, had I known what was headed my way, I reckon I'd a been whistlin' a different tune.

Pullin' up into the meadow, I could see right off that Ma'd been right. Why, some o' them apple trees were nearly draggin' the ground, they had so much fruit on 'em. It was quite a sight.

I didn't need a ladder either. I just pulled up next to a tree and stood in the bed of the wagon. If the fruit was too high, I balanced on the sideboard.

Worked so well, I must have had a half dozen bushels resting on the straw covered bed before I made it to the fourth tree.

That's when I got a surprise. I was standing there, stretching way up high, tryin' to reach a particularly juicy lookin' apple, when I heard, "Hello, Billy."

Well now, I like to've fell off the sideboard. Ain't every day you're out in the middle of nowhere all by yer lonesome and a voice goes to talkin' to ya.

When I got my heart reswollered, I looked back and saw Ally Haggen standin' there.

She was sorta teetering on her toes, lookin' up at me with her silky black hair hangin' down and her hands clasped behind her back like I'd seen in a picture book one time. She must o' been pinchin' her cheeks like they say them big city gals do, cause they was all rosy and looked real nice, framin' that pretty smile she was flashin'.

"Hey, yourself," I croaked when I could speak.

"You tryin' to get that big apple for me, are ya?" she asked in a voice sweet as molasses.

"If'n you want it, I am," I said.

She brushed back an imaginary strand of hair and bit her lower lip while she considered my offer. Then, with her head slightly tilted and her sparkling eyes gazing into mine, she smiled and said, "You know, I been hungry a-l-l day."

Suddenly I felt like I had an apple core stuck in my throat.

'Course it was obvious that Ally knew just what she was doin' cause when my discomfort got about as discomfortable as it could, that's when she winked.

I ain't sayin' my next move was pretty, and I ain't sayin' I done that tree much good, but I assure you, I got that apple.

And held on to it all the way to the ground.

Standing up from where I'd landed after snapping off two limbs in the process of proving Newton's theory applies to more than just apples, I handed it to Ally.

"Oh, Billy, are you okay," she gushed as she took the apple with one hand and tried to brush me off with the other.

"Yeah, I'm fine," I muttered, blocking her hand, and taking a half step back. I'd never met a gal quite so familiar with folks.

She looked me in the eye and said, "Don't be shy, Billy, you're my hero."

With that, she threw her arms around my neck and kissed me right on the lips.

I don't reckon I gotta tell ya how shocked I was. That wasn't no bashful, "I'm thinkin' yer a real sweet kinda guy," kiss like Mary gave me. That was a slap ya upside the head, "What'd ya think of that?" sort o' thing.

I didn't know what to do.

Of course, it wouldn't have mattered if I did, 'cause all of the sudden the nearby underbrush exploded with laughter and jeerin'.

"Ally kissed a boy!"

"I'm gonna tell Pa!"

"I'm gonna tell him first!"

"Un-uh, I am!"

Ally spun around, fear in her eyes. "Where are you little monsters?" she screamed.

All we heard was laughter, hoots, and snappin' twigs. Whoever it was, they were making a beeline across the forest floor.

Ally stood transfixed. Panicked.

"He'll kill me!" she said.

"Who?" I asked, looking around.

"My Pa."

I had no idea what was going on. Fact is, I'd been in a haze ever since Ally showed up.

"Who was that?" I asked.

"That was my twin brothers, Jonathon and Jaden," she said, "The monsters! When they tell Pa what they saw, he'll kill me."

"It can't be that bad," I said, reaching out to squeeze her shoulder.

She actually jumped back.

"You ain't never met my Pa." she said.

She put the palms of both hands on either side of her head and squeezed.

"Eee! "she screeched. "He'll skin me alive, and then ground me till I'm eighty-five."

She looked into my eyes for a moment as if trying to decide what to do, then with a groan and a shake of her head, said, "I got to go."

I only nodded.

With that she ran, dropping her apple before reaching the edge of the orchard.

≈

The first thing Pa noticed when he and Ma rode into Long Star's front yard, was two men sitting on the ground, tied to the large oak tree in the back pasture. Two Hand was standing nearby, using his staff to chip embers from a stack of burning logs placed between two heavy, forked sticks, planted upright in the ground. The swaying of a dead limb soon revealed Henry coming through the long grass, dragging more fuel for the fire.

Pa hopped off Mac and helped Ma down from Joleen as Long Star hesitantly stepped from the cabin to see who had arrived.

"Hey there," said Pa.

Long Star dropped the rag she'd been twisting in her hands and rushed over to hug Ma and then Pa.

"I'm so glad you're here!" she blurted out.

Pa was shocked by Long Star's obvious distress. She was a strong woman, and seldom showed fear. It had to be whatever was happening in the field.

"What's going on?" he asked, looking out back.

"Them two tried to force me and Henry off our land," She said. "Threatened to kill us. If not for Two Hand, there's no telling what they would have done."

Pa instantly felt his Scottish ire come bubbling to the surface. A rage he had spent a lifetime trying to contain; even to the point of denying his own heritage.

"I'll . . ." he started to step towards the gate, his back stiff and his hands balled into fists.

"No," pleaded Long Star as she placed a hand on his chest to stop him. "That's not what I want."

Pa stopped and looked into her brimming eyes. He was confused.

"I'm listening," he said. "What do you want me to do?"

"I want you to let 'em go."

"Let 'em go?" cried Pa. "After what they done?"

"Yes," said Long Star taking Pa's huge hands in her own and keeping his eyes focused on her face. "Two Hand has already threatened to roast 'em for what they did. He made a display of measuring 'em both with his staff and buildin' a spit large enough to do the job. That's when the younger one got all belligerent and started screamin' and shoutin' and beggin' and carryin' on. He demanded to know what the fire was for."

Long Star paled.

"Two Hand told him it was to roast pig. He laughed and said, 'Indians call human flesh long-pig.'"

Pa smiled. He'd heard the term before and knew about Two Hand's flair for the dramatic. He also knew

Two Hand would never actually do such a thing. At least he didn't think he would. Of course, after what these two had done? Well, he prayed he wouldn't.

"If he doesn't stop," continued Long Star, "his troubles will return. This time they won't stop till they've killed him."

Pa could see the anguish in her eyes.

"And what about Henry?" she said. "I don't want him to go through what Two Hand did. What kind of a life is that?"

Pa stood unmoving. Thinking about all the lost years. A single act of kindness had cost Two Hand a lifetime of hardships. What Ma called, 'The Sacrifice."

He shook off his reflections and focused on Long Star. "Tell me what you want me to do?" he said.

"I want you to cut 'em loose," she said. "But I don't ever want 'em coming back."

Pa considered what she'd asked. Two Hand surely didn't need any more trouble. Nor did Henry. But most of all, these heathens had to be convinced they didn't want any part of Black Gum Shoals.

"Okay," he said to Long Star. "I'll take care of it."

"Thank you," she said. "It was a comfort to Jim, before he passed, knowing you'd watch over his son."

Pa was startled. Indians rarely mentioned a lost loved one. He was also honored. Jim Rainwater had been a true friend.

"I'll tell Two Hand and Henry you want to talk with them," he said.

Knowing Pa would take charge, Long Star turned to Ma.

"Let's have tea," she said. "I hear you've become a businesswoman."

Ma laughed and squeezed Long Star's hands. They entered the cabin talking like neither had a care in the world.

As Pa entered the gate and started across the field, Two Hand told Henry to throw more wood on the fire and then follow him.

To the Haggen brothers he looked like a Norse god of vengeance with his massive frame, chiseled features, and wisps of long white hair fluttering around his face in the blowing wind. Though Caleb had tried everything from threats to begging, nothing seemed to squelch the rage burning within the man. A hate deep and smoldering, as if tempered by a lifetime of persecution. Neither brother had ever faced such unadulterated animosity, or ever felt such fear and utter despair. They knew without doubt he was death personified. The question was, what horrors would they face before it came?

Two Hand walked beyond earshot of his captives to meet Pa. The two men looked into each other's eyes.

225

"She told me what happened," Pa said.

Two Hand stayed silent.

"She's worried about you."

No emotion. A face of stone.

"It can't be this way my friend."

Pa laid his hand on the chest that had once seemed as broad as a mountain to him. As powerful as a hickory. The chest of the only man he had ever looked upon as a father. His truest friend.

"They'll never forget," he continued. "Not in this life. Think of Henry."

Two Hand closed his eyes and after a moment nodded.

"Good," Pa said. "She'd like to see both of ya. I'll take care of things here."

As Two Hand and Henry walked toward the cabin, Pa picked up a long stick and drew near to the fire.

"Names Zebulon Banion," he said. "Looks like you boys are in a fix."

Caleb was ecstatic as he watched the big Indian walk away. Spittle gathered at the corners of his mouth, and he nearly giggled with joy.

"Untie us," he said in a hushed whisper as if he feared Two Hand would hear him from all the way across the field. "Hurry, before he comes back. That old Injun is crazy."

226

Pa stood poking the burning logs with his stick; clumps of glowing embers cascading into the fiery coalbed. He slowly turned to face the brothers.

From the looks of the younger one, he hadn't arrived any too soon. A large goose egg protruded from his forehead and blood pooled below his left eye before coursing down his cheek and dripping onto his collar.

Caleb thrashed about wildly, pulling at his restraints. "Come on man," he sputtered, "untie us. Do you know what that old coot is fixin' to do?"

"Way I hear it, he's got cause," stated Pa.

"What?" gasped Caleb. "Now, hold on there a minute." He looked exasperated. "You can't be believin' what that old Injun told ya. Why . . . we was just funnin' the gal."

He looked at Barnabas and said, "Tell him Barney. We was just funnin' her. We'd never dream o' seeing no harm come to the little lady . . . or her brat."

"That so?" Pa asked as he raised the tip of his now burning stick from the fire and blew on it.

"I swear it mister," Caleb was near to tears. "Just cut us loose and you won't never see us ever again."

Barnabas sat quietly, waiting to see what would transpired next. He'd had his reservations about this entire escapade from the beginning. Now he knew there was nothing for it but to face retribution, however it came.

Pa watched as the flame died out on the stick leaving nothing but a glowing ember. He blew on it as if contemplating what to do.

"I don't know," he said. "Be mighty cruel to my way of thinkin', cuttin' ya loose to face him out there in the wilderness all by yourselves."

"What are you talkin' about?" cried Caleb. "He's fixin' to roast us alive. Even said he's got a name for it. Lost pig or lone pig or somethin' like that. What more could he do to us?"

Pa solemnly shook his head. "I reckon you boys don't know who—or what—you're dealing with."

At that, Barnabas looked up at the man who held both their lives in his hands. He looked as hard as the Indian. If by some miracle, they survived, he'd never cross either of 'em again.

Caleb sat open mouthed, ignoring the long strands of drool dampening the front of his dirty homespun shirt. Had they went from one lunatic to another?

"Legend says he's a shaman and a shapeshifter," Pa said, "and immortal."

Both brothers sat stunned. Not moving.

"Now I ain't sayin' I buy into every tall-tale told 'round a campfire," Pa continued as he dropped his

228

stick into the fire and lowered down onto one knee to look the brothers straight into the eyes. "But I know for a fact he's lived three lives and ain't died yet."

He removed his hat with his right hand and drooped it over his knee.

"And according to a band of Creek Indians, they saw him change into a bear right before their very eyes." He shook his head at the wonder of it all. "It's even said he knows everything that happens in the mountains 'cause he soars as a hawk in the daytime, and as an owl at night."

"Remember that hawk that was eyein' us when we was fixin' up Pa's place," Caleb said to Barnabas. "And there was an owl, near scared me to death as I was watched this place."

"Shut up, Caleb," Barnabas said.

"'Course, I can't attest to none of that," Pa continued, "but there's been times I've had a wolf shadow me in the thick timber only to come to a clearing where Two Hand sat waiting on me. How he knew I was in the region, I don't know. But I can tell ya this. When I looked around, the wolf was gone."

"You figure he was the wolf?" Caleb asked.

Pa didn't answer.

"So, there's my dilemma, boys. Would it be kinder to let him do what he's gonna do and get it over with, or turn you loose to face his wraith when he comes huntin' ya down?"

A stunned silence followed. Even Caleb seemed to be considering the alternatives. Then his eye fell on the roasting spit.

"Cut us loose!" he cried. "Cut us loose! We'll take our chances."

Pa looked at Barnabas and said, "That your decision too?"

"Yes sir," Barnabas said.

Pa considered their requests for a moment, then stood up and walked over to where their rifles leaned against a maple tree. Taking each in turn, he used a rock to hammer a long stick into the barrel and broke it off, then he tossed their ramrods into the fire.

"Hey!" shouted Caleb.

"Shut up!" growled Barney.

Pa then came over and stared each of them in the eye before reaching out and cuttin' their bonds.

Caleb immediately jumped up and grabbed his rifle, desperately trying to pinch out the lodged stick.

Barnabas looked Pa in the eye. "You won't ever see us around here again, mister."

Then, looking at his brother, he said, "Either one of us. I guarantee it."

Pa gave Barnabas a look that sent shivers down his spine. "Your life depends on it," he said.

Fleeing through the forest, certain the giant Indian was right behind them, they nearly collapsed by the time they reached their horses.

"He-he-he," Caleb gasped as he untied his reins. He bent over and placed his hands on his knees as he gulped in air. A stabbing pain ripped through his side. "He had no right to jam our rifles."

"Are you too dense to realize he just saved our lives?" Barnabas croaked.

As fatigued as his brother, Barnabas suddenly felt the acrid burn of bile as it flooded his throat. Spewing the foul-tasting filth, he stumbled to the stream and plunged his head into the cold water. Slurping and spitting, he cleansed his mouth and soothed his gullet, unaware of the morsels still clinging to in his beard.

Sitting back with his eyes closed, he struggled to control his breathing. How had he become so out of shape, he wondered. Following one last deep breath, and a long exhalation, he opened his eyes . . . looking straight into those of a massive wolf standing on the far bank.

The wolf's jaws parted releasing a low rumble.

Standing up, Barnabas eased back, never looking away from the cold yellow eyes that chilled him far deeper than any mountain spring ever had. Backing, step by step, he tried motioning with his hand behind him to get his still grumbling brother to shut up.

Caleb finally noticed Barney's frantic waving and followed his line of sight.

Two Hand, he thought. *He is a shapeshifter.*

Before Barnabas could reach his reins, Caleb was in the saddle, whipping his mount through the scrub. The fact that his brother may need help never entered his mind. 'Course it wouldn't have changed his actions even if it had. Not even the throbbing knot on his head impeded his mad dash through the shrubbery.

Miles passed beneath his horse's pounding hooves as he raced for his life. Each time he heard Barnabas draw near, he pushed his steed all the harder. In his terror, he was sure it was the shapeshifter gaining on him.

All the way to the gap, the brothers fled without slowing. Neither would return again.

The wolf had followed at an easy lope until it was sure the intruders were no threat to its den. Standing atop a rock-strewn hillock, it surveyed its domain. Many a time over the months it had shadowed interlopers, always vigilant in keeping its mate safe during her time of gestation and while the pups were young. Now, with the days of summer shortening, the pack would soon be strong enough to hunt together. Soon, no creature of the forest would dare challenge their home again.

THIRTEEN

On Thin Ice

A S I SAT at the base of an old apple tree, snacking on the light lunch I'd brought along, I contemplated the strange events that had just transpired. How I'd been minding my own business, collecting a few apples one minute, and had a gal hangin' 'round my neck kissin' on me the next. I just couldn't quite figure out how that had come about. I do have to admit though, I was woefully unprepared for the wiles of a headstrong young firebrand like Ally Haggen. Truth be told, she plumb scared me, is what she done.

I sure wished Mary would come home.

While I was sittin' there tryin' to make sense of it all, Ally was scramblin' and crawlin' for everything she was worth, tryin' to claw her way up the steep ridge their homestead sat on. She hoped she could reach her pa before the twins did, figuring they went the long way, up the pond trail.

It was a futile gesture. She didn't stand a chance.

As Ally came rushing into the yard, she saw her pa talkin' with the wildly animated twins. They were standing over by the pigsty wavin' their arms and jumpin' around, playin' out the whole scenario. They were huggin' themselves and makin' smoochy faces and, all in all, actin' like idiots.

But what frightened Ally most was, the more the little monsters carried on, the redder her pa's face got. Even from where she stood, she could see the big vein in the center of his forehead begin to throb. When that happened, everybody knew things were headin' south in a hurry.

She desperately looked around for an ally. Avery stood in the doorway with a drink in one hand and Hanna on the opposite hip. She'd made it perfectly clear, she thought her little sister was a shameless tease and deserved whatever came her way. The three older boys were all gone tryin' to find Barney and Cal their own homesteads. Only her Ma could stop the tannin' she had comin'.

It was then that she noticed the wagon was gone.

She'd forgot her Ma said she needed to get Buck's plow back to him. Her and Avery had spent three days breakin' an acre of ground in preparation for next spring's garden, and she felt that was long enough to have her brother's equipment tied up. She was probably headed over there and took Cole and Hiram J with her.

Ally's last hope for a reprieve had vanished.

"I didn't do it!" Ally screamed as her Pa came stomping her way with a red face and closed fists.

Bein' his favorite was mighty nice when it came to gettin' them little extras the others didn't get. A hug, a tickle, an extra piece of rhubarb pie after supper. It made her feel special to see the looks of jealousy her siblings gave her. But if she disappointed him, his fury knew no bounds. It was as if the offense was against him personally.

She held her hands out in front of her as if to stop his advancement and cried out again, "I didn't do it."

"What are you sayin' girl?" he roared. "You sayin' them boys is lyin'?"

"No Pa," she gushed. "I'm sayin' they didn't see what they thought they saw. I didn't kiss that boy . . . he kissed me. I didn't even know he was gonna do it."

She suddenly realized, she just might be onto something. She may get out of this thing yet.

"I's just tryin' to get some apples so me and Ma could make you a pie for yer birthday."

Her inner child had to smile at that one. She'd learned long ago how to manipulate the man. A little sweet-talkin' and exaggerated adoration and she could make him to do whatever she pleased. He was putty in her hands.

"You know your birthdays comin' up the month after next."

Hiram had to think for a moment. He couldn't read a calendar, but he could cipher the seasons pretty well. *Reckon that ought to be about right,* he thought.

"Billy said I could have some," she continued. "Then he went and fell outta his wagon tryin' to get you a good one. Well, naturally I went to help him get up, and that's when he grabbed me and kissed me. That's what he done Pa. Weren't no fault of mine at all. You know I'd never dream of doin' such a thing."

Avery 'bout choked, spewing her drink into Hannah's curly hair. Ducking into the kitchen, she grabbed a towel and dabbed it off. Hannah laughed and slapped Avery on the mouth.

"Icky," she said.

Hiram's face was like stone. A muscle bulged in his right jaw and Ally heard his teeth grind together.

"Say he done that all on his own, do ya?" Hiram glared at Ally.

"I wouldn't lie to you, Pa," Ally blurted.

"Don't believe her Pa," shouted Jonathan.

"Ya, we saw what we saw," joined in Jaden. "I'll fetch ya a switch."

"Oh, shut up!" bellowed Hiram.

He flung a roundhouse backhand at Jaden who ducked out of the way, leaving Jonathan to take the blow on his left ear. The boy was dazed and hearing church bells as he stumbled back a few steps before crashing to the ground on his rump. Jaden stood in stunned silence for a moment before pointing at his red-faced brother and laughing. Jonathon leapt up, lost his balance, nearly fell on his face, then regained his footing and chased after his twin.

"You best not be lyin' to me, girl," Hiram said, ignoring the boys and looking Ally straight in the eye.

"I wouldn't do such a thing," she cried. She hung her head and took his right hand in both of hers. Lifting it, she kissed the base of his thumb. "I love you, Pa."

Avery, who had returned to the doorway, shook her head knowing Ally had wiggled out of another one. She then stepped aside as Hiram came charging into the kitchen. He reached up and removed his rifle from where it rested on pegs above the door and grabbed his possibles bag from the wall.

Ally's eyes lit up when he came out, rifle in hand.

"What are you gonna do?" she cried.

"Go in the cabin," he ordered as he brushed past. "And stay there."

"But Pa," she called.

"I said get," he roared without looking back.

Within moments he had disappeared down the pond trail. The orchard laid less than two miles away.

"You done got that boy kilt," said Avery.

Ally screeched and covered her face with both hands. She rushed into the back room, collapsing on the bed. She hated this life. Being stuck out here in the back of beyond. No dances, no parties, no pretty dresses. It just wasn't fair.

As Pearle, Colton and Junior neared the Wheeler farm, Buck's dogs came rushing out to greet them. Being excited and curious about the new arrivals, they leapt up and down—yapping, and barking, and putting on a display.

Colton scooted to the center of the seat and shrank down as if slipping into a shell. He crossed his arms and tucked both hands out of sight. A shiver ran down his spine as he remembered the one-eared dog his pa used to own that liked to nip at young fingers.

Junior stood in the wagon bed holding the seatback and watched his brother cringe. He thought it was funny from a ten-year-old.

"They won't hurt ya none," Pearl said. "Them's Buck's dogs. He introduced me to 'em, so they know we're okay."

238

Cole nodded but didn't remove his hands. In his world, it was better not to tempt fate: no matter who said it was okay.

Pearle was pleased to see that Eunice was working in her garden. It was amazing what a couple short months had done for her.

"Pearle," Eunice called after dropping a handful of okra pods into her hand-woven basket. Placing the basket on the ground, she trudged across the freshly turned garden soil on dirty, bare feet. "I'm so happy to see ya."

She nudged dogs out of the way as she drew near the wagon. Several leapt up, licking at her face and arms, wanting to play.

"Get back there," she ordered. "Get down. Go find Buck."

At the mention of Buck's name, a couple hounds spun in circles before racing off toward Buck's work shed. Soon, the rest of the pack followed suit. One, being no more than a pup, nearly tripped over his own floppy ears trying not to be left behind.

"So, who do we have here?" Eunice asked as she smiled at the boys.

"This is my boy, Colton," Pearle said as she laid a hand on Cole's shoulder. And the troublemaker in back is Hiram Junior.

Eunice noticed Cole flinch at the touch.

"Don't need to be asking him anything 'cause he won't answer ya," said Pearle. "Been silent since he was a toddler."

She went to rough his hair, but he jerked his head away. "Strangest thing. He up and disappeared out of the yard and was gone for nearly a week. Ain't spoke a word since we got him back. Now his brothers pick on him so bad, I can't leave him alone with 'em, for fear they'll hurt him. Oh, they don't mean nothin' by it. Just funnin' like boys will do. But sometimes they get a bit carried away with the rough housin'."

Junior crossed his arms and said, "He just can't take it. Not like I can."

"Yes Junior," Pearle said. "I know you're getting' to be a big boy."

Eunice watched Cole. He just blinked a few times as he studied the wagon's floorboard. No indication that he was even aware they were talking about him. It was as if he didn't exist.

Just then Buck poked his head around the shed and waved.

"There's Buck now," Eunice said, waving back.

Looking at Pearle she said, "Why don't you and Junior go visit with your brother? I'll show Colton around."

"That'll be nice, won't it, Cole?" Pearle said as she climbed down the wagon wheel.

240

Cole didn't budge.

"Now, you be good," Pearle said.

She then lifted Junior down and they hurried off to greet Buck.

Eunice looked up at the boy as he continued staring at his feet. He wouldn't make eye contact.

"Would you like to get down and walk with me?" Eunice asked.

No reaction.

"I got something special for ya," Eunice said. "But it's in the house."

It was as if he couldn't hear. Reaching up, she held out her hand. "Come with me," she said, "I know you'll like it."

In reality, Cole could hear just fine. He simply didn't know how to respond. His insides squirmed when people spoke to him. He was tortured with indecision. He feared strangers, yet so wanted to please adults. He knew it was impolite to ignore this woman his ma said was his aunt, but he didn't understand what she wanted from him. He certainly couldn't bring himself to touch her hand. Finally, turning his back, he began climbing down. His head swiveled back and forth as he took care to avoid all contact.

"That's okay," Eunice said, seeing how he flinched anytime her hand came close to him. She stood back.

"I didn't like being touched when I was your age either."

When he was settled on the ground, she said, "Let's go to the house and I'll give you your surprise."

As they walked, Eunice talked about her life when she was a little girl. She had six siblings, all from her stepfather's first marriage. When his first wife died, he married her mother, who was also a widow, because he needed someone to care for his children. No one seemed to notice that from that day on, she felt second best. Left out. Everyone else had someone of their own. She had no one. Not even her mother, who was woefully unprepared to take over such a large family.

"So, you see, I understood what it's like to be lonely even when surrounded by family," she said.

As they entered the house, Eunice told Colton to sit at the table. She then placed a tin cup of milk in front of him and turned to retrieve a cloth covered plate.

"I think I know how you feel," she said. "Like there's nothing special about you. Nothing special *for* you. Well, when I was a little girl, I dreamed of having something that was just mine. Something I didn't have to share, and that no one could take away from me. And so," she pulled the cloth off the plate, "this is just for you."

Colton's eyes widened as Eunice sat two slices of blueberry pie down in front of him. Two slices! Never in his life had he been offered such a treat. And it was his . . . his alone.

It broke Eunice's heart to see the joy in the boy's eyes; in his smile. He had such a beautiful smile.

He picked up the fork laying on the plate and started to stab the treat . . . then stopped. His face slackened. Sliding the plate slightly toward Eunice, he indicated, she should take a slice.

"No dear," she said, resting her hand on her chest, marveling at the gesture. Moisture clouded her eyes.

"That's all for you."

As Colton ate, Eunice talked more about her own upbringing. To lighten the mood, she inserted humorous anecdotes that made him chuckle. On one occasion she remembered gettin' a tanning for tellin' her orneriest stepbrother that a week-old cow patty was a loaf of Russian Black Bread that their neighbor had givin' her. He grabbed the "bread" from her and ran off thinkin' it was great fun. At least until he took a bite from it.

Colton sprayed crumbs across the table. They both laughed 'til they had tears in their eyes.

By the time Colton was done with both slices of pie, he had blueberry smeared on both cheeks and milk coating his upper lip. He didn't even flinch when

Eunice reached out with her apron and dabbed at the sticky mess. He did, however, go ahead and use the back of his sleeve to finish the job.

Eunice smiled. Boys will be boys.

After the milk was recorked and the plates placed in the dry sink, Eunice took Colton out back.

"See that stream down there," she said as she pointed out the wide stretch of white-water cascades that flowed past their property.

Colton nodded.

"That's the same stream your daddy's property is on. If you ever need me, just follow the water and it will bring you right here. It's a long walk, three miles or more, so I don't want you ever trying to do it without tellin' your ma first."

She got down on her knees and held his hands in hers as she looked into his eyes.

"I just want you to know, you're never alone. I'm right here."

Colton suddenly threw his arms around Eunice's neck and hugged her. Tears filled both their eyes.

Buck had removed his plow from Pearle's wagon and Pearle reckoned it was time to be gettin' home. She was amazed when Colton hugged Eunice before climbing aboard the wagon. As they clattered down the trail she said, "Looked like you took to your aunt Eunice just fine."

Colton stared straight ahead and said nothing.

Junior paid no attention as he dropped ants on the rear wheel to see if they scurried to the side before gettin' scrunched.

After supper that night, Buck was surprised that Eunice didn't offer him a piece of pie. It was her routine to bake one on Saturday, and they each ate a piece Sunday through Wednesday.

When she went out to get a bucket of water to do the dishes he got to poking around and found the pie plate in the sink. Scratching his head, he picked it up and looked it over. He was sure there should be two slices left.

Oh, well, he thought, dropping the plate back in the sink. *Come to think about it, Eunice did seem to have put on a little weight lately.*

≈

I'd 'bout decided I had all the apples I needed. I should have settled onto the seat of my wagon and headed on home. Would o' saved myself a heap of trouble if I had. Problem is, that's when I happened to see the finest lookin' bunch of apples I'd seen all day. They were just hangin' there, all together, way up high. Funny how it seems anytime you see something you figure you just can't live without, it's way up there, nearly out of reach.

So, there I was, standing on the sideboard of my wagon, trying to keep my balance by grasping a twig between my left thumb and index finger, stretched out as far as I could reach, fingers mere inches from a half dozen plump apples, when I heard, "Don't move."

Now, the first thing a body does when someone says, "Don't move," is they turn to see who said, "Don't move."

Don't ask me why. I don't make the rules. I'm just sayin'.

The second thing a body does when they're standing on a narrow sideboard, using a twig for balance as they turn to see who said, "Don't move," is they move way more than they intended to.

For the second time that day, I stripped tree limbs bare as I ungracefully plummeted to the ground.

Corn Pone looked back and whinnied, ending with a hee-haw. Gabby just looked the other way and hung her head. I guess she felt a second tumble was a bit humiliating, even if I was just her human.

When I rolled onto my back, I saw nothing except the massive black bore of an unwavering rifle barrel planted firmly in my face.

"She weren't lyin' none about your coordination, boy," I heard a gruff voice say.

With that barrel in my face, I wasn't about to move. Didn't take offense about the comment either.

246

"I come here to kill ya for what ya done," the voice said.

Now, that caught my attention real quick. I had no idea what I might have done to be shot for. Only thing I could figure was . . . *that guy must really like apples!*

I let my eyes refocus past the rifle barrel to the man standing over me. He was a medium sized fellow with lank, salt and pepper hair, a scraggly unkempt beard, and dirty work clothes. Deep furrows etched his face seeming to deepen the dark hollows in his cheeks and around his slate gray eyes. A musky odor emanated from the cracks in his worn leather boots.

"I'm mighty sorry, mister," I said. "If I'd known it was yours, I never would have touched it."

The creases in his forehead deepened even more.

"What'd you say boy?"

"Well," I said, "most folks round these parts figure if somethin's left to go wild in the backwoods, there ain't no claim on it. It's free for the takin' if you got a hankerin' for it."

He stood with his mouth agape and his eyes boring into mine. "You must be plumb loco," he said.

"No, sir," I gulped.

Right then, I didn't figure I'd ever fancy a piece of apple pie again. "It was my ma told me to collect all I could find."

"Your ma told you that, did she?" He shook his head in disbelief.

"Yes, sir," I said. "Figured we'd clean 'em up and sell 'em at my sister's store."

I reckon I might o' seen a more confused and agitated fella in my life, but I can't rightly say I remember when. He was kinda sputterin' and spittin' and what not but couldn't seem to pry out of his mouth what he was tryin' to say. All I knew was, that gun barrel was swayin' back and forth with every heavy breath he took, and I was twitchin' and duckin', tryin' to keep it from clippin' my nose off.

"You can have the whole batch of 'em," I blurted.

That seemed to help him focus. The barrel quit swayin' as he growled, "The whole batch of what?"

"Apples," I said. "If I'd o' known they were yours, I never would o' picked them in the first place, but since I did, you tell me where you want 'em and I'll even deliver 'em for ya."

"Who said anything about apples?" he roared.

Now, it was my turn to be confused.

"Didn't you say you was gonna shoot me for takin' your apples?" I asked.

"What kind of a man would shoot a kid over takin' an apple?" he bellowed. "I said I was gonna kill ya for disrespectin' my daughter."

"Your daughter!" I cried. "What daughter?"

"Ally Haggen," he seethed. "You tellin' me, you done what you done and don't even know who she is? Boy, your traipsing on some mighty thin ice."

I didn't know what to think. Here I thought we was talkin' apples and come to find out we was talkin' Ally.

"Sir," I said, tryin' hard to sound more composed than I felt. "I'm mighty sorry about all the confusion, but I still don't know why you want to shoot me over Ally."

"You don't, don't ya?" he sneered. "Here I come marchin' down here to defend my daughter's honor, and you up and tell me you and your ma was fixin' to clean her up and sell her at your sister's store!"

I was taken aback by that. I'd never say such a thing. But then I recollected my comments when I thought we was talkin' about apples. I reckon with what he thought we were discussing, that didn't sound the best. Fact is, Pa would a shot me himself over such a comment.

"I didn't mean . . ." I started to say before he bellowed "Shut up and crawl out of there."

He stepped back and I scrambled out of the broken tree limbs and overgrown grass. My torn shirt, stained pants, and scratched face and arms didn't exactly give me the appearance most folks would look for in a suiter for their daughter. If that's what he thought I was. I could see he'd come to lookin' me over close.

"What I was sayin' is..." I began as I brushed off my clothes.

"Shut up," he said. "You think I wanna hear your lies?"

"I just . . ."

"I said, shut up," he repeated. "And what do you mean by manhandlin' my daughter?"

"I didn't . . ." I 'bout bit my tongue when he stabbed that rifle barrel into my innards.

"You got a real problem keepin' your mouth shut, don't ya, boy?" One eye twitched as he glared at me. "What ya doin' out here anyway?"

I didn't know what to do. Every time the man told me to shut up, he asked me a question. I kept my mouth shut.

"You want me to teach ya some manners, boy," he said as he popped me under the chin with the barrel. "Answer me when I ask you a question."

I gotta tell ya, I was gettin' real unfond of that rifle of his.

"I was just pickin' apples to sell in the Cove," I said.

He spit, unaware or uncaring that most of it spattered into his beard where it clung in small brown droplets.

"Alone?" he asked.

"Ya," I said. "My folks and brother are all out of town, so I figured I'd pick a mess of apples to sell while they're away."

"Home alone, are ya," he queried.

"I'm old enough," I said.

"Reckon ya are," he replied as he looked me over. "How long they gonna be gone?"

I was startin' to get a bit nervous about the direction that conversation was takin'.

"I don't know," I muttered. "Maybe three days."

"Three days," he said, running his hand over his beard then looking at his palm as if wondering where the dampness had come from. "I'm thinkin' I may have found a solution to our little problem."

"What problem?" I asked.

"The problem that 'bout got you laid low," he glared. Then with a snicker, he said, "Reckon it still could."

Backing off several steps, he said, "Unharness them critters."

Not wanting to rile the man any more than he was, I went to work pulling the trappings off Corn Pone and Gabby. Within minutes they stood freed from the wagon.

He pulled a skinnin, knife from its sheath and cut the reins short.

"All right," he said, leading Corn Pone far enough away to get mounted without fear of me trying something stupid. "Jump aboard, and let's get going."

I climbed onto Gabby's bare back and set off leading the way as Ally's father instructed me where to go. I could almost feel his old Kentucky rifle prodding me along.

For sixty minutes or so we topped steep ridges and passed through dark hollows. The sun was well past its zenith and an eerie silence had settled over the woodlands. Shadows gathered in the underbrush beckoning night creatures to stir in their secluded sanctuaries. I shivered as we passed near a hidden grotto emitting a cold breeze that saturated my sweaty, torn shirt. Finally, exiting a laurel thicket, we came to the banks of a clear stream.

"Cross at that wide spot," Mr. Haggen said, "where the swift current is. Stay shy of the still water, there's some deep holes in there."

I reckoned I could read a stream as good as most, but I didn't mention it.

Just beyond the far bank of the stream, we skirted around a tranquil pond of reflective water. About as pretty a spot as a person ever saw, if you asked me.

At least under different circumstances.

I saw a quick flash of color and a small ripple on the surface as a startled fish plunged into the depths.

We then began ascending a long, narrow trail up a cliff face. To our left, a smooth rock wall towered above, interspersed with lichen and the waxy leaves of clinging rhododendrons. On our right, a steep drop-off fell away to jagged rocks far below. A number of springs trickled from the rock face making the stony path treacherous and slick. Even so, perched upon the backs of Corn Pone and Gabby, we couldn't have been safer.

When we reached the top of the trail, we entered an old homestead with a newly repaired cabin, and several dilapidated outbuildings.

"Hop down, boy," Mr. Haggen said as he climbed off Corn Pone.

When I did, he pointed towards the open door of an old log corn crib.

"Inside," he ordered.

I wanted to protest, but that pesky barrel in my face kinda drove the point home. Ducking my head low, I stepped through the heavy doorway. As clouds of dust swirling around my feet, a heavy cross bar fell in place behind me. It was soon pinned shut in a way that prevented me from dislodging it.

"Welcome home, boy," Mr. Haggen said. "Welcome home."

FOURTEEN

The Crib

AS TWO HAND walked out to where Pa was standing, he watched the brothers frantically race across the pasture. Leaping small bushes and tripping in the long grass, they furtively glanced over their shoulders as if to see if that crazy shaman was watching them from the cabin.

"That younger one's gettin' along pretty fair for a man with a walnut sized knot on his head," Two Hand said.

Pa nodded as the men disappear into the tree line.

"I gonna have to take care of 'em when they come back?" Two Hand asked.

"Reckon not," said Pa, keeping track of their advance through the woods by the occasional bird that took flight. "They seemed to have an aversion to long pig."

Two Hand grunted.

Pa studied his friend from the corner of his eye. Even with all they'd been through over the years, he still could not be sure just how far the man would go if pushed beyond reason. He reckoned them boys were lucky they hadn't found out.

"Still got a roastin' pig in the wagon," Two Hand said. "Just got back from Charlie's with it when I saw them yahoos harassing Long Star. Reckon we best be gettin' it on the spit before it 'goes off'."

Pa nodded. He was happy to employ the spit for its original intent.

He and Two Hand headed out front to retrieve the pig. By mid-morning of the following day a gathering of friends and relatives would be stopping by on their way to the Green Corn Festival and were sure to be plenty hungry. This year, Long Star was being honored by hosting two days of games and feasting. When the assemblage departed for their ceremonies, Ma and Pa would return home.

While Pa was occupied attaching the pig to the shaft and cross pins at Black Gum Shoals, Diver and Delma's were busy with their new businesses in the Cove and Casey had not yet returned from Kentucky.

Sarah May was concerned about me being alone, but Forrest assured her I was fine and didn't need nosey relatives checking up on me.

"He's near a grown man," he said. "Let him enjoy his freedom."

Freedom?

Under normal circumstances he would have been right. As it was, while I was truly on my own, I was a long way from being free.

≈

"Ow," I cried when I felt a stabbing pain in the small of my back. Flipping onto my hands and knees, I looked between the timbers to see what had poked me.

A cloud of dust, disturbed by my movements, swirled in the light-shafts piercing the gloom of the crib. I sneezed.

As the dust settled, I saw two tow-headed boys I took to be twins, laughing and fighting over a long stick.

"It's my turn," one claimed as they wrestled.

"Un uh, it's my stick," the other grunted.

"Oh yeah, well who made you 'stick sheriff' of the yard?"

Whack! The first kid clubbed the other over the head snapping the stick in two.

"Ow," his brother yelped.

"Ha!" the first one laughed, "Now we both have one."

The injured one picked up his half of the stick and swished it around a few times as if testing a sword. He then grimaced as he rubbed his head trying to decide if he'd won the tussle or not.

"What are you two up to?" An older girl asked as she stepped around the corner of the crib.

"Ain't none of your beeswax," the original stick holder shouted as they both ran off swinging and flailing as if they were sword fighting.

"Sorry," the girl said as she turned to me. "My names Avery. I brought ya some water and a piece of cornbread."

She handed me a bowl of water and placed the bread in a gap between the timbers.

"I wish I could let ya go, but Pa would plumb skin me alive."

I could see in her eyes that she meant what she said, but I somehow didn't take much comfort from it.

"It's all Ally's fault," she continued. "That girl's flirtin' was bound to come to no good."

"I didn't do nothin'," I said.

"Reckon that's not how Pa sees it," she said as she waited for me to finish the water and hand the bowl back. "He's mighty short sighted when it comes to his precious Ally. But you hang in there. I reckon we'll get this straightened out when Ma gets home."

I slid the bowl back through the timbers.

She flicked out a few lingering droplets before tucking it under her arm.

"I gotta get back in the house 'fore Hanna gets into somethin' she shouldn't oughta," she said. "Ma won't be long."

"I'll be here," I said.

A sudden crash, followed by the high pitched squall of a toddler filtered through the open doorway of the cabin. The girl hurried off to see what Hanna had done now.

Left alone, I was still shell-shocked by the sudden turn of events that had led to me sitting captive in an ancient corn crib. Around me, the dust covered floor was scattered with every kind of rodent droppings you could imagine. I wondered when sanity would return to my world. How I had went from blissfully collecting apples one minute, to finding myself as Mr. Hiram Haggen's prisoner the next, was beyond me.

Hoofbeats drew my attention.

Peeking through the gaps, I saw a thin, unshaven man of perhaps twenty-years-of-age, ride a bay horse into the yard. Close behind followed a younger man in his upper teens riding a black mule.

The girl who had fed me stepped from the cabin doorway with the toddler on her hip.

"Caleb," she said to the older man. Then looking at the younger one she sneered, "'Bout time you got back, Clay. You got chores that need tendin' to."

"You ain't my boss," Clay blurted.

258

Caleb chuckled. "Don't be gettin' too high and mighty, little brother. It comes to head knockin', I ain't protectin' ya."

"I don't need protectin' from her," Clayton said. Course, it didn't go unnoticed that he pulled his mule around to give his sister a wide berth while heading to the barn.

Caleb grinned. "Where's Pa, Avery?" he asked.

Avery hitched Hanna a bit higher on her hip as she watched Clayton ride by. "Last I knowed, he said somethin' 'bout a possum in the blueberries. Might try there," she said.

Caleb raised his reins as if to ride off, but before clicking his tongue nodded towards the corn crib. "Caught yourself a man, did ya?"

Avery stared daggers at him. "Reckon Pa can fill ya in on that," she said.

Caleb grinned and rode away as Avery returned to her chores in the cabin. He'd only came back to get another tent tarp from his wagon but couldn't resist teasin' his sister when he got the chance.

I sat in wonder. A man rides up to find a stranger locked in the corn crib and the best he can do is quip about his sister catchin' herself a man. What kind of a lunatic family was I involved with here?

As Caleb rode up to the blueberry patch, he saw Hiram pock his rifle into a tangle of dead weeds.

"Yo, Pa," he said. "What ya up to?"

Hiram glanced back, then straightened up and shaded his eyes from the sun.

"What happened to you, boy?" he said.

Caleb was taken aback at first, not knowing what his Pa was referring to. Then he realized the knot on his head must look worse than he'd figured. Self-consciously, he touched it with his fingertips.

"Oh, nothin'. I had a mishap with a rock."

"Well, looks like the rock won," Hiram snickered.

Caleb chose to drop it there and begrudgingly grinned.

Hiram turned back to the blueberry patch debris he'd been probing,

"You see a possum from up there?" he asked.

"No, Pa, I surely don't," said Caleb.

Hiram crushed his hat in his fist as he pulled it from his head. He then wiped his brow with his sleeve. "Shame," he said. "I was lookin' forward to a baked possum pie."

Caleb shuddered. He never had cared for the nasty critters. Like slurpin' down a mess of rancid lard dumplin's, to his way of thinkin'.

"Yeah, that's a shame, Pa," he said. "A plumb shame."

Hiram stood shaking his head for a bit before stuffing the hat back on and reaching down to dig a bothersome twig out of his boot. He then turned and headed toward the house.

"I see we got a guest in the corn crib," Caleb said, his horse falling in beside his pa.

"Yep," said Hiram. "And I got a chore for you. Let's get some cider and I'll tell ya all about it."

Twenty minutes later, Caleb had been given Ally's version of the great orchard fracas and been told that the only solution was an immediate hitchin'.

"I want you to ride east on Parson's Branch into North Carolina to find a preacher man," Hiram said. "We can't trust 'em yonder in the Cove, so you find me a Carolina man and fetch him back here."

Ally, standing in the bedroom doorway stamped her foot and screamed, "No! No! No! I won't do it! You can't make me marry that boy."

Hiram leapt from his chair, sending it crashing to the floor. He charged the frightened girl like an enraged bear, driving her up against the wall.

"You will do as I say!" he bellowed. "And I'll not hear another word about it."

He flung his mug of cider against the wall sending shattered shards of glazed clay streaking past Avery and Hanna. Avery winced as a thin line of blood oozed from her cheek. She quickly turned away and checked Hanna for injuries.

Hanna gazed back, sucking on two sticky fingers.

"Once the vows is took," he continued, "you can be a wife or a widow. I don't much care which."

Putting a dirty finger in her face, he growled, "But you will get hitched, my dear. That, I guarantee you."

Ally seemed to shrink in upon herself. Never in her short life had she seen her father so out of control. Never had she felt so helpless before his fury. This time, she realized, she had gone too far.

His eyes bored into hers as he slowly pulled away. White spittle had gathered in the corners of his mouth. Without looking at Caleb he said, "Get going boy. I don't care how you do it, but don't you dare show your face on this property again without havin' a preacher man at your side."

"Sure Pa," Caleb said. He turned and gave Avery a bewildered look, then grabbed a half tin of cornbread off the table before rushing out the door. As he dropped the bread into his saddlebag and mounted his horse, he had no idea how he was going to find a preacher, but find one, he would. And when he did, the man was coming back with him even if it meant at gun point or gagged and hogtied. The one thing that would never happen was him coming home alone.

It was then that Pearle and Junior rode into the yard on Hiram's draft horse. Colton was walking behind, having refused to ride crammed in so close to his ma and brother. The wagon had been left down the way with a broken singletree.

The first thing Pearle saw was Caleb sitting his horse looking like he didn't know which way to turn. Clayton was crouched low peeking into the kitchen window, and Avery, with Hanna on her hip, was just slipping out the door while wiping something red off her check.

"What's going on here?" Pearle demanded.

Everyone froze.

"I said, what's going on?" she repeated.

Even the twins who had been rolling around, wrestling in a batch of nettles, stopped and scratched as they sat on their backsides staring at their mother.

Avery stepped forward. "Pa's got a boy locked in the corn crib," she said.

"What!" Pearl blustered.

Climbing from the horse and helping Junior down, she stormed over to the crib. Cole stood silent, hands clutched behind his back, staring wide-eyed at my filthy face as I sat in the cage staring back and forth between him and his mother.

Junior laughed. "Got him caged, don't they Ma?"

"You shush," she said. "What's that man done now?"

With a grunt, she pulled the peg from the hasp and threw open the door.

I scooted to the doorway and stepped out. It felt good to stretch to my full height after hours of being cramped in the confined space.

"What are you doin'?" bellowed Hiram from the cabin doorway.

We all jerked around and stared at the enraged man.

"Run," whispered Pearle. "Run and don't stop."

I didn't need no second tellin'. No siree bob. I fled across that yard like 'ol Slewfoot himself was on my tail. Comin' to the slope leading down to the stream didn't slow me a bit. I reckon I tumbled as much as I ran down that hillside, but whether afoot or ridin' my backside, I kept my momentum goin'.

Hiram was furious as he charged across the yard.

"What did you do, woman?" Hiram shouted.

Pearle stood her ground, hands on hips, and faced the onslaught of her enraged husband.

"You can't hold no boy caged like he's some sort of animal," she yelled.

"He done abused our girl," he blurted. "Now he's gonna make things right."

"What are you talkin' about?" asked Pearle.

Hiram just stood there for a moment, wild eyed and breathing heavy. Then he shouted, "Go get him boys," before taking Pearle by the arm and propelling her towards the house.

"I'll let Ally tell you what he done her own self," he growled.

At their pa's command the twins leapt up and grabbing their imaginary swords, roared at the top of their lungs as they started down the hill behind me. Clay fled to the south where he knew of an easier descent and Caleb guided his steed down the treacherous cliff trail. Only Colton and Junior remained standing in the yard, not sure what to do.

Finally, Junior reached down and snatched up some of the nettles the twins had been rolling in and threw it in Colton's face before running away laughing.

Colton went to sit on the woodpile, his checks already beginning to sting.

As I fled, Ally stood petrified before her parents. She wanted to tell her ma the truth and end this whole business, but she was already in too deep. If she admitted now that she was the one who kissed me, she would break her father's heart. And who knows what he would break. So, she held to her story. I was the aggressor and she bore no fault at all.

Pearle pleaded with her husband. "You can't do this, Hiram," she said. "Folks won't let this be."

"Ain't nobody's fault but the boy's," he said. "He done did what he did and's gotta make things right.

When we get him back, Caleb's goin' after a preacher and we're havin' us a hitchin'."

"But Hiram," Pearle started.

"Enough," screamed Hiram. "I won't hear no more of it."

Grabbing his rifle, he headed out back. Who knows, maybe that critter had returned, and he could have his baked possum pie after all.

When I reached the bottom of the hill I leapt as far as I could into the stream. Being calm water, it was deeper than it looked, but even as it filled my shoes, I only needed a few strokes to bring me to the other side. Clawing my way up the muddy bank, I plunged into the thick underbrush at a full run. I hoped my pursuers weren't quite as agile in water. I needed as much of a head start as I could get.

Rushing through the forest greenery, I could hear the boys giving hoots and catcalls as they fell further and further behind. They didn't know it, but I was outdistancing them by the moment. If I could only reach more familiar ground they'd never catch me. I reckon even Pa would be hard pressed to find me in my old haunts.

I was leaping bushes, dodging trees, and slapping bristled limbs out of my way as I fled through the forest. My heart was pounding, but my muscles were fluid. This was my element.

Then I saw movement off to my left.

I stopped cold. Waited. Watched. There it was again.

A flicker of color crept through the slanted sunbeams filtered by the tree limbs. It was Clayton. His alternate route down the hillside had somehow allowed him to get ahead of me, and I'd nearly ran right into him. I should have known better. I should have noticed the stillness of the woodlands ahead of me. In my headlong rush to escape, I'd neglected the most rudimentary lessons Pa had taught me. Always be aware of your surroundings. The wild things of the forest will warn you of danger.

I sank to the ground and crawled under a dead limb lying at the base of a shagbark hickory tree. Pain coursed through my chest as I tried desperately to bring my breathing under control. A stitch burned in my side.

I could hear Clayton crushing brush under foot as he scanned his surroundings. A woodsman, he was not. But more concerning, the barks and howls of the twins were drawing nearer. I couldn't stay there long.

Shimmying up to the hickory tree, I carefully stood up. Peeking through open spaces between the lose fitting bark, I could see Clay. His back was to me, and he was slowly moving further away. He glanced from side to side as he went as if I might magically appear at any moment.

Lowering back down, I crawled as quietly as possible on hands and knees in a direction I hoped would get me out from in-between Clay and the twins. It was a painful trek with rocks and stickers piercing my knees and the heels of my hands, but I made good time. I figured, barring an unwanted meeting with a rattler or a copperhead, I was home free.

It was then that I came to the edge of a clearing.

Pulling my knees up under me, I slowly rose to get a better look. It was the apple orchard. The same place this whole nightmare had begun. I had no idea I'd traveled so far.

Snap! A limb cracked somewhere behind me.

"Swift move, klutzo," I heard.

"Shut up and help me out of here."

"Get out yourself. It's not my fault you can't stay on your feet."

"Jaden, I'm gonna..."

"Yeah, yeah, yeah. Grab a hold of this."

I wasn't as far ahead of the twins as I'd thought.

Carefully looking around, I didn't see anybody in the clearing. The orchard looked empty. My best bet was getting to the other side as quickly as possible.

Taking a deep breath, I placed both hands on the ground in front of me, raised one knee into a set position, counted to three, and burst out across the orchard. I ran for all I was worth.

Apple trees flashed by. I nearly lost my balance as I mashed rotten cores underfoot leaving scattered streaks of fragrant, brown mush smeared through the long grass. Great clouds of fruit flies erupted with my passing and swirled in my wake. At the far end of a tree row, I could see my wagon still waiting to make its journey to the Cove. The flower field came into view. Another two minutes and I'd be home free in the confines of the tree line on the far side.

Then I heard a "Yip".

Caleb came charging out from behind a massive tangle of brush, riding high on his bay horse. His rifle was sheathed but he was thrashing the air with a couple piggin' strings as if to let me know, if I ran, I'd feel the sting. I dodged here and there several times trying to avoid his mounts heaving chest and cutting hooves. The strings stung my cheeks and hands. My legs weakened. In my heart, I knew I didn't have a chance. Finally, I collapsed to the ground exhausted.

Caleb pulled up short and sat back grinning. His horse blowing from excitement.

"You done good, boy," he said. "Almost made it."

He then clamped two fingers in his teeth and let loose a long warbling whistle. Within minutes his brothers emerged from the woods; scratched and dirty, but eager to get me back to their pa.

Handing a piggin' string to Clayton, Caleb said, "Tie his hands behind his back. Don't reckon he'll be so anxious to run with limbs slappin' him in the face."

Clay smirked and prodded me onto my stomach with the toe of his boot. He then planted a knee in the small of my back as he tied my hands behind me.

"That ought to slow ya down a bit," he said as he stood up.

Yanking on my shirt collar, he helped me struggle to my feet.

"You know the way," he sneered as he pushed me, nearly sending me back to the ground. "And hurry it up. I'm gettin' hungry."

It was a long walk with the twins happily poking me with their sticks and Clayton shoving me along from time to time if he felt I wasn't moving fast enough.

Caleb rode well back making any attempt at escape impossible.

By the time we climbed the incline and I stumbled into the corn crib, it was well past dark. The hasp slapped shut and Caleb jammed the pin home.

"Get some sleep," he said. "You want to look good fer your hitchin', don't ya?" He chuckled as he retreated into the light splaying across the yard from the open kitchen doorway.

I slumped back to my previous position on the filthy floor with my back propped against the rough-hewn timbers. I didn't know what tomorrow would bring, but it didn't look promising.

A cacophony of chatter, clanging dishes, and the occasional peel of laughter carried on the night breeze. I heard Hiram's harsh voice say, "Too late to find a preacher tonight, son. Head out first thing in the mornin'."

He then burst into an off-key rendition of 'Little Bess the Ballad Singer'. Several voices joined in along with the grating screech of a poorly played fiddle.

I hung my head and gave into exhaustion. So much for having the farm to myself. Closing my eyes, I prepared for a long, restless night.

Two Hand kept Pa and Henry company till well into the night. Old times were rehashed, and long-ago stories retold. Many of them about Henry's father, Jim Rainwater.

Jim had died when Henry was quite young, and he never tired of hearing about his father's exploits. But the pain he saw in the men's eyes when they spoke of their fallen friend was beyond his comprehension. What unspoken bond had existed between them.

Pa and Jim were close in age and obviously best of friends, as were Henry and me. That, he could understand. But what connection did they have with the old shaman? That was the mystery.

Two Hand had always been part of his life, but a part that was never questioned. He was a protector, and provider: an entity that appeared and vanished at will. A friend who anticipated their needs, and a fierce and terrifying foe to any that would harm them.

Was he somehow the embodiment of his father's benevolence come back to watch over them? Even with the myriad of stories told that night, Henry's unasked inquiries went unanswered.

By noon of the following day numerous guests had arrived by horseback, wagon, and afoot.

Chief Charlie appeared in a raven colored long-tail coat with tan breeches, leather moccasins, a beaver skin top hat adorned with two long feathers from a red-tailed hawk, an intricately carved eagle's head walking stick, and driving a shiny black carriage pulled by a black gelding with three white stockings.

Some questioned his newly acquired wealth, but most considered his mores beyond reproach.

He had Ahyoka sitting beside him, dressed in her traditional buckskin garments.

Long Star welcomed her guests and hurried about making sure all were comfortable. She understood the high honor that was being bestowed on her and refused to let anything mar the experience for the attendees.

As for Ma, she did what she could but later told Pa the younger woman had plumb worn her out.

"You ever decide to throw a Green Corn Festival," she quipped, "you can pick me up at Sarah May's when it's over."

Pa laughed and said that would be no problem seein's how he'd be there before she was.

Everyone enjoyed the festival and Henry later told me that Pa seemed to be held in nearly as high esteem with the Cherokees as Two Hand was.

By noon of the following day, the assemblage was packing up to leave and Ma and Pa bid everyone farewell. Clambering aboard Mac and Joleen, they drifted away into the forest, looking forward to the long ride ahead, and time spent together. The world seemed hushed and clothed in splendor as husband and wife rode side by side. Each was unaware that the other was reflecting on the first time Pa had led his young bride to their home in the mist. Ma smiled when Pa reached over and took her hand.

As they rode, little could they imagine what dangers laid ahead.

FIFTEEN

Colton's Eyes

I AWOKE TO the sensation of something scratching and nibbling at the soles of my shoes and licking my ankle.

"Quit it, Baby," I said as I pushed it aside with my foot and rolled over, not ready to face a new day.

I heard a soft hiss and wondered why Baby's hair was so bristly against my lower leg. Prying one eye open, I looked down the length of my body.

Another hiss.

There, crouched low but staring me straight in the face, was a long thin snout with jaws stretch wide displaying several sharp, pointy teeth. Unblinking, black, beady eyes watched me as if I were the intruder.

It took a moment for my sleep muddled mind to register what I was seeing. It was the fat, ugly possum that Hiram Haggen had been thrashing about in the bushes for. The one he was figurin' on makin' possum pie out of.

It had its thick, hairless, prehensile tail wrapped firmly around my foot and one long-toed paw grasped my pant cuff.

I have to admit, I was a bit startled there for a moment. I'd never heard of a possum tryin' to eat a near growed man before.

Then I noticed the bits and pieces of apple pulp hanging from his whiskers and smeared along his jawline. He'd been in the process of scouring my shoes and cuffs for tidbits of rotten apple core that I had mashed while running through the orchard.

"Sorry 'bout that fella," I said as I drew my feet away, "but with those sharp teeth of yours, your gonna have to find a less apprehensive dinner plate."

The possum pulled back, still wide jawed. He didn't seem pleased at having his snack taken away. On the other hand, not willing to push the point, he soon lumbered around and slipped through a gap between the timbers. The last I saw of him, he was disappearing into a hole beneath the woodpile.

The morning was cool but quickly warmed as an orange and yellow glow filtered through the tops of a distant tree line. A light breeze arose with the rising sun, then settled into an post-dawn calm. By the time I heard commotion coming from the cabin, the dew had mostly dissipated leaving the air crisp and clean.

Early rising bees and fluttering butterflies were already making wide sweeping excursions among the myriad of newly opened wildflowers interspersed across the yard. Another day of collecting nectar and spreading pollen had begun.

One by one, the cabin's occupants dashed across the yard to visit the necessary as was their custom upon greeting a new day. With a bit of discomfort, I realized I wouldn't mind making that trip myself.

Soon the aroma of bacon and eggs washed across the homestead. Chairs scrapped on worn floors, pans clanged on iron grates and dishes clattered as they were passed around. Voices rose as if trying to talk over one another. Yelps and shouts were followed by scoffs and laughter, and a high-pitched screech from Hannah was quickly squelched. Probably by a tasty tidbit shoved into her mouth. Morning for the Haggen family was a far cry from what I was accustomed to back home.

Things quieted down a bit after a while, though not much. I figured they must be eating.

Not long after, Avery appeared at the crib with a plate of eggs and bacon along with one lumpy drop-biscuit and a cup of cold spring water.

"Sorry, kid," she said as she passed me the food, "I hoped Ma could talk sense into Pa, but he ain't havin' it."

It was then that Caleb came out, glanced at me and Avery, then walked to the barn and began saddling his horse.

"Looks like you and Ally is gettin' hitched after all," she continued.

I got mighty queasy in my stomach after that remark, I can tell ya. Kinda felt like I had a ground squirrel in there tryin' to bury his winter's stash among my innards. Last thing I felt like doin' was eatin', but I figured I might oughta cause I didn't know when I'd get something again.

As I ate, I tried one more time to explain what happened.

"I believe ya, Billy," Avery said.

The clacking of iron shod shoes on bedrock drew our attention and we both watched as Caleb rode away.

"I just don't know what I can do for ya," she continued. "Unless Ally fesses up, Pa ain't gonna listen to nobody." She smirked and shook her head. "And I know my little sister. She'd let our whole family burn if it meant she wouldn't have to face Pa when he's angry."

I nodded and slid the dishes back through the gap.

"I ain't faultin' you none, Avery," I said. "Fact is, I ain't even all that worried about what might happen to me. I'm just mighty feared at what's gonna happen when my Pa hears 'bout this. I don't reckon these old mountains ever seen what's a comin'."

Avery's eyes looked puzzled. A cold chill gripped her heart. Taking the dishes, she walked back to the house.

"I'm afeared Ma," she said as she passed Pearle. She dropped the dishes into the dry-sink and picked up Hannah. Hugging her close, she looked at her ma. "I ain't never knowed it before, but I'm plumb afeared."

"Why child?" Pearle asked. "What brought this on?"

"I've lived among deceit my whole life but refused to see it," she said. "Now, I'm afeared if I open my eyes I'll see ol' doom himself glarin' straight into my soul."

Pearle was stunned. She looked up and saw Hiram standing in the doorway.

"What kind of nonsense is this?" he sneered. "Get yourself together, girl." He then thumped a chair on the floor and hollered, "Come here, boys!"

When his boys gathered 'round, he said, "Your sister can't be marryin' nobody that looks like he crawled out of a pigsty. I want you to take him down to the fishin' hole with a bar o' soap and see to it that he gets cleaned up. Clayton, get him some of your clothes to put on."

"But Pa," Clayton whined, "he ain't big enough to wear my clothes."

"Don't sass me boy," Hiram roared with a raised backhand.

Clayton dodged out of the way and shoved Jaden in front of him. "I ain't sassin' ya Pa," he said. Jaden jerked out of his hands. "I just wanted him to look good fer the hitchin'."

"Just shut up and do what I say," growled Hiram. "And don't be lettin' him get away."

"I won't let him get away," said Junior, placing both fists on his hips.

Turning to Pearle and Avery, Hiram said, "Sweep out and mop the corn crib while he's gone. I want him to be presentable when the preacher man gets here."

Grabbing his hat, he headed for the barn. "I gotta fix that singletree," he grumbled. "Serves me right for lettin' a woman use the wagon."

Avery grabbed the broom and inspected the warped and tattered bristles. She figured it would be fine for what they needed to do, but she'd need to trim back the ends of the broom corn when they were done to restore a flat edge. Handing the broom to her ma, she propped Hannah on her hip and picked up a bucket in the other hand.

"You wanna get to sweepin' out the crib, I'll run get water," she said.

Clayton and Jonathon headed out to release me from my prison, but Jaden said he had something to take care of, then he'd be right along.

"Don't you be laggin'" Clayton warned as he eyed his little brother. "You heard what Pa said."

"Yeah, you heard what Pa said," repeated Junior.

"I won't," said Jaden before he stuck his tongue out at Junior. "I'll be right behind ya."

Pearle stood, broom in hand, as Clayton unpinned the crib door and ordered me out. Avery sat Hannah in the side yard well away from the crib and pulled a corn husk doll from her apron pocket for the toddler to play with.

It didn't slip my notice that Avery refused to look at me as she headed toward the spring with the water bucket in hand.

Colton stood quietly out of the way, watching.

"Turn around and put your hands behind your back," Clayton barked as he pushed me up against the crib wall. He then pulled Caleb's piggin' string from his pocket. "Glad I had a mind to keep this," he snickered.

After I turned, Clayton tied my hands painfully tight, then snatched a fist full of my shirt to pull me from the wall and push me toward the cliff trail.

"Get to movin'," he ordered.

Stumbling, I nearly fell. If I had, having no hands to cushion the fall, I can only imagine what would have happened landing face first in that rock-strewn yard.

"Behave yourself, Clay," Mrs. Haggen admonished.

"Yes, Ma," he muttered. "As long as he don't give me no trouble."

Jonathon giggled.

As we neared the descending trail, movement in the shadows behind the cabin caught our attention. There stood Jaden, peeking around the corner as if checking to make sure that the coast was clear. In his hands he held his pa's longrifle. The weapon looked massive in the clutches of a thirteen-year-old.

Assured that no one was watching, he crouched low and dashed to the sheltered confines of the trail.

"What are you doing?" hissed Clay.

"Who ever heard of guarding a prisoner without a weapon?" asked Jaden, a big smile on his face.

Jonathon laughed as he stared at the rifle. "Yeah, what do you want us to do? Throw rocks at him if he runs?"

"Well, Pa catches ya, he's gonna skin ya alive," spat Clayton.

"Skin ya," agreed Junior, giggling.

"Un uh, not if I keep Billy from escaping," Jaden said. "'Sides, I'll put it back 'fore he even knows it's gone."

"Yeah," Jonathon cut in, "he won't even know it was took."

Reaching for the rifle he said, "Let me hold it a while."

"Un uh," said Jaden, spinning away from Jonathon's reaching hands and trotting a few yards down the trail, "I snuck it, I'll carry it."

"Oh, come on," pleaded Jonathon, "we can take turns."

"Okay," laughed Jaden, "I'll let you know when it's your turn."

"You will not," shouted Jonathon as he chased after his brother. "You'll just hog it all to yourself."

Clayton ignored his brothers as he pushed me along. "Get goin'," he said, "we gotta get you cleaned up for your hitchin'."

It wasn't long before we had left the scuffling twins far behind with Colton standing there watchin' 'em.

"You gonna behave if I untie ya so's ya don't drown while yer bathin'?" asked Clayton.

I looked at the deep, cold water and figured I'd just as well not get in there with my hands tied behind my back.

282

"Yeah, I'll not cause no trouble," I said.

Clayton reached down and picked up a heavy stick. "You best not, or I'll club ya," he warned.

"And I'll clunk ya with a rock," Junior said from were he stood, rock in hand.

Turning me around, he struggled to release my hands. As soon as I felt the cutting binds ease, a foot was planted in my back, and I found myself plunging into the frigid water. The unexpected cold felt like the flat of a giant hand slapping every inch of my flesh all at the same time. My lungs constricted and a torrent of liquid fire burned my throat. I was sure my heart had seized as I shot to the surface, coughing and retching. I was slapping the water with outstretched arms as if I could clamber out of it like climbing the limbs of a tree.

"Ha," I heard Clayton laugh. "That ought to take the rabbit out of ya."

"He ain't gonna be no rabbit no more, is he Clay," echoed Junior.

I struggled to my feet. Standing chest deep in cold water, shivers rippled down my back and threatened to clamp my legs in charley horses. Wrapping my arms tightly around my chest, I waited for my body to acclimate to the cold.

"Here," called Clayton, as he took a bar of lye soap from his pocket and threw it to me. "May as well wash them clothes while you're in there, then strip down and get that muck off ya."

Kerplunk! I heard a splash next to me. Looking up I saw that Junior had tossed the rock in his fist.

"I'll keep the snappers away from ya," he laughed.

I fumbled for the soap but couldn't grip it with my numbed fingers. Luckily it had a high ash content and floated. I'd have hated to take my eyes off Junior to dive for it.

"And Billy," Clay said in a high pitched, motherly voice, "don't forget to wash behind your ears."

"Ha," cried Junior, "Wash yer ears Billy."

They both laughed as if that was the funniest thing they'd ever heard.

While I was suffering through the indignation of having the brothers watch as I turned bright red from cold and lathered up to become presentable enough for a wedding I wanted no part off, the twins were at an impasse half way back up the trail.

"I got just as much right to be a guard as you have," Jonathon groaned as he and Jaden rolled around clutching and punching each other on the rocky ledge.

"Didn't say ya ain't," Jaden croaked as he tried to get a grip on Jonathon's ear. "But I'm the guard with the rifle."

Jonathon twisted his head before Jaden could get a firm hold and bit his brother on the fleshy part of his thumb.

"Ow!" cried Jaden, pulling his hand back and nearly taking Jonathon's tooth with it.

"Therves ya right," Jonathon muttered, as he tried to talk while pressing his tongue against his newly loosened tooth.

While the boys wrestled, the rifle laid across the trail with its crescent shaped, bronze butt plate and intricate metal firing mechanism being splattered by the trickling water of a natural spring.

Colton stood back watching, neither willing to interfere in the struggle, nor pull the rifle from its potentially damaging location.

Jaden suddenly felt a loosening of Jonathon's grip and used the opportunity to pull away and run for the weapon.

"No, you don't," Jonathon cried as he grabbed Jaden's ankle sending him crashing back to the ground.

Jonathon then jumped up and made a dash of his own toward the rifle.

Jaden kicked out, knocking Jonathon off balance long enough for both of them to gain their feet.

Pushing and shoving, they charged the prize. At the last moment, Jaden stooped low and rammed a shoulder into Jonathon's side sending him crashing to the ground on his back directly into the trickle of water that flowed from the rifle's butt plate, across the trail and down the side of the sheer rock cliff.

Jonathon screamed as he slid uncontrollably across the slick surface and plunged into the depths on the other side.

Jaden was stunned. He stood as if in a trance, staring at the empty ledge before him. His face paled. A dark stain traced down his inseam. He began to release a deep moan that emanated from the bottom of his soul.

Then, a weak and panicked voice drifted from the beyond.

"Help, help," it cried, "I'm slipping."

Jaden rushed to the edge and looked over. His brother was hanging by his fingertips nearly six feet down the water slickened cliff face. He had one tenuous toehold on a nub of stone and was desperately feeling around with his other foot for another. Looking up with terrified eyes, he spotted Jaden and mouthed, 'Help me'. Then, gulping in a breath, he whimpered, "I'm slipping. I can't hold on."

Jaden quickly looked over the situation.

Jonathon had somehow miraculously managed to secure a grip on the slick rock face—though temporary it may be. He dangled over a thirty-foot drop with large boulders scattered across the ground below. He was too high to survive a fall, but too low to reach from the ledge.

"Hang in there, brother," Jaden said. "I'm gonna go get Pa."

"I can't," gasped Jonathon. "I can feel myself slippin'. Please, don't leave me."

"I gotta go," yelled Jaden. He turned around and started to run. "I'll be back," he called over his shoulder.

After Jaden left, Jonathon laid his face against the cold wall and whimpered. He'd finally found another toehold that helped a bit but knew in his heart it wouldn't be enough. He had never felt so alone in his life. Never realized how truly cruel the world could be.

Then, not even registering it at first, he felt a few small pebbles pelt his bare hand and land in his hair.

Looking up, he saw the expressionless face of Colton staring down at him.

"Help," he uttered.

Even as he said it he knew how absurd the notion had been—help from the idiot.

Colton's face disappeared.

Standing alone on the trail, Colton hung his head and wondered what he should do. He knew he didn't matter to no one, but his older brother Jonathon was surely meant to be somebody, someday. Even if at times, he could be selfish and mean.

Noticing he was standing with one foot in a small stream of water, he let his eyes follow it back to the abandoned longrifle lying on the trail.

An idea struck him.

More pebbles showered down. Jonathon looked up.

Colton had sat on the edge of the ledge above Jonathon with his legs dangling down on either side of a protruding rock. He twisted at the waist and grunted as he pulled something across his thighs.

It was Pa's rifle.

Careful to keep a firm grip on the cold iron barrel and long wooden stock, he lowered the weapon, butt first, down between his legs. When it reached a small ledge in the cliff face near Jonathon's left hand, he grunted as he hooked the tip of the crescent brass butt plate into a crevice.

Jonathon looked at the weapon, firmly latched into the stone. He then let his eyes follow up the length of it to where Colton sat, tightly gripping the end of the barrel with both hands. It was the perfect climbing pole. He'd climbed less stable tree limbs hundreds of times. But it still scared him half to death. Doubt flooded his mind nearly paralyzing him. What if? . . . What if?

Suddenly his right toe slipped from the slick rock. His body shifted, pulling his right hand away also. In terror he screamed and grasped out. His palm slapped the curly maple of the butt stock allowing him to grip it with the first two joints of his fingers. He frantically reached up and grabbed the narrower part of the stock, just below the action, with his left hand.

Having lost all contact with the wall, he hung free over the abyss.

The sudden motion nearly tore the rifle out of Colton's hands. He tightened his grip and strained to pull the weapon back toward him. If not for the rock he had straddled, he would have been yanked from the ledge along with Jonathon.

As both brother's hearts settled in their throats, Jonathon glanced down at the awaiting rocks below him. Colton stared into the deadly bore of the rifle pointing at his chest.

"Don't let go," yelled Jonathon.

Colton nodded.

Jonathon felt around with his feet until he found new toeholds. With a grimace on his face and a whimper in his throat, he used them to help climb the makeshift ladder.

Rising slowly, he cried out when his hand slipped on a slick surface. Snatching at anything available, he inadvertently grabbed the rifle's hammer, pulling it down into halfcocked. He yelped at the inch and a half drop but quickly got a more secure grip above the frizzen.

Colton grunted. Sweat burned his eyes and tickled his nose as it coursed down and hung in long droplets from his nostrils. In his intense state of concentration, he puzzled at how the drops seemed to hover for just a moment after snapping loose, before plunging down to dampen the cuff of his shirt sleeve.

He desperately needed to wipe his face but refused to loosen his grip on the rifle.

Jonathon ran his fingers along the smooth surface of the weapon and secured a grip where the groove for the ramrod enters the stock. With a grunt, he heaved himself up and got his feet reset. Then, reaching between his brother's hands, he grasped the muzzle of the barrel, not even noticing when the front site gouged a piece of flesh from the heel of his hand.

"Almost there," he whispered, encouraging his body not to give up while falling rocks clattered among the moss-covered boulders far below.

Colton closed his eyes and willed himself to give it his all as the rifle tried to pull away from his grasp. The higher Jonathon climbed, the more pressure he put on his little brother's arms.

Finally, with his tongue clamped firmly between his teeth, Jonathon reached over and got a handhold on the edge of the cliff. A tear slid down his cheek as he brought his other hand across and grasped the solid stone next to it. His heart felt like it was going to pound out of his chest. Flexing his knees and scraping his ankles, he sought out any niche that might give him a toehold.

After what felt like an eternity, he found firm footing, heaved up and got one elbow onto the ledge. He then shifted and brought the other one up. With a giggle of desperation, he grasped at cracks and crevices in the hard-rock trail and pulled himself onto solid ground.

What neither boy knew, was that in the final moments of Jonathon's thrashing, he had kicked the rifle's hammer into fully cocked.

Hiram always kept the weapon primed and loaded in case it was needed in a hurry. Now, with the hammer fully set, all that was required for it to be fired was a pull of the trigger.

Jonathon rolled over onto his back in the trail sobbing, laughing, and gasping for air. He couldn't believe he was alive!

Colton grunted as he tried to lift the heavy rifle. His cramping fingers and sweat-soaked hands made it hard to grasp. He stared down at the black muzzle as he pulled, not knowing a clinging vine had got caught up in the trigger guard. With each heave of the weapon, the trigger depressed farther. Frustrated, tired, and not knowing what was holding the rifle back, he gave it one hard pull.

Snap!

The trigger released the mainspring sending the flint tipped hammer smashing down along the rough tooled surface of the frizzen. Sparks flashed as the frizzen jumped, exposing the powder filled flash pan below. A weak fizz and a small tendril of fowl smelling smoke flickered and wafted up into Colton's face. He jerked his head back and closed his eyes, expecting the firearm to discharge.

Nothing!

The spring dampened powder in the pan had failed to ignite the rifle's charge. The very conditions that could spell disaster for a man in the wild, had saved young Colton's life. He finished pulling the weapon up and let it lay across his chest as he collapsed on the cold trailway. The rifle raised and lowered with each of his labored breaths.

"What's going on here?" Hiram roared as he came charging around the bend to find both boys laying on the damp ground. In his hand was a section of rope. Jaden was close behind him.

Jonathon propped up on one elbow and said, "Hi, Pa." He was about to explain how Colton had helped rescue him from the cliff when Hiram saw his rifle.

Charging at Colton, Hiram bellowed, "What are you doing with that?"

Snatching up the weapon with his left hand and Colton with his right, he looked over his pride and joy before passing it to Jaden.

"I told you boys not to mess with my gun," he growled as he twisted the back of Colton's collar in his fist. "Now I'm gonna make a believer out of ya."

He thrust an arm down over Colton's back bending him at the waist and proceeded to whip him with an open hand.

Jaden looked on startled. *It wasn't him*, he thought. Then realizing he'd somehow got let off the hook with Colton getting the blame, he laughed.

Jonathon, now propped up on both open hands, wanted to say something. Protest. Explain what had happened. But the fear of his father's rage was too much. He simply watched as Colton suffered Hiram's fury without as much as a whimper. Jonathon cringed, knowing firsthand how painful their pa's beatings were.

Then Colton looked up and stared Jonathon straight in the eyes. Tears flowed down his cheeks. Pain and sorrow were etched across his face.

Jonathon was stunned. It had never occurred to him that Colton could have feelings like everybody else. He'd always assumed that since he didn't show emotions, he didn't have any.

Not being able to keep eye contact with his brother, he looked away. Guilt washed over him, but even then, he held his tongue. Suddenly, Jaden's laughter invaded his consciousness. It was like cold spikes twisting in his guts. Jumping up, he screamed at his twin to shut up as he ran toward the house. He needed to get away. To be alone. To find a spot to burrow down out of sight and hide his shame.

≈

As I was scrubbing up for my nuptials, and the Haggen brothers were living out the drama on the trail, Pearle and Avery had finished cleaning the corn crib and come to a decision. Getting ink and paper, Pearle scratched out a note.

> Deer Buc,
> This is Pearle. Need Help.
> Hiram has kidnapt Billy
> Banyon. Tel his Pa. Hurry.
> Pearle an Avery

They waited till after lunch, when Hiram customarily took a nap, then lead Colton out behind the old smoke house to talk with him. Neither was aware of what the boy had already been through that day.

Avery knelt down in front of him and held his shoulders as she looked him in the eye.

She was the only one in the family that he would let touch him.

"Do you know how to get to Uncle Buck's place?" she asked.

He just stared for a while, then looked at his ma. She nodded.

He walked to the edge of the yard where he could see the river and pointed downstream.

"That's right," said Avery. It's about three miles.

She took the note from her apron pocket and put it into his hands.

"Can you take this to Uncle Buck?"

He hung his head looking at the note. He then, once again looked at his ma. He waited for her to nod. When she gave it, he turned and began scooting down the hill on his backside. He held the note well out in front of him so as not to damage it.

Neither Avery nor Pearle could see the moisture in his eyes. The last time he had been alone in the wilderness was when the hairy man had took him. He was nearly paralyzed with fear, but he so wanted to please.

SIXTEEN

The Note

AS MA FOLLOWED Pa through the rugged trails on their homeward trek, she reminisced. The little girl she remembered playing with her dolls in her father's parlor or sashaying around the house in frilly bonnets and pretty dresses with lace lined collars, could never have imagined bearing and raising a family in the primitive backwoods of Tennessee. It went without saying that she would marry a banker, or a wealthy merchant, or a sea captain with a whole fleet of ships. She'd live a life of luxury and ease, never having a care, or even a cloudy day.

In reality, she'd followed this man, (no more than a boy at the time), into the wilderness. She'd lived through the most humiliating honeymoon a woman could imagine. Fed and nursed her children for months on end not knowing where her husband was, or if he was even alive. Then, welcomed him home upon his return, never once begrudging him his trade.

And through all that, she couldn't help but feel how much poorer her life would have been, had her childhood dreams come true.

As they came out of the buckbrush and dropped into the valley with the apple orchard, the first thing they noticed was the abandoned farm wagon loaded with fruit.

"Strange," Pa said, looking over the wagon and not seeing any obvious damage. "Could be something happened to one of the mules."

"What could have happened, dear?" Ma asked, concerned.

"Stepped in a hole . . . snake bite. It's hard to say. Let's not worry about it till we get home."

Continuing down the now well established path between the orchard and the Banion homestead, Pa tried to keep the conversation light. He knew that Ma's fertile imagination was conjuring up every possible scenario it could conceive.

But I don't reckon even she could have dreamt up what had really happened.

The sun had just settled beyond the western hills as they came through the back gate of the pasture. A yellow light glowed in the barn. Pa pointed it out.

"There he is," he said. "Nothing to worry about."

As they neared the front gate, Pa hopped down and helped Ma dismount.

A Home in the Mist: On Thin Ice

"You go on in and get some coffee started," he said. "I'm gonna see to the mules. We won't be long."

Relatching the gate after Ma went through, Pa entered the barn expecting to see me milking Tilly. Instead, he saw Casey.

"Casey," Pa said as he began stripping the tack off the mules, "welcome home. I thought you were Billy." He plopped the saddles on the breezeway railing before hanging the bridles on the wall. "How'd the auction go?"

Casey glanced over his shoulder and gave Pa a nod as he continued milking. "Auction went great," he said. "Got me a fine Mammoth Jack. Stands fifteen-two. He's in the pasture out back."

Pa whistled as he massaged his left shoulder. He then scraped the side of his boot on a stall post trying to remove a bit of cow patty Tilly had gifted him.

"Fifteen and a half hands, that's sixty-two inches," he said, "That's a whole lot o' jackass."

"We'll look him over tomorrow," grinned Casey. He knew Pa was itchin' to see him.

"As for Billy," he continued, "I ain't seen hide nor hair of him. I got back a little bit ago and saw Tilly standin' out here with her utter 'bout to bust. She wasn't a happy girl either, I can tell ya. Didn't look to me like she'd been milked in a day or so. Figure I better go ahead and get the job done myself."

Pa snatched his hat off his head and bent down to examine Tilly's utter for bruising. Any farmer knew, not adhering to a strict milking routine could cause serious complications. Luckily, she looked okay.

"Somethin' ain't right," said Pa. "Even if Billy got distracted somewhere, he'd never let the animals suffer."

"That's what I was thinkin," said Casey.

"You seen Corn Pone and Gabby?" asked Pa.

Casey thought about it for a moment. "No, guess I haven't," he said. "They weren't about when I turned the jack loose."

Pa thought for a moment. "You need any help out here?" he asked.

"No, sir, I got it," Casey said.

Pa shoved his hat back on his head and tapped the toe of his boot on the post a few times to dislodge whatever droppin's he may have missed.

"You come on in, when you're done," he said. Turning, he headed for the house.

"How's Billy?" Ma asked as Pa entered.

Pa tossed his hat on the table and sat down after taking the cup coffee she offered him.

Picking his hat up, Ma hung it on the peg where it belonged.

"Don't know," said Pa. "Billy and the mules ain't here."

"Ain't here," said Ma. "Where are they?"

"Don't know that either," he said. "That's Casey in the barn. He said when he got home, Billy was gone, and he noticed Tilly needed milkin'."

Concern creased Ma's forehead as she bunched her apron in her hands.

Pa noticed and got up, berating himself for being a fool. He could have been more discreet in breaking the news. Taking her in his arms, he said "Now, don't get yourself worked up. There's a hundred reasons why Billy could be gone."

"With both mules?" Ma asked.

"Well, perhaps one got hurt, like I said," he gently pressed her head against his chest and hugged her in his arms. "He may have rode one while he led the other to go get help."

She nodded but didn't say anything. Pa made a good argument, but her innards were tied in a knot anyway.

Pa didn't mention Casey saying Tilly hadn't been milked in a day or so. No reason to imply he'd been gone longer than need be.

"Why don't I ride down to Diver's place and see if he's there?" Pa offered as he retrieved his hat.

"Would you?" she asked.

"Sure," he said, "I'll bet they're nursin' ol' Corn Pone or Gabby and plumb lost all track of time."

≈

While Ma and Pa were contemplating where I could possibly be, Colton was tangled in a rosebay rhododendron bush, trying desperately to extract his entrapped foot.

No one had thought to tell him that when he came to tributaries along the way, simply cross over them and continue. His understanding was, he should follow the water. Which he did. When he came to a brook flowing into the stream, he turned and followed the brook as far as he could. Sometimes it led to a spring flowing from a hillside, at others a marshy groundswell with runoff wending through the forest. Whatever the case may be, upon reaching the source, he went around it and returned to the mainstream on the far side.

The river caused a wide gash in the upper foliage, allowing massive thickets to grow along its fertile banks. Wherever the sun penetrated the open canopy, great tangles of lush shrubbery grew. In areas the water loving rosebay was nearly impenetrable.

If Colton had walked parallel to the watercourse, at a distance, he would have been in relatively open woodlands. But not willing to lose sight of the water, he pushed through the tangles.

A Home in the Mist: On Thin Ice

What should have taken an hour or so, had lasted all afternoon and well into the night. He was cold, lost and frightened. His body ached, and he had never been so tired in his life. All he wished for was a safe place to hide. Somewhere that the hairy man, whom he was sure lurked behind every dark tree trunk and shadowy bush, could not find him. Somewhere to shelter until someone came to get him.

Unknown to Colton, his mother and Avery assumed he had long ago reached his destination. As for Buck, he wasn't even aware that Cole was coming. No one was looking for him.

As Cole fought to free his foot from the tangle of rosebay, he could feel the letter scratching against his belly were he had placed it in his shirt. Deep down inside, he knew that even if he found somewhere to hide, he wouldn't do it. Hairy man or not, he'd promised to deliver the letter, and he could not break his promise. He had to continue his trek.

Tears streamed down his face as he struggled to free his foot. Anger and frustration burned in his chest. He was stretched out in a nearly horizontal position, pulling and yanking, vines and stems chafing his ankle. Then, suddenly, the vine broke.

Propelled backward by the unexpected freedom, Colton flopped seat first into the cold water. Though only his backside, legs, and feet got wet, he loosed a raspy scream. Never having learned to swim, he was petrified of water. To be thrust into a cold, dark, cascading stream, alone in the wilderness at night, was a terror beyond all comprehension.

In his panic, he wasn't even aware that he had screamed. It was the first sound that had escaped his throat in nearly eight years.

Scrambling up the muddy bank, he crawled into the tall grass and collapsed into a fetal ball. Clutching his knees tight to his chest, he gasped-in ragged breathes of air, and wept. *Why?*, he wondered for the millionth time in his life. *Why was he different? Why wasn't he be like everybody else? What had be done wrong? All he wanted was to be normal... and loved.*

As tears moistened the soil beneath Colton's face, he tried to imagine what it would be like to belong. To be accepted. To be family.

Though a shiver racked his body, the memory of his Aunt Eunice talking with him as if he were a real person engulfed his heart in a warm glow. A smile etched his lips. *Blueberry pie.* Exhaustion overtook him. He closed his eyes and slept.

It was a long, slow day, living in the confines of my cage at the Haggen place. Though I have to admit being cleaned up and not sitting in rodent droppings and corn dust was a vast improvement.

Though I didn't know what had happened, I could see there was a strain in the Haggen household.

No one was talking.

Hiram spent the afternoon with a hatchet, shaping a new singletree for his wagon.

Clayton got a pole and headed back to the fishing hole having noticed a good-sized Rock Bass as I bathed.

Avery and Pearle both went about their chores but seemed jumpy and nervous.

Oddly, I didn't hear a snide remark or see a single tussle between the twins all afternoon.

And as for the quiet one, Colton, he seemed to have disappeared. Though, truth be told, I figured that I might have been the only one who noticed.

As the sun sank and twilight gathered, I was pleased that Caleb had not returned with a preacher. Every delay was like a reprieve, giving Pa time to track me down, and get me out of this nightmare.

≈

When Pa rode onto the McCoy place, the first thing he noticed was a second carriage parked next to Diver's. He climbed off Mac and tied him to a fence post before walking over to get a better look.

"Well, I'll be," he said to himself, "Pastor Wilson is back in town."

Walking up to Diver's front door, it opened before he could knock.

"Hello, Zeb," Diver said as he shook Pa's hand. "What brings you out so late?"

"Well, I was hopin' Billy was here," Pa said.

"Billy?" said Diver. "No, I ain't seen him since before y'all left. I thought he was takin' care of the farm."

Diver moved back and said, "Come on in."

Pa stepped through the doorway and immediately greeted Pastor Wilson.

"Pastor," he said, shaking Wilson's hand. "Welcome home. When'd y'all get back?" He then nodded at the women, "Charlotte, Mary."

"Just this evening," said Wilson. "Our house needs to air out a bit and our pantry's bare, so Charlotte and Diver generously offered to let us stay here tonight."

"Well, I'm mighty glad to see ya," said Pa.

"Ya say ya don't know where Billy is?" asked Mary.

"No," Pa said. Then looking back at Diver, he said, "We just got back a short while ago and found Casey milking Tilly. He said when he got home she looked like she was about to bust. He had no idea where Billy was, so he figured he better go ahead and take care of things himself."

"That don't sound like Billy at all," said Diver. "He'd never neglect his chores. Especially with wantin' to show you he can handle the place by himself."

"I agree," said Pa. "But Billy and two mules are missing. I know he was at the orchard cause the wagon is there, loaded with apples. I thought maybe something happened to one of the mules and he brought 'em here for help."

Charlotte came over and took Diver's arm in her hands. Her face was pale with apprehension.

Pa hated to see her fret so. He knew how concerned she and Diver were about her condition. Especially after Dennis.

"No, sorry Zeb," Diver said, putting his arm around Charlotte and rubbing her shoulder. "We haven't seen him, and Delma just left here about an hour ago, so I'm sure she hasn't either. Fact is, I doubt he would have passed by without stopping in, so I don't think he's in the Cove at all."

Pa considered that for a moment.

"You know," he said. "I didn't pay much attention to it at the time, but it does seem like the grass in the orchard was mighty torn up. Too much for one boy and two mules. I think me and Casey'll go out there at first light and see if there's tracks leading anywhere."

"You want company?" Diver asked.

"No, you got plenty to do with your new mill," Pa said. "But I promise you, if I do need ya, I'll send Casey in a hurry."

With another round of handshakes and welcome homes to Wilson and Mary, Pa made an exit and headed home.

Diver, Charlotte, and Wilson sat around the kitchen table debating what could have happened to me. No one noticed when Mary excused herself and went to stand on the dark front porch, all alone.

Now if you recall, Colton was in quite a fix: lost, cold, and frightened, in a labyrinth of jungle-like undergrowth. Terrified beyond comprehension, his young body had finally given into exhaustion, and he passed out among the twisted vegetation.

Though no one witnessed what happened next, from the story I got, this is how I picture it.

The eastern hognose snake slowly advanced. It flicked its black tongue to collect scent particles to be delivered to a special smelling organ in the roof of its mouth. He could detect his prey; a lungless salamander, hiding deep within a crevice under a strangely warm, and humid log.

Confused by the unfamiliar object before it, it paused for several minutes with its head held high, swaying back and forth, trying to detect danger. It bobbed its upturned nose, its dark, soulless eyes unblinking as it studied the scene. A light hiss escaped its mouth. Its tail whipped in the leaf litter imitating a rattle snake as its thick, twenty-six inch body coiled beneath it.

No cause for alarm was detected. Three weeks had passed since its last meal. Hunger won out. Lowering its body to the ground, it slithered forward.

Not being a constrictor, and not having hollow, penetrating fangs with pressurized, lethal venom to immobilize its prey, it relied on small, strong, teeth placed far back in its mouth. It used them to puncture and deflate its favorite meals: toads, frogs, and salamanders, making them easier to swallow.

It did have mildly toxic saliva that was effective on most amphibians, but useless for defense. A hognose hunted by speed and entrapment. It tried to block any avenue of escape until it could get a firm grasp on its prey. Then, with crushing force, it chewed its way down the victim, drawing it into its stomach.

Moving forward, constantly testing the air with its tongue, the snake slid its head into the crevice.

Though normally a slow moving creature, the bright orange salamander suddenly burst into a flurry of motion. From birth, it had had an overwhelming fear of snakes. Twice before it had faced such danger and each time managed to escape through a crack in the wall of its shelter.

The hognose was determined to see that same trick did not succeed again. He thrust his coils into the space, blocking all exits. As the salamander tried to flee, the reptile whipped about, looking to get a death grip.

Colton's eyes flew open. It was if the earth beneath him had come to life. He jumped to his feet.

Startled by the sudden commotion around him, the hognose quickly snapped back and thrust its head high above the grass, poised like a cobra. Upon seeing the tall creature before it, it sucked in air, flattened its head, and hissed.

The salamander quickly fled through the grass and disappeared into the water.

Colton, standing with his back to a tangle of brush, couldn't move. He stretched both hands out in front of him as if to ward off danger.

The snake reacted by thrashing the tip of its tail wildly in the dry leaf litter and opening its mouth wide, hissed anew. It then struck with lightning speed.

Colton flinched.

It reset as if to strike again.

It was then that Colton realized the snake hadn't bit him. It had simply struck his palm with its upturned nose and closed mouth. In disbelief and wonder, he reached out and snapped off a long twig to use as a weapon.

The snake, eyes locked forward, watched as the menacing stick draw near. Its threat had failed. It suddenly collapsed and rolled onto its back.

Colton was shocked. He hadn't even touched it.

Lowering the twig, he took a tentative step forward and gazed down at the apparently dead reptile. Its mouth was agape, its tongue hung out and its upturned white belly looked to be cold and stiff.

The only giveaway was as Colton moved, he could see the eyes watching him.

He reached down with his stick and flipped the snake onto its belly. It immediately rolled back over, this time emitted a foul odor.

Colton smiled. *Once you commit to playin' dead, you insist on playin' dead, don't ya?* he thought. *Well, it's a good thing my brothers ain't here cause you wouldn't just be playin'.*

Still not trusting the snake to stay *dead*, Cole gave it a wide berth and continued on his way. He was surprised to see the sun was up, not realizing he had fallen asleep on the riverbank.

Ten minutes later a roof and chimney came into view, perched atop a high ridge. It was Uncle Buck and Aunt Eunice's house. Five minutes after that, he had climbed a path up the hillside and stood at their open kitchen doorway.

"Colton!" Eunice blurted as she scooted back her chair and stood up. She'd been having breakfast with Buck and happened to look up and see Colton.

"Where'd you come from?"

Buck looked up. "Hello, son," he said. "Is your Ma out there? Is something wrong?"

Colton looked down as he undid a button on his shirt and pulled out the note. He stepped through the doorway and handed it to his Uncle Buck.

Eunice grabbed a damp cloth from a bucket of water sitting on the counter and knelt before the dirty and disheveled boy. "

"Are you okay," she asked, as she looked him over for wounds. Even as she cleaned his superficial scrapes and bruises, she glanced out the door looking for Pearl's wagon.

"Did you come all this way by yourself?"

Colton nodded.

"Why, you poor thing," Eunice said. "She finished washing his scratches and pulled out a chair. "You sit down here and let me make you some flapjacks."

Colton smiled as Eunice uncovered a bowl of blueberries and sat a jug of cool goat's milk on the table.

Buck had hurried into the bedroom where he reappeared pulling a long shirt over his union suit.

"Got trouble," he said.

Eunice turned to look at him as she stirred an egg into her cornmill, butter and goat's milk mixture.

"According to the note young Cole there was carryin'," Buck said, "Hiram's done kidnapped Billy Banion."

Eunice nearly dropped her bowl.

"Pearle wants me to fetch his pa. Says to hurry."

Eunice was dumbstruck. She looked at Buck, then at Colton, then back at Buck.

A body would be hard-pressed to find a person in the mountains that didn't know Zebulon Banion, she thought. *And even fewer would want to cross him.*

"You better go," she said. "But, you be sure to let him know, kin or not, you ain't got no doin's with Hiram Haggen."

Buck grabbed his hat and said, "I'll let him know," as he hurried out the door.

Minutes later, Eunice watched through the kitchen window as Buck trotted away, bareback, down the trail that leads to Parson's Branch. Sitting atop his big draft horse with its massive, feathered feet, he reminded her of one of them knights of old trotting off to war.

"God's speed," she thought.

Placing her skillet on the grate, she asked, "Honey or molasses?"

Colton pointed at the jug of molasses and smiled.

≈

Pa and Casey arrived at the apple orchard a half hour before first light. By the time false dawn had surrendered to the full rays of the bright morning sun, they had determined that two confrontations had taken place in the clearing. One at the wagon, and the other near the wood line on the far side of the flower field.

Ripped and tangled tall-grass, and freshly plowed divots in the loamy soil, gave testament to a short-lived struggle.

Tracks leading from both encounters led east. Not far into the shadowed woodlands they merged into a single pathway. Disregarding *my* footprints, which Pa would recognize anywhere, he determined there was one female, two small people: probably kids, and perhaps three adults, one on horseback.

What made less since, was the two encounters didn't seem to be from the same incident. How I could have been taken twice from the same field was beyond him.

"Billy and the mules didn't go of their own free will," Pa said as he pointed out the jumbled tracks to Casey. "And, whoever took 'em weren't mountain folk or Indians. I reckon even your ma could follow that trail."

Climbing aboard their mules, Casey fell in behind Pa as he followed the flattened tuffs of grass, rolled over stones and broken or twisted limbs and twigs that talked as plain to Pa as a road-sign on a byway would to a seasoned coachman.

A half hour later Pa pulled Mac to a stop.

"I know where their headed," he said as Casey pulled up next to him. Pointing out a smattering on white speckles in the distance, he said, "'Bout half a mile past that dogwood yonder, lies Black Gum Shoal. Ol' Dan'l Ross had himself a homestead on a ridge just the other side. Got run out by Cherokees back before I married your ma. Way I hear it, them Haggen's from Kentucky took it over."

"Haggen's," said Casey, "I know the two older boys: Barney and Caleb. They're bad company."

Remembering the names from the Long Star fiasco, Pa said, "Yeah, I reckon I met 'em myself. But how do you know 'em?"

Casey didn't answer right off. Then he said, "That's a story for another time."

Pa nodded, "Fair enough," he said.

Pa then explained the layout of the homestead to Casey. "The trail up the cliff-face to the north is too easily defended," he said. "We'll leave the mules here and climb the ridge to the south."

Casey nodded. "After you," he said.

Diver and Pastor Wilson were sitting on the porch drinking coffee as the gals enjoyed each other's company in the kitchen. Even with the early hours kept by most farmers, the slow moving wagons from outlying farms wouldn't start arriving before nine or so, giving Diver a couple hours to relax before he put his grinding stones into motion.

While Wilson rambled on about deeds and trusts and will provisions, Diver nodded and 'yepped' and 'hmmed' in all the appropriate places.

Truth be told, Buck's arrival was plenty welcome.

"Preacher, I need a word with ya," Buck called as he slid from his blowing farm horse.

Diver and Wilson both stepped from the porch and hurried over to Buck.

Buck handed Diver the note.

"I just got this about an hour ago," he said.

Diver read the note then handed it to Wilson.

"Where's this Haggen place?" he asked Buck.

"First trail to the left past the overflow on Parson's Branch," Buck said. "Can you take the note to Mr. Banion? My horse is played out."

"He ain't home," said Diver. "He's on the trail."

Taking the note back from Wilson, Diver rushed to the house and gave it to Charlotte. "I'll be back as soon as I can," he said. He then ran out to saddle Aristotle.

She glanced it over. "You be careful," she called. "And bring Billy home safe."

Wilson rushed to harness his horse. "I'll be right behind you," he shouted.

"Not without me, you're not," Mary yelled as she hurried out and climbed aboard the carriage.

Within minutes, Charlotte stood on her front porch, apron in hand. As the dust settled, she could see nothing except Buck Wheeler gently leading his big, worn-out draft horse down the road.

"Dear Lord, watch over Billy," she prayed. *That boy could find trouble at a church social.*

SEVENTEEN

The Reckoning

I CAN'T SAY I was lookin' forward to another night in the corn crib even if bein' cleaned up the way it was made for a little more comfort. Then again, I reckon that ol' possum may not have agreed. He didn't bother with coming back for a second visit that night. Made me fill unwelcome in the neighborhood.

Course, come to think about it, I don't recollect invitin' him back neither. Maybe it was my fault.

Anyway, it was a long night. Just me, the crickets, and the fireflies. Long and lonely. But, truth be told, if I'd a known what was comin', I'd a opted for it to be a whole lot longer.

I reckon it couldn't have been more than a half an hour or so after sunup that Caleb and the preacher came ridin' in. Why they hadn't showed the night before, I couldn't tell ya. Must have camped within five miles of the place.

After tyin' their horses to a pawpaw tree near the smoke house, Caleb walked over and beat on the cabin's door jamb with the side of his fist.

The sound split the morning stillness loud enough to frighten several birds out of nearby trees.

I heard something crash to the floor in the cabin, followed by ragged coughing and Hannah screeching.

"Shut that brat up!" Hiram bellowed.

"Yeah, shut that brat up," I heard from a young voice that must have been Hiram Jr.

A clanging sound followed as if a tin bowl had been kicked across the bare wood floor. Hannah's screaming stopped. I guess somebody put something in her mouth.

"I'm coming!" a rough voice bellowed. "Don't beat the door down."

Moments later, the kitchen door flung wide, slamming it against the wall.

Hiram stood there, rifle in hand, wearing his threadbare, sweat stained union suit. Matted hair jutted out in all directions and a foul stench emanated from his unwashed body after a long restless night, twisting in hot, soiled blankets.

Caleb grimaced as he took a half step back, recoiling from the unexpected odor that drifted out the kitchen door.

His bay horse stood hipshot as the preacher's stout, long faced roan tried in vain to reach a tasty looking clump of bush clover. Neither seemed fazed by Hiram.

"Got the preacher, Pa," Caleb said.

Hiram looked over the portly man dressed in black from head to foot.

"You're a preacher, are ya?" he asked.

"Brother, I must protest the brutish handling of my person by this, this, this… heathen!" he began.

"Shut up," Hiram growled as he poked the man's ample midriff with his rifle barrel. "I said, are you a preacher?"

The man's face turned bright red, and his eyes bulged. He sputtered for a moment before taking a deep breath and composing himself. Straightening his clothes, he pulled back his shoulders and said, "I am a minister of the word and sacrament, duly ordained by the presbytery in accordance with the ecclesiastical polity of the Presbyterian church…"

Hiram raised the rifle's barrel to the man's nose.

"For the last time," he said in a slow, menacing voice. "Are you a preacher, or ain't ya?"

The man's wattles quivered as he swallowed.

"Yes," he said, "I am a Presbyterian Pastor. You can call me Brother Pike."

Hiram eyed the man, then looked at Caleb.

"Couldn't ya find a plain old Methodist?"

I took a shot and called out, "Guess we'll just have to wait for somebody else. I'm a Baptist."

"Shut up," roared Hiram.

I shut up.

By this time, everybody was up, and those not watching the interrogation of the Presbyterian pastor, were taking turns at the necessary.

Suddenly, Jaden came rushing over to Hiram. "Pa," he shouted, pointing across the stream, "there's somebody comin' through the woods."

I hurried to the far wall of my cage and tried to get a view of the landscape beyond the stream but couldn't see anything. From my vantage point, only the treetops were visible.

"Caleb," Hiram ordered, as he pulled on a pair pants and settled the suspenders over his shoulders, "get your rifle."

Caleb hurried to his horse and untied his long rifle. Quickly pulling the buckskin cover from it, he primed the flash pan and set the frizzen. Out of habit, he always kept the chamber loaded.

Starting to go over to where Hiram had prodded Brother Pike into the front yard, he paused.

Clayton was standing ideally by the corn crib.

If worse, came to worse, Caleb reasoned, *we may need all the firepower we can get.*

320

Looking at his saddle bag, indecision creased his face. He knew letting his pa see what he had would be a gamble.

He shook his head. *If whoever was in the woods was coming to recue Bill, they had no time to waste.*

"Clay, come here," he said.

Loosening the bag strap, he reached in and pulled out a cloth covered package that looked to be nearly twenty inches long.

"What ya got there?" Hiram asked, looking over his shoulder.

Caleb hesitated. This was one possession he wasn't giving up. Not to any man. Pa included.

Reaching in the cloth, he extracted the finest dueling pistol Hiram had ever seen.

Hiram whistled.

"It's a Phillip Creamer," Caleb said. "Same pistol Andy Jackson and John C. Calhoun own."

Even at a distance, Hiram couldn't help but admire the exquisite workmanship of possibly the finest gunmaker in America.

"Where'd you get it?" he asked.

Caleb smiled. "Seems that senator's son that came up missin' back in Kentucky ordered it special all the way from Dupo, Illinois. Said it was for his daddy's second inauguration. Claimed he'd kept it secret for a whole year. Not a living soul knew about it but him and Phillip Creamer himself. Problem is, once he picked it up from Creamer's St. Louis shop, and saw how pretty it was, he got to hankerin' to show it off."

Caleb shook his head at the stupidity of some people. Pride and trust are deadly companions.

"The further he traveled across Illinois, the stronger the itch got. By the time he got to Pott's Tavern, where I happened to be havin' lunch, he got to talkin' so much I couldn't hardly get him to shut up. We finely went out back so he could show it to me.

"Now, don't that beat all. A weapon like that, and only two people in the world knowin' about it. When you think about it, there's only one way a situation like that *could* have ended."

Caleb shrugged. "Fact is, that saddle and bridle were just topping on the cake. I'd o' kept his Arabian too, if I could have thought of a way to disguise the brand. Well, at least it gave me something to try the pistol out on. Kind o', kept it all in the family, if you know what I mean."

Hiram eyed the boy. He always had known he was devious, he just hadn't realized how much so. With the knowing came respect. But, with respect came trepidation. Trust wasn't in the cards.

Caleb hurriedly dug a ball and patch from his bag and loaded the pistol. He then charged and primed it from the horn on his side. After tapping the iron ramrod home and replacing it in its slot, he handed the weapon to Clayton.

"Be careful with that," he said. "I've seen the damage it can do."

Clay rubbed his hand along the highly polished stock and gazed at the gold inlayed barrel. His voice wouldn't come, so he simply nodded.

"Here they come," called Jaden, as he and Johnathon hid behind the old smoke house. All that could be seen of the twins were their heads and shoulders bobbing in and out from the corner of the building as they shoved and jostled each other, trying to get the best view of the coming confrontation.

I strained to get a good look as Pa and Casey topped the hill. They each had their Hawkins in hand, and fight in their eyes.

"Hold it right there," yelled Hiram, raising his own weapon. "You ain't got no call to be on my property."

"I hear you got my boy," returned Pa. "I come to fetch him home."

"I'm right here, Pa," I shouted. "In the corn crib."

"You shut up," threatened Hiram.

"You okay, son?" Pa called.

"I'm okay," I replied.

"I said shut up," Hiram blurted, cocking his rifle.

A Home in the Mist: On Thin Ice

At the snick-click, sound of the weapon being readied, Pa and Casey instantly set their hammers and drew a bead on Hiram's chest. The action was so swift it seemed to pull the oxygen from the air.

Brother Pike gasped and stumbled back a few steps before plopping down onto his generous backside. He clutched his chest and began hissing like Ma's copper tea kettle as he gulped and blew massive amounts of Smoky Mountain air. My first thought was that he'd been shot, but of course, no weapons had been fired.

I reckon he must have thumped that ground mighty hard, cause just then that ol' possum vacated his hole in the woodpile and scuttled across the yard to the safety of the forest.

Guess he truly believed that discretion is the better part of valor.

Caleb was caught completely off guard. Not only from the quick actions of Pa and Casey, but also from realizing that Pa was the friend of that crazy Indian shapeshifter.

All the sudden, them mountains seemed awful small.

He glanced around to make sure the shaman wasn't sneaking up on him. The far-off screech of a souring hawk made him shiver. With his rifle only half-cocked and the barrel pointed over his shoulder, he'd lost all inclination for pushing the fight.

If that meant his pa was goin' under, then so be it. Him and Ally were the instigators in this whole mess anyway.

A short pause followed. Both sides waited to see what would happen next. All was silent except a long nasally whine emanating from Brother Pike with each labored breath.

Amazingly, it was Clayton who broke the stand-off. Pointing the Creamer through the timbers, and directly at me, he screamed, "Don't move or I'll shoot him."

Hiram cautiously swiveled his head to see what was going on and saw Clayton pointing the dueling pistol at me.

He smiled.

"You done good, boy," he said.

He then looked at Caleb. "What's with you?"

Caleb snapped out of it and pointed his rifle at Casey.

It was then, with tension as thick as blackstrap molasses, that Diver came riding up the trail with Pastor and Mary Wilson trailing close behind. He reined in Aristotle directly between the combatants.

"What's going on here?" he demanded.

"Who are you?" snapped Hiram.

"I'm Homer McCoy," said Diver, "but people 'round these parts call me Diver."

"Well, Mr. Diver," Hiram sneered, "if it's any of your business, we're gonna have us a hitchin'."

"A hitchin'?" blurted Brother Wilson from his carriage. "Well now, that sounds just fine. Who's the happy couple?"

By this time, Pearle, Avery, Ally, and the kids were all gathered in the doorway.

I noticed that Ally was wearing her bonnet pulled mighty low.

"My girl there," Hiram said as he pointed toward Ally. "Ally, you step out here. Her and that boy in the corn crib is getting' hitched."

Everyone looked my way.

Diver, Wilson, and Mary hadn't even noticed me in the dark crib.

"Billy, is that you?" Diver asked.

"Yes, sir, it is," I said, "and I didn't do nothin'."

"I told you to shut up!" bellowed Hiram.

"But I didn't do it," I said. Looking back at Diver, I said, "I didn't." Then looking at Mary,...*What was Mary doing there?*...I repeated, "I didn't."

"Don't you be tryin' to weasel your way out of it now," yelled Hiram. "You know good and well what you done. You snatched a holt of my little girl down there in that apple orchard and went to kissin' on her.

Plumb took advantage, is what you done. All the while, her just a fightin' and tryin' to get away from ya. Then, when she come runnin' to me, cryin' and tremblin', why..."

He stood in silence for a moment, shaking his head as if the memory of it was too much to bear.

"Well, I marched down there like any lovin' father would a done and inquired as to what your intentions were. And what did you say?"

I was dumbstruck. It hadn't been nothin' like he was sayin'. Nothin' at all.

"Why, you told me that you and your ma was fixin' to clean my little girl up and sell her in your sister's store."

Well, now, I can tell ya, that 'bout sat everybody back on their heels. I felt my ears get hot as them eyes looked at me like I was a three headed snapping turtle that just came crawlin' outta the swamp. Even Pa and Diver had a mighty peculiar look in their eyes.

Poor Brother Pike like to o' fainted as he went into a whole new round of flutters.

"That's not...Ma wouldn't...Apples," I said. "We were gonna sell *apples* at my sister's store."

"I ain't listenin' to no more of it," Hiram snapped. "Ally told me what you done, now you're gonna get hitched and make it right."

"But I didn't," I insisted. "She kissed me!"

"Are you callin' my little girl a liar?" Hiram exploded as spittle spewed from his mouth and he began to point his rifle my way.

Pa and Casey both placed a finger on their triggers and took up the slack. Hiram was a hair's breadth away from death.

Diver flung out both arms with palms out and stood between the combatants. "Now, just calm down," he said.

"I'll call her a liar!" we all heard a feminine voice call out.

Turning, we saw Mary, who had climbed down from her pa's carriage, marching straight toward Ally.

"I know Billy," she exclaimed. "He wouldn't take advantage of *any* girl. Why, he's so bashful, he'd near wet his britches if a girl was to take his hand."

I appreciated the help. I truly did. But I wished she'd o' found another way to go about it. As you can imagine, it was more than just my ears that were red at that point.

As Mary closed in on Ally, fists tight and eyes blazing, she said, "You tell 'em the truth!"

Ally was glancing this way and that, trying to decide which way to flee. How to get away from this crazy, wild girl, headed her way. Then her eyes happened to settle on her pa's hard glare. She knew in an instant that no beating from any foe could be half as bad as facing her pa if she dared to run.

"The truth," Mary said, as she got in Ally's face.

Ally pushed Mary back a step or two and shouted, "I don't have to tell you nothin'."

That wasn't the brightest move she could have made right then.

To the amazement of everybody gathered 'round, Mary had Ally by the hair in an instant. Pulling her away from her mother and sisters, she shook her like a terrier with a rat.

"I said, tell the truth," she demanded.

"Yeow!" screamed Ally.

Bent at the waist, she desperately tried to loosen Mary's grip and wildly throw roundhouse punches at the same time.

They pushed and pulled and twisted and shoved and soon wound-up tumbling to the ground.

Wilson, not knowing what had come over his peace-loving daughter, started to rush in and stop the fight.

"Back!" Roared Hiram, swinging his rifle Wilson's way. "Let 'em settle it themselves."

Wilson held up his hands and backed off.

"Tell 'em," Mary repeated. "Tell 'em."

Avery was having a hard time keeping the smile off her face. She'd waited a long time to see Ally get what she had coming to her. She planned on enjoying every minute of it.

Pearle turned away and took Hannah and Junior back inside the house.

As soon as she let go of him, Junior raced back out and stood grasping Avery's skirt. He didn't plan on missing anything.

As for the twins, they didn't care who won. To them it was about the fight itself. They leapt about, hootin' and cheering and throwing wild punches every which way. Directly Jaden whipped out a backhand that smacked Johnathon on the ear. Not to be outdone, Johnathon clocked Jaden on the jaw. Soon the boys were thrashing around on the ground in a brawl of their own.

Ally tried punching and scratching and kicking, and everything she could think of, but just couldn't dislodge Mary. Unlike the other Haggen kids, anytime she'd had a problem with a sibling, she'd simply ran to her pa. She'd never had to fight for herself.

Mary deflected most of Ally's punches, got her turned onto her stomach, and sat astraddle of her.

Ally screamed and cried and clawed the ground but was completely defenseless.

"Tell the truth or I'll sit here all day," Mary said.

"No!" Ally screamed in defiance and frustration.

Mary grabbed Ally's ears and squeezed. "Tell the truth."

"Ow!" screamed Ally. "Ow!" It dawned on her then that no one was going to help her. She was on her own. Through racking sobs, she finally cried, "Okay, okay, I did it! I did it! Just get off of me."

"What?" bellowed Hiram as Mary stood up and helped Ally to her feet.

Ally looked at her pa, tears streaming down her dirty face.

"What did you say?" he hissed.

Ally hung her head and quietly muttered, "I kissed Billy, Pa. It was just an innocent kiss. Billy didn't even know I was gonna do it. If it hadn't been for them monsters running off to tell you and making such a big deal out of it, it would have meant nothing at all."

Hiram lowered his rifle.

"I couldn't tell the truth, what with you claimin' I was your favorite and all," she continued.

The weapon slipped through his fingers and clattered on the ground.

"I's feared of hurtin' ya." She'd suddenly reverted to her corn syrup, little girl voice. "And feared of what you'd do to me," she finished.

Hiram was defeated.

Caleb lowered his weapon also.

A Home in the Mist: On Thin Ice

A calm settled over the Haggen homestead. No one moved and no one spoke.

It was then, as tensions eased and concentration lessened, that Clayton inadvertently flexed his finger.

The greatest of actions begin with the slightest.

Twice in my life I've heard a sound so loud, it was as if a physical entity had ripped the heart from my body.

The first time was when a bolt of lightning struck Ma's cast-iron kettle where it sat in the yard.

It was on one of those dark, stormy nights that I so enjoy. I was lazily propped up on my pillow, quietly rereading about one of Lemuel Gulliver's fantastic adventures, when suddenly a thunderous blast ripped the book from my hands. It was dashed against the wall as if I'd flung it in a rage. In that same instant, every ounce of breath was expelled from my lungs and I found myself gasping for air a good three or four feet from the sleeping mat where I'd been a split-second before. My nerves were inflamed and seemed to writhe beneath my skin like a million ants running in every direction. My hearing was lost and only returned over the next half an hour or so. All in all, it was a terrifying experience.

The second time was when Clay pulled that trigger.

I can't say I truly remember being hurled face first into the heavy, pinned door of the crib, breaking my nose and loosening several teeth. But I'll never forget that thundering crash of sound. It was an auditory immersion as real and tangible as being washed over a towering cascade into the bottomless depths of a swirling pool. A crushing force that constricted every fiber of my body. What I imagine to be, the acoustic embodiment of the Liberty Bell's clapper making contact with its bronze counterpart. A noise too loud for the human ear to comprehend.

Then all went black, and silence followed.

$$\approx$$

I awoke three days later, somehow knowing I was lying on Ma and Pa's bed back at the Banion cabin. I couldn't remember how I got there, but it seemed to have something to do with a thunderstorm.

"You awake, Billy?"

I struggled to open my eyes, only half succeeding. As a mist cleared, I saw the sweet, smiling face of Mary Wilson looking down at me.

"Welcome back," she said.

"Hi," was all I could utter.

I tried to touch her face, but before I could lift my hand from the sheet a searing pain racked my body.

"Now, don't you move," she admonished. "You've been hurt real bad."

I closed my eyes.

"Time to wake up, Billy."

It was a male voice, but I didn't recognize it. I felt a cool cloth dampen my forehead and cheeks. It felt good. I opened one eye, then the other.

"There you are."

It was Doc Dulaney. Over his shoulder, I could see the worried but smiling face of Ma.

"Hate to bother your slumber," he said, "but it's about time for you to return to the living."

"Hello, ahem," I loosened a weak cough. "Hello, Doc. Ma." I said. "How long I been here?"

"Four days now," Doc said. "I hear you had a nice visit with Mary Wilson yesterday."

Was that yesterday?

As he talked, the doctor checked over my wounds. I hoped he wouldn't touch my nose cause it hurt something fierce. He didn't.

"You was real lucky," he said. "That ball happened to graze a timber as it passed through the wall of that crib and deflected through your right shoulder. Not a pretty wound, but a broken collarbone is a lot better than a hole in the heart."

I nodded and wished I hadn't.

"Course that ain't all," he continued. "Two chunks of shattered wood got ya too. One was a piece about twelve inches by four, and three inches thick. It slapped you flat sided on the back. Did a lot of bruising and may have cracked a rib or two but it could have been a whole lot worse. Another piece about six inches long and half an inch square pierced three inches into your right side. I got it out and don't think it hit anything vital, so mainly we're gonna have to keep an eye out for infection."

He nodded at Ma who was now sitting on the bed with a hand on my leg. "From what I hear, you got the best nurse around. I think you'll pull through just fine."

The doc patted my arm and stood up to leave.

"By the way," he said, "thanks for the business. My family was about to starve before I started carin' for you. I was beginnin' to think this must be the heathiest town in Tennessee. Now, all the sudden, I've got more business than I can handle."

I grinned and nodded.

He smiled as he put on his hat. Placing a hand on Ma's shoulder, he said, "I think he's gonna be just fine. I'll find my own way out."

Diver came to see me every evening after he closed the mill. Turns out, he'd been there every day, but I'd been sleeping. He said Casey had retrieved the wagon full of apples and delivered them to Delma's store. They put up a sign that read, 'Billy's Beauty's, no girl included'. In two days, they sold out.

That kinda tickled me but it hurt to laugh.

The next day, Diver said a group of men from the Cove had formed a posse to confront Hiram Haggen. On their way to his place, they met Buck Wheeler headed for town. Buck told 'em that Pearle had showed up the night before last and asked if he and Eunice would keep Colton. She said Hiram figures it was Cole that ratted him out, and she's plumb scared for the boy to ever come home again. How he figured Cole had told anybody, seein's that he don't talk, was beyond her, but she'd brought his clothes anyway. Eunice was thrilled and said she'd be proud to have the boy.

Colton seemed happy too.

Pearle also claimed the entire Haggen clan was headed out. They'd be gone by morning.

The posse went ahead and checked Hiram's place, but the Haggen's were gone. All that was left was a red tail hawk eyein' an old possum sittin' on a woodpile.

I gotta say, I wasn't in the least bit sorry to hear they'd lit a shuck. I figured there was nothing but peace and quiet for the Cove from here on out.

Boy, oh, boy, was I wrong. And it all started with one little misspoken statement to Mary. But then, that's a story for another time.

One odd thing happened a day or so later though I'm sure it was unintentional. As Diver was rising from my bedside, I saw moisture in his eyes. I was a bit puzzled but didn't say anything. Then, just before he turned to leave, I noticed he had a faraway look in his eyes. That's when he patted me on the arm and whispered, "Good night, Dennis."

I'll admit, I cried for my friend's loss that night.

A Home in the Mist: On Thin Ice

Aug. 16, 1849

Deer Buc,

I ts y or sister Pearle. Hope you are well.
An d Un ise an d my preshus Col e to. I thot id
rite to tell you what becam of the Haggen s.

Barn y said a old in dian in the mon tan s
helped him chan g. I did n ot n o he n ew n o
in dian s. He becam a cotton broker. Sadly
we lost him when the steemboat Lucy
Walker blowd up at New Albany, I n diana.

Caleb did n ot chan g. He is wan ted in 3
stats. He took my Clayton with him.

Ally run d off an wen t back home to
Ken tucky. Her an that Rollin s boy Sammy
got marry d. He becam a docter an d she is his
n urs. Emagin that. I wish her well.

The twin s is somthin chan gd. They are
both good famly men. They work at the
lokal lumber yard an d John athon is a
decun at the Babtist Church.

As for Hiram Jr. hes a lawyers aprin tus
in St. Louis. I thin k sumday he may be
presiden t.

Hiram Sr. wen t west on a wagon tran

led by x Senater Worthington. Said hed send for us wen he got land. I think he was jus run in off. I got a lettr said he got in trubl and tryd to by his way out with 1 of them silvr things off that sadl. He never coud reed an thot the WWW on it was a fancee dezin. It stood for William Walter Worthington. The Senaters son! They said the rok calld Scottsbluff is his headstone.

Avery met a man namd Buckman Fischer with a farm near Forsyth, Missouri. We call him Buc same as you. He does not have a lot but is a good man. They maryd and have 4 kids with 1 more comin this fall. He bilt me an Hannah a small cabin overlookin the White River. It remins me of our plas in the Smokees. We ar happy.

Tel Colton I mis him an to com visit if he can.

Yor lovin sister

Pearle.